Shoed

by

J L Wilson

*Remembered Classics Romance,
Book Twelve*

The Wild Rose Press, Inc.
PO Box 708
Adams Basin, NY 14410-0708
Visit us at www.thewildrosepress.com

Publishing History
First Edition, 2024
Trade Paperback ISBN 978-1-5092-5800-0
Digital ISBN 978-1-5092-5801-7

Remembered Classics Romance, Book Twelve
Published in the United States of America

Chapter One

I was off my late afternoon shift at the Emergency Animal Clinic and was driving home when I saw a haze of exhaust smoke in the distance, drifting into the clear autumn sky like a disgusting belch. The sight added to my crappy mood. I knew this would be the lowlight of a lousy day that started with our well on the fritz. Then I had a stint at the clinic, which was always stressful, and now I had to deal with these construction assholes.

"Those rat bastards. They weren't supposed to do any work until the environmental impact study was done." I slammed my hand against the steering wheel of my nineteen-year-old pickup and gunned the motor.

The construction site was a little more than a mile from my farm and on the other side of a big hill north of me. I couldn't see the site from my house unless I climbed to the top of the hill. That was a tricky proposition given the heavy rains we'd had recently. Add to it the fact the pastureland was rented out and in use by cows which meant it was messy. Very messy. Oh, how I wish I had a drone so I could spy on those creeps. They weren't supposed to be doing any more work until my appeal was heard. That wouldn't be done for at least two weeks.

"Rat bastards," I muttered again, glaring at the gray ribbon of road in front of me. I was coming at the construction zone from the north, using County Road 97 which wound south and west from the larger four-lane highway. It was an old road lined with maples, sumac, and oaks, brilliant with fall foliage. The frost we had the night before had sharpened the colors, one of October's gifts for those of us in the Midwest who were expecting winter soon.

That made the shock of the site even more horrible when I came over a hill. Heavy construction equipment had flattened the rich Iowa soil, gouging out a road to where trees were hacked down and lay uprooted in mud and muck. The contrast of the gorgeous trees near the paved road with the wholesale slaughter in front of me made my stomach churn.

This had once been thirty acres of bucolic hillside and trees with dirt paths through it worn by hooves and paws. The deer who populated those woods often found their way south to my farm and now they had nowhere to go with the land being torn up around them. Consequently, we saw more and more herds moving through our area, only to have them boxed in by the suburbs south of me, the Interstate to the east, and burgeoning construction on the west. This piece of forest had been their remaining refuge.

But now the area was denuded, like a bald man with a fringe surrounding his pate. It gave a nod to being environmentally friendly by retaining a semblance of the former beauty and keeping a windbreak of trees around what would eventually be yet another shopping center.

I inched my ancient truck forward on the packed earth, careful to avoid deep ruts and mucky spots where water pooled from the rain and sleet we had the day before. I spied the heavy equipment ahead of me, earth-moving machinery dwarfing the two men standing near it. I drove toward them at a snail's pace, heading for the fancy sports car parked next to the muddy pickup truck off to one side.

I recognized one of the men. It was the site boss or foreman. I wasn't sure of his title, but he was always there when I showed up so I assumed he had a leadership role. Mike Parsons was a stereotypical Construction Guy, a big burly man in Carhartt clothing with creased and tanned skin and a perpetually angry expression. He always seemed like he was in a hurry and Mother Nature was just jerking him around with her antics.

I didn't know the other man. He was shorter than Mike and he wore jeans and a sports coat over a black turtleneck sweater. When he turned to watch me drive in, I saw he had a thin, smooth face with dark eyes and silver hair that was curly but short around his face and ears. His hands were jammed into his pants pockets, his jacket pushed back. Unlike Mike, he didn't appear to have a beer gut. In fact, he looked like a model with his stylish clothes, unmuddied boots, and the cool, assessing way he watched me while I parked the truck.

I'm accustomed to surprise when people see me. The way his eyes widened and his head tilted told me his reaction. First of all, I'm short, barely five feet tall. Secondly, I'm part-Asian thanks to my Japanese grandmother, and my facial features reflect it. Third, I have long, thick wavy dark hair with an overlay of gray that makes it shimmer.

Most people saw Small and Pretty. After they got to know me, they amended the description to Small, Pretty, and Takes No Prisoners.

I slid out of the truck and the breeze met me from the top of the hill. I'd released my hair from the confining braid I used at work and now it blew around my face. I pulled an elastic band from my jeans pocket and dug my hands into my hair, dragging it into a ponytail. Then I straightened my denim coat over my flannel shirt while I considered the morass of mud in front of me.

The site was a mess, torn up with puddles God knows how deep. Boards were laid down to make a semblance of a walkway, but it was iffy. The boards slid around on the muck, making it more like a tightrope than a walkway. I was only a few yards away from the men, who stood on some kind of platform. I sucked in a deep breath and headed to them, keeping my attention on my footing. Luckily, I'd worn my barn boots, an ancient pair of cowboy boots so well-worn another layer of mud wouldn't hurt them. I hopped from one plank to another until I was a few feet from the two men, who had turned to watch me wend my way on the maze of planking.

"What the hell are you doing?" I demanded as soon as my footing didn't demand all my attention. "You're not supposed to have heavy equipment in here until after the study is reviewed."

"Aw, shit," Parsons muttered. "It's her."

"Yeah, shit, it's me." I maneuvered my way toward them, slipping once and almost losing my balance. The man with Parsons made a move to help me. I waved him away and finally got to where they stood on a wooden platform. It was an island in the sea of mud around us. "You're breaking the law."

"You have no right to be here." Parsons flung out an arm, pointing to my truck. "Get that piece of junk off this property. You're trespassing."

"It's not junk. It's a well-cared-for antique. And I have as much right to be here as you do." The breeze was stronger here, bringing with it an odor of muck and diesel fuel along with cold air and moisture. "In fact, I have more right to be here, asshole. This used to be my land."

"Used to be," Parsons sneered. "And it wasn't yours. It was your husband's mother's land."

"Listen, you know as well as I do this land was sold under false pretenses. If it wasn't for—"

"Actually, the city requested we move in to stabilize the site." The stranger regarded me with calm, cool brown eyes, his gaze flickering over me in one quick up-down motion. He had an odd voice, low and husky, sort of whispery, like he had a cold or a sore throat.

"Who are you?" I swung my attention to him, prepared to do battle with yet another macho construction dude. When I focused on his face, though, I saw intelligence and perhaps respect. Or maybe it was only wariness.

He held out his hand. "Aden Kingsley. My family's company is working with the city and the people who own the land to develop this property."

I ignored his gesture of friendship. "Was it your father who made a presentation at a community information meeting several years ago? He made it clear what his plans were. He wants to clear-cut this land, bulldoze it down, and put in another Big Box Farm Store." I surrounded those last four words with air quotes.

"What's so wrong with that?" Parsons snarled.

"We don't need a damn store here. There's one twelve miles away. It's easy to get to if people would get off their lazy asses and go there. Plus, we have a perfectly good hardware store in town. We don't need a store that's thousands of feet big and a parking lot with a car wash and gas station and—"

"I'm sorry. I don't believe we've met." Kingsley held out his hand again.

I regarded it and him suspiciously, but he met my gaze without blinking. "I'm Ashley Schone." I took his hand and gave it a brief squeeze.

He had other ideas, though. He held on to my hand, staring into my eyes before releasing it and saying, "I take it you live near here?"

"I run F.T.E." I gestured at the south end of the site. "Past the road and downstream from here. Our farm is there." When I gestured I noticed a knot of men standing not far away, watching our conversation. When I glared at them, they made a show of working, lifting boards and shuffling around the equipment parked there.

"F.T.E.?"

"Fairy Tale Endings. It's a wildlife rehabilitation clinic."

"Yeah, she takes in beat-up coons and releases them. They're trash rats. Waste of time." Parsons shook his head. "Waste of money, too."

"We don't only take in raccoons. We currently have two foxes, four squirrels, a rabbit, a possum—" I stopped. These men didn't care about injured wildlife. Why argue with them? "Needless to say, we're busy because of the destruction that's been going on in this area, what with the Interstate construction project, a new subdivision, and this." I flung out an arm. "This monstrosity."

Kingsley looked as though he agreed. "This is an up-and-coming part of the metro area, Ms. Schone. Dasdorf is close to Iowa City and the university. Once the new Interstate exit gets finished, it'll be a natural stopping place for people on their way to and from the university. It's a perfect location for more retail development."

He was repeating the time-worn phrases I'd heard from people who favored this so-called Metro Boom. "You know what else comes with retail development? Traffic congestion, pollution, wildlife injuries, and tax increases."

"That's part of progress." His patronizing smile fueled my anger. "Although I'm sure it's caused an increase in your business." He made it sound like that was a good thing.

"I run a charity operation." I leaned forward, glaring up at his face. "I rely on donations and grants. My patients don't have the means to pay. So don't give me any crap about benefiting from the turmoil. Have you ever been in town? I'll bet you haven't. I'll bet you haven't even seen how nice it is. North of the highway where the houses are, the east-west streets are named for birds and the north-south streets are named after flowers. There's one stoplight in town and it turns off at six at night. It's a little bit of peace and quiet in the middle of the university hustle-bustle."

"I know. I live at the corner of Nightingale and Lilac."

I was momentarily speechless. So this was the person who bought the old house and was renovating it. The project was the talk of the town at the coffee shop and gas station. Whoever owned it, apparently this guy, was restoring it to its Craftsman glory. The guys at the lumber yard were full of tales of oak woodwork, stained glass, and Frank Lloyd Wright touches.

"So you know what I'm talking about." I gestured around me, almost falling off the precarious platform that was our sanctuary amongst the mud. "We don't need this. We don't need your father coming in here and telling us what to do."

"Several people did want him to come in and tell them what was possible." Kingsley's tone was neutral, calm, and reasonable, which pissed me off even more. What an arrogant, over-confident asshole. "That's why he was asked to submit a bid for development of this property." His gaze swept over the barren earth and the chopped-up trees. "But my father is no longer running the company."

"Seriously? I had the impression he loved his job and would never give it up."

"Loved it?" Kingsley shook his head. "My father was obsessed with success."

"Why did he give up control?"

"He died."

The flat statement caught me by surprise, and I made no pretense of hiding it. "I didn't read anything about it."

"We haven't advertised it widely. My mother tried to run the company, but it was too much for her. She and the shareholders asked me to step in and reassure our partners the company will continue on sound footing." He said it without inflection or passion, like a repeated mantra.

"What do you know about the company? I mean, did you work in the office or something?" I gave him an up-down look, like he had done for me. He appeared to be one of those front-office types, with his manicured hands and shiny new work boots.

"I have experience in managing difficult projects." He said it absently, his gaze fixed on the landscape around us.

"Well, I won't say I'm sorry about his death, but I know it can be tough to lose someone you love, so you have my sympathy." I tried to say it with sincerity, but I don't think I succeeded.

"That's one of the rudest things I've ever heard anyone say," Parsons muttered.

"I won't sling bullshit about how I'm sorry for the loss. That old man made my life miserable for the last twenty years." I wrinkled my nose, remembering the times I faced down Kingsley Senior, either in his office, in court, or here on the job site. "I sometimes thought he enjoyed making my life miserable."

"Oh, I doubt he thought much about it," Kingsley murmured. "My father didn't concern himself with other people when he was working on a project. People were minor inconveniences who occasionally got in his way."

"And you'll concern yourself?" Now I know I sounded skeptical, but I didn't care. I had a faint glimmer of hope. Maybe this guy might be more amenable to working out a compromise. Maybe I could find a loophole big enough to salvage something.

His next words dashed any hope. "That's why I'm here. To discuss this property with Mara Colby and Emily Blake, who I believe are the owners of record for this parcel."

"The evil stepsisters," I muttered. There went any chance I had for a reasonable compromise. This guy would be putty in Mara's hands. She loved to toy with men.

He turned his attention to me. "Are you related to them?" He studied my slightly upturned eyes, probably comparing me to their polished WASP prettiness.

"They're my sisters-in-law. My husband's

stepsisters."

Parsons bobbed his head. "This is the crazy no-chemical lady I was telling you about. She's the one who's filed the petitions to get construction stopped."

"As I have said, ad infinitum, I am not opposed to chemical use." I kept my tone calm and non-confrontational, but it was tough. "I am opposed to the widescale use of herbicides in order to accomplish something that can be done as effectively with less chemical use."

"Like what we're doing here," Parsons said. "Clearing the land without using chemicals."

"Bullshit," I retorted. "You are using chemicals. I know you are because I live downwind of this site and some of my plants and crops are suffering."

"You have no proof that's coming from us." Parsons took a step toward me. It took all of my resolve not to move. Well, resolve and common sense lest I step into the mud.

"Does your husband share your feelings about his family?" Kingsley asked.

"He did share my feelings."

"Did?"

"He died twenty years ago. Of herbicide poisoning, from the same kind of chemicals used on this site." I was mildly gratified by the look of astonishment on Kingsley's handsome face.

"There's no proof of that," Parsons sputtered. "You're spreading lies now."

"Bullshit I'm spreading lies." I longed to take a swing at him, but my balance was precarious and I knew I didn't dare. I turned my peevishness on Kingsley. "You don't know the half of what your damn company has done to try to drive us off this land."

"You're right. I don't know."

Kingsley's calm voice soothed my anger and common sense took over. "I don't blame you. You weren't around when it happened."

"That's good to know. Thank you." When he saw me getting ready to blast him with a reply, he said, "I mean that sincerely. I try to be open-minded about this company and what it has and hasn't done in the past. If you have a legitimate complaint, please tell me."

"I doubt your shareholders would support you in that." I edged past him and pointed at the construction equipment, which was moving to and fro, pushing down the earth. "You're not supposed to be doing any work."

"As I said earlier, the city managers asked that we try to stabilize the site. The rains have caused runoff." Kingsley scowled at Parsons. "We moved too quickly to clear the trees. We should have waited until after a hard frost."

"If we waited until after hard frost, it would have taken twice as long," Parsons shot back. "Who knew it would rain so much this fall?"

I belatedly realized I had stepped into the middle of an argument between the two men. Here was Office Boy Kingsley, coming out to the field to berate Construction Guy Parsons about the work he did. Parsons looked like he'd like nothing better than to pick up Kingsley and toss him into the nearest mud hole. He was bigger than Kingsley and could probably do it easily.

But something about the way Kingsley stood, his gaze fixed on Parsons, made me wonder if the smaller man might not have a trick or two up his sleeve. He reminded me of my father-in-law, Frank Goddard.

People underestimated Frank, too, because Frank was old now and somewhat stooped. But there was power in Frank's grip and cagey intelligence in the way he managed the animals we worked with. Kingsley had the same kind of craftiness about him that told me he could handle himself in a fight.

"Any idiot would know it was going to rain," I said. "We've had a screwed-up growing season this year. The long-term forecast from the Extension Service said we'd have a wet harvest. Why didn't you bother to check with them?"

"Nobody can predict the weather that far in advance." Parsons dismissed the combined knowledge of university-trained agronomists with a wave of his hand.

"They're pretty good at evaluating monthly trends. They were saying harvest this year would be messed up. I sent you those reports in July and August." I kept my eyes fixed on Parsons, daring him to deny it. "If you'd waited a few weeks to clear-cut the land, we wouldn't have a sea of mud moving toward the sewer system, which hasn't been upgraded to handle the runoff from your damn parking lots and store, much less able to handle cleared acreage like this." I tossed my hands in the air and the platform under our feet shifted.

Parsons swayed and struggled to stay on his feet, but Kingsley kept his balance like a cat riding a skateboard. I staggered, nearly tipping off our island. Kingsley put a hand under my arm, and I shook him off. He shied away from me, probably afraid I'd hit him.

"We'll do our best to mitigate the problems," he said. "We'll put down straw for now and move the chippers in so we can spread the mulch faster."

"Mulch," I muttered. "Grinding up perfectly good trees."

"We'll do what we can to keep the area stable until the court decides how we can proceed." Kingsley moved to the edge of the platform. "I'll be back later this afternoon to see how much progress we've made."

"We won't make any progress today. It'll take all day to get the chippers in place." Parsons pulled a grimy rag from his back pocket and wiped his hands with it, shooting Kingsley's crisp jeans and sports coat a disdainful look. I could almost see the thought bubble above his head. *Office jerk comes in here and doesn't know shit about real work.*

"I'll check in with the crew before I leave for the home office. If they start at the road, we should make progress quickly because that part of the site is already compacted. Ms. Schone, I'd appreciate it if you would share those extension reports with me." Kingsley pulled a leather business card case from his inside coat pocket and handed me a card. "Would you email them to me? I want to get a better sense of what might be coming our way."

I studied the card. The Kingsley logo—a crown jauntily perched on a bulldozer—was in bright red next to his name and contact information. "I'm curious. Why did you move to Dasdorf? It's just a pokey little town. Why not move to Iowa City? That seems like more your speed. It's a happening place."

"Really? I doubt if you know my speed."

I eyed the shiny blue sports car. It was like a sleek predator hemmed in by two stodgy old workhorses. "You're wearing a Harris tweed sports coat not off the rack, you drive a BMW sedan that costs at least fifty-thousand, and your Timberland boots don't have a scratch on them. I can guess at your speed."

He smiled slowly, the tanned skin around his brown eyes crinkling into little fan lines. "Maybe you can. Or maybe not. I meant what I said earlier. If you have a complaint, I'd like to hear about it. I've been out of touch with the business for several years. I'm only now getting caught up on the history."

"A lot of dirty tricks have been done to get this land and get this project driven through."

"That's crap and you know it," Parsons said. "This land was purchased fair and square. We can do what we want with it."

"That's not exactly true." Kingsley put his business card case back in his pocket. "We have to answer to the city, the county, and the state. As I understand it, there is still a question about what project will be designated for this land."

Parsons waved his hand. "That's crap. She filed an injunction to put things on hold, but it won't win in court. Everybody knows this corner will be a shopping center."

Kingsley stepped off the platform, balancing easily on the makeshift sidewalk of boards. "I don't count any battle won until it's fought. I'll be in touch later today about the progress with the chippers. It was a pleasure making your acquaintance, Ms. Schone."

I tried to follow him, but Parsons made a grab for my arm. "You're messing around where you don't belong," he hissed in a low voice.

I dodged away. "You don't scare me. I've taken all the crap I'm taking from you and your bully boys. You leave me alone or the next time somebody comes by my house at midnight with firecrackers, I'll call the cops.

I'm coming out with my shotgun and scaring you for a change."

"What's that?" Kingsley paused, balanced on the board leading to our cars.

"You heard me. Your construction crew is trying to scare us." I glared at Parsons, whose face was mottled red with anger. "The last few nights somebody's come on our lane and tossed out cherry bombs, scaring the hell out of me and the animals we've got in recovery. The next time it happens, I'll be ready."

"Ms. Schone, I can assure you, if my crew is involved in that, I'll see to it they're handled."

"Yeah, right," Parsons muttered. "You and who else?"

Kingsley's gaze shifted from me to Parsons. He stared at the foreman for a long moment before resuming his balancing act toward his car. I started after him, but Parsons pushed by me, striding off the platform and making it shift so badly I lost my footing. I managed to stay upright but had to flap my arms to do so. I stretched out a foot toward the wooden walkway. Just as I did, Parsons pushed it away so I overbalanced and slid off the platform, my left foot slipping into the mud.

The men standing near the equipment not far away laughed. I flapped my arms, struggling to stay somewhat upright and not go face-first into the goo around me. I glimpsed them watching while I twisted and turned. "Damn it," I snarled. I tried to pull my boot away from the muck, but instead my foot slipped out of the boot. I was left standing on one foot, my Sock Monkeyed foot held above the mud, the red heel a bright splash of color against the shit-colored brown muck.

Parsons looked over his shoulder at me and grinned.

"Nice socks." The men nearby laughed even louder. Parsons moved to his truck, parked next to Kingsley's sedan.

I didn't stop to think about it. I stepped back to get both feet on the platform and bent over to pull off my other boot. I scooped it through the mud and threw it at Parsons as hard as I could.

Kingsley turned when the boot hit the rear of Parsons' pickup. Mud splattered the side of his pristine blue car, leaving a big glob of mud on the rear fender.

"Hey! You can't do that!" I thought Parsons might come after me, but common sense got the better of him and he ducked into his truck. I was already stomping off, the cold mud soaking into my socks when I made my way along the boards to my truck, goo squelching between my toes.

I passed Kingsley, who stood next to his car with my boot in his hand. "You want this back?" He held it up.

I ignored him. I got to my truck, slammed open the door, and pulled myself up by the overhead handle. My feet were so cold it was like driving with frozen stumps. I managed to back out, spinning my tires for good measure and splattering Kingsley's car and Parsons'. Kingsley wasn't in sight, so I assumed he got into his car before the mud came his way.

I fishtailed my way off the job site, praying I wouldn't get stuck. God was watching out for me because I managed to get to the road after bottoming out once. I put the heat on full blast on my feet, but the poor truck was elderly. All that came out was a feeble trickle to warm my petrified tootsies. I clung to the steering wheel, shaking from cold and anger and pissed off that I'd lost a good pair of boots. Well, not a good pair, but at least a usable pair. Shit. I had backup boots, of course, but those boots still had another year in 'em.

Oh, well. I finally felt warmth again when the heater kicked in. At least Kingsley would try to do something about the sea of mud and grime, even if it meant he'd chop up a few acres of trees to do it. I had experience with muddy fields. I doubted they'd get enough mulch from those downed trees to stabilize the land, especially since we were due for more rain in a day or two.

It wasn't my problem. I could report it to the city engineer, but if he'd already talked to Kingsley, they knew about the mess. I'd continue to take pictures of the crap coming downstream to my property, documenting the problems the stupid construction site was causing. Okay. I had a plan. I began to settle down, anger seeping away.

I viewed my mental DIN-DIL list (Do It Now or Do It Later). On the DIN was re-test the well and make sure the water was okay. Frank had tested it this morning, but sometimes Frank got confused about the results. Frank was getting confused more often lately. That was at the top of my DIN list. I had to try to get him to see a doctor to make sure it wasn't just forgetfulness on the part of an eighty-two-year-old man.

After the death of his second wife, mother of the evil stepsisters, Frank built a tiny house next to the farmhouse I once shared with his son. Between the two of us we were able to keep FTE a going concern, but there were a few years where we only scraped by. I was worried about Frank not only because I loved him but because he was an invaluable part of FTE. If I lost him, I'd lose FTE. I couldn't handle the work on my own.

First things first. Get him to a doctor and make sure

there wasn't anything serious to worry about. I realized if I could put my mind at ease about Frank, some other worries would dissipate.

I was so caught up in my thoughts I was driving on autopilot. It wasn't until I got to the intersection I noticed the gray SUV behind me, tailgating so close I saw the steam coming off the engine. I slowed for the four-way stop coming up, spying a car to my right that didn't appear to be concerned about traffic.

I was at my stop sign when the SUV behind me laid on the horn, sounding a blast so loud I automatically swerved, narrowly missing the stop sign and the car that braked and skidded into the intersection. My head slammed back into my seat rest and for a minute, all I saw was stars.

Chapter Two

When my vision cleared, the stop sign swam into view. My front bumper had apparently nudged it because the sign seemed tipsy. Or maybe it was me that was tipsy.

I started to get out but the SUV had pulled up next to me on the driver's side, and I didn't have enough room. I peered groggily at the vehicle and that's when I saw Mara Colby, elder of the two stepsisters-from-hell. She waved merrily at me and the window on her passenger side rolled down.

"Are you okay, Ash?" she called. "I've been trying to get your attention for the last quarter-mile. You were daydreaming."

I was agonizing about your damn stepfather, I almost yelled. "I'm fine," I said. "Only bruised." I touched my forehead and winced.

"We need to talk. Meet me at Kathy's Kafe." Without so much as a *sorry I scared the bejesus out of you*, she drove off, pausing momentarily at the stop sign before making a left turn and heading for town.

I considered ignoring her preemptive summoning, but I knew if I did she'd show up at the farm and Frank would get upset. When Frank got upset, the animals got upset and nobody got any rest. I went left on the county road. Mara was already far ahead of me, her pricy SUV gobbling up the road like Ms. Pac Man.

I followed at a more leisurely pace, praying my feet

would dry enough to slip them into my rubber boots stowed in the truck bed in my toolbox. Those were my Last-Ditch Boots, used only if I was stuck someplace. They were patched with duct tape and a size too big, but at least they were usable and might keep my feet somewhat protected.

As I expected, when we got close to town Mara turned onto busy Highway 6, which bisected Dasdorf east-and-west. I preferred driving in on the old Creek Road, which brought me to the downtown district south of Highway 6 via a tree-lined, winding street. It took longer, but it was a prettier drive.

I glimpsed Mara leaving her dark gray SUV when I approached the shopping district, a three-block-by-three-block square south of the highway. Most of the residences in town were north of the highway, although a couple of new subdivisions were being planned south of the highway and town. I parked at the corner of First Avenue and Main Street, reaching back through the truck's port window to find my rubber boots. I dragged them on, wincing when my cold feet touched the cold rubber.

I hopped out of the truck and headed for Kathy's, the only coffee shop on Main Street unless you counted the four pots brewing at the Gas-and-Go station down the street. The café was warm and smelled of pumpkin spice when I entered. It was an odor I found sickeningly sweet, but which was redolent at this time of year. Kathy's was a tiny shop with only twelve tables. The lunch crowd was gone, and the store closed at four on Saturday, so it had a postprandial feeling.

Mara was at the counter, undoubtedly buying a high-priced coffee drink that required the barista to have a

PhD in mixology to make. That was Mara's style: order something amazingly complicated and criticize how it was done.

I got in line and watched my stepsister-in-law while she ordered and paid for her beverage. Mara was Chic with a capital C, her short black hair artfully fluffed, her black leather coat collar tugged up against her flawless complexion. I had once seen the array of beauty products on Mara's vanity and blanched at the sight, recognizing one jar of potion that would have fed my entire animal hospital for a month. I bought the cheapest cruelty-free over-the-counter beauty products with the fatalistic certainty that genetics trumped cost.

At least I hoped it did.

Mara was surely getting her money's worth. She had sculpted cheekbones, big dark eyes, and full lips which I suspect were artificially plumped. She was such a contrast to her younger sister, Emily, who was outdoorsy, rough, and more Annie Oakley than Angelina Jolie. Both had plenty of money, or so it seemed. Mara got hers through her divorces and Emily from her business sense.

I reached the front of the queue and ordered a coffee with room for cream, joining Mara at the far end of the counter to await my beverage. "Honestly, I don't know why it takes them so long," Mara grumbled. "It's only a venti caramel frappe with extra drizzle and light nutmeg powder with an extra shot and dark chocolate curls. How hard is that?"

"I have no idea. I don't even know what most of it is. You're speaking in a foreign language to me." I took the coffee cup the clerk handed to me and moved past Mara to get to the cream and sugar bar. "What did you want to talk about?"

Mara took the drink from the barista and joined me. "Look at this. It's not right."

I eyed her drink, which had a layer of white frothy stuff overlaid by swirling lines and chocolate sprinkles. "Seems okay to me."

"Like you would know. I suppose I shouldn't expect quality service in a town like Dasdorf." She headed for a small table set against the windows facing the street. I trailed after her, my rubber boots sticking to the flooring and making me feel like I was back on the raft in the sea of mud at the job site.

"What are you doing in town?" I asked, plopping down across from her.

"Emily and I had a meeting with Aden Kingsley about the land." She tapped the table with one bright red fingernail. "He's an attractive man, don't you think?"

"How would I know?" I sipped my coffee, my gaze straying to the world outside. I glimpsed the sign for Herold's Home Store and made a mental note to get another water testing kit.

"You were at the job site, and Aden mentioned he was going there this afternoon. So I assumed you and he talked." Mara sipped her coffee, her gaze fixed on me.

"Yeah. I saw him there."

"He's handsome."

"That's your hormones talking." Mara was my age, fifty-five. I knew all about hormonal uproar.

Her lips pursed, giving her a pinched appearance, not the expression she wanted. "My hormones are fine, thank you."

"We're getting older. It's a fact of life. I personally am welcoming menopause." I sipped my coffee. "The hot flashes sure keep me on my toes."

"Speak for yourself," she snapped.

I smiled through my coffee steam. I loved getting up in Mara's face about her age. I know it stuck in her craw that I still had great skin and hair, more thanks to my parentage than to any beauty ritual on my part. She had to rely on regular visits to the spa to achieve the same rosy glow I had plus her hair was brittle and overworked. Mine, which had never felt a curling iron or chemical, was still bouncy and shiny.

"It's the little things in life that make me happy," I murmured.

"What's that supposed to mean?"

I shrugged. "Nothing. Anyway, Kingsley is probably married."

"He isn't. He's divorced. He's been divorced for fifteen years."

"How do you know?"

Mara simpered. "I asked his secretary. He's a retired police officer."

"What?" I nearly dropped my coffee cup. "I thought he was a front-office minion."

"He was with the St. Louis police department for more than thirty years. He retired. A couple of years later he was asked to step in and lead the company."

"You got so much detail from his secretary?"

"Among other people. I like to know who I'm working with."

"Is Kingsley what you wanted to talk about?" I wouldn't put it past Mara to stalk me on the assumption I was trying to poach a guy she had her eye on. The idea was ludicrous. I didn't have time or the inclination for man-poaching.

"Of course not. We need to discuss the construction project."

I sighed. "Mara, we've had this talk a dozen times. I won't change my mind. It was stated specifically in Bryan's will that the land he gave me be used for an environmentally responsible purpose. What you're doing with it is exactly the opposite."

"But the land is ours. We can do what we want with it. No one disputes that."

I grabbed a napkin and sketched a big square on it with a pencil stub I dug from my denim coat pocket. "Don't play stupid, Mara. Frank inherited a huge parcel of land from his first wife." I drew a horizontal rectangle at the far end of square. "He gave his second wife, your mother, the part where the construction site is." I drew another, bigger horizontal rectangle adjacent to the first one. "He still owns the part where the farm sits. It was given to Bryan in Frank's will, and he's told me when he dies, I'll inherit that."

I drew a line down the side of the square sharing the border of the first two rectangles. "There was also this odd rectangle abutting the road. He gave it to Bryan separately, as a land deed. Before Bryan died, he deeded it to me, and I refuse to allow any construction there. And unless I allow access, you cannot have a huge shopping center north of here because I will not cede rights to create roads and sewer lines there." I drew a big X through the vertical rectangle. "Never."

Mara studied my crude drawing as though she'd never seen it before. I knew damn well she had. We had examined far more precise drawings than mine and the result was always the same. "Never is a long time. And speaking of property inheritance, have you set up a trust fund in the event of your death?"

Mara's tone of voice chilled me despite the hot coffee in my hands. "What are you suggesting?"

"Nothing. It's just that life is uncertain. You're the owner of an extremely valuable piece of property. It makes sense you'd want to protect it in the event of your death."

I examined her through the steam. Her eyes, flawlessly outlined with dark blue color, didn't meet mine. "Yes, as a matter of fact, I set up a document for the treatment of the land in the event of my death. I had a lawyer in Des Moines draw it up."

"Des Moines?"

"I know how gossip flies around Dasdorf. I decided it might be best to go out of town to have it done. I have someone acting on my behalf in the event of my death or disability. Someone in addition to Frank, I mean."

"Frank is getting along in years," Mara said. "That's a wise idea. How is he doing?"

"He's your stepfather. Why don't you ask him yourself?"

Mara sipped her coffee, foam dimming the shine on her perfect lips. "As you well know, Frank and I aren't on good terms and haven't been for years. He never acted as a father to Emily or me, so I see no need to act as a daughter to him."

"Maybe the reason he didn't act as a father was because you made it clear you wouldn't pay any attention to him if he did. You weren't exactly a doting daughter."

She smiled sympathetically at me. "I'm sure your view of the circumstances is different than mine or my sister's. Our relationship to Frank is irrelevant. That's in the past. What we need to think about is the future and what's best for this town."

I sighed. "I've heard it from Kingsley, so you don't have to repeat the marketing bullshit to me."

She drew back. For an instant, I was sure she was surprised. "You discussed plans for the site with Aden Kingsley?"

"Not in detail, no. But he parroted back at me the usual crap about retail development being a boon for the town, yada yada yada." I made puppet motions with my hand.

"Yes, I'm sure he's aware of the benefits of retail development." She tapped the table again but this time it was a thoughtful sort of tapping, not impatient like before. "It's interesting he discussed it with you."

"It wasn't interesting to me. In fact, it was boring." I slid back my chair. "Well, it's been fun talking like this, but I have chores to get through. I hope I've put your mind at ease. It won't do any good to kill me because you won't get your hands on the land even if you knock me off." I stood, bumping into one of the clerks, who was clearing off the table next to me. Her shocked expression told me she heard my words. "You're my witness," I joked. "If I die an untimely death, you'll know who to blame."

"Don't be stupid, Ash." Mara waved away my words with a wave of her hand. "I wouldn't do the deed myself. I wouldn't be caught if I hired someone to have you killed."

I laughed. "Yeah, you are devious, but I'm sure you wouldn't want to get your hands dirty. Give my regards to Emily." I jammed the lid on my coffee and headed for the door.

What a waste of time. I fumed while I got into the truck and trundled down the street to Herold's. I'd had the same conversation in a variety of settings and times with one or both of the stepsisters. They wouldn't get it through their thick skulls I wouldn't budge on selling the property. There was no way in hell any retail development would come in and use it for their access.

I parked at the side of the hardware store and went inside, the odor of lumber a welcome change from the cloying scent of pumpkin spice in the coffee shop. Harold Herold, third generation of that name, peeked out at me from the nuts-and-bolts aisle. His son, H2-4, did most of the administrative work, but Harold still liked to clerk now and again. He was a buddy of Frank's, also a widower. Like Frank, he was stoop-shouldered, gray-haired, and sharp as a tack. "Hey, Ash, how's it going? You getting ready for the party in a week?"

A guilty pang shot through me at the reminder. "You bet, H2-3," I called back. "Can't wait for it!"

"You folks have a solid presentation. You'll knock 'em dead. Anything I can help you with today?"

"I think I know where I'm going, but thanks anyway." I wended my way along the long narrow aisles of shelving stacked high with all kinds of helpful hardware gadgets. I'd shopped at Herold's most of my life and knew the store better than many of the clerks.

I scanned the shelving, using that to distract me from the panicked thoughts stewing in the back of my mind. The "Harvesting the Future" Charity fundraiser, an annual event, was coming up a week from today. I was responsible for attending and shilling for donations to FTE by doing a presentation demonstrating what we did.

The problem was I didn't have a costume yet, I had

no idea what kind of dog-and-pony show I'd put on, and I didn't have a clue about how to accomplish either task. I was praying a couple of my good friends were working on it for me as they'd promised they'd do. I needed to call them and light a fire. The event was a week away. If I had to practice anything, I needed to start doing so.

I found the water testing kits where I remembered. The official test, which I sent to a state laboratory, cost a hundred dollars and was something we only did once a year. This home test kit would be acceptable for now, especially because I tested last month and things seemed fine then.

I wandered toward the back, where lumber and fencing were stored in the big building attached to the storefront. I was always looking for cast-off pieces of wood and wire to use on the cages at the farm. Harold was good about letting me dig through his scrap bins. He also kept his wood shavings for me to use as bedding for the critters, bagging them up for me in old gunny sacks in the back.

I opened the door leading into the blocked-off space where lumber was tossed, willy-nilly. I spied scrollwork trim pieces which might serve as reinforcement on a cage and some other oddments I could use. I loaded up my arms and backed out just as Harold came into the back room.

"…here somewhere," he said. "It came in the other day, and I set it aside special."

"I'm taking some stuff, Harold." I turned awkwardly with the oddly sized wood scraps teetering in my grip. I almost whacked into Aden Kingsley, who had followed Harold into the back room. "Look out!" I wheeled, the lumber shifting and sliding.

Kingsley caught the bigger pieces before they upended and hit me in the face. "Let me help." He tugged on the rest of the load in my arms.

"I've got it. Drop those off to the side, I'll come back for 'em." I staggered toward the exterior door.

"I can help," he said in his hoarse, low voice.

"Yeah, I'm sure you can, but I don't need it." I nudged the door open and maneuvered outside, staggering to my truck. I fumbled with the tailgate, the wood shifting in my arms.

"It won't kill you to take help." Kingsley popped open the tailgate and tossed in the wood I'd left in the store.

"I'm used to doing for myself." I let the load in my arms tumble into the bed. "Thanks." I headed back to the store.

"Hey, Ash, I got a bale of chicken netting here somebody ordered but decided they didn't want. They said I could donate it to you." Harold tugged out the cylindrical roll of mesh metal netting. "Four-foot tall by hundred-fifty-foot. You want it?"

"I'm sure I can use it." I grabbed the bale and slung it onto my shoulder. "Nice and lightweight, too."

"Here's the wainscoting plate rail you ordered," Harold said to Kingsley, who watched us from the doorway. "It came in the other day."

Kingsley joined Harold at a lumber rack where special cuts of lumber were neatly stacked. He pulled out a beautifully detailed trim piece with a maze-like design worked into the wood. "This will sit on top of the wainscoting in the dining room," Kingsley murmured. "I found a set of paintings I want to display on it."

"That's a lovely piece of wood. I heard you're

restoring the house. It's nice to see the old places getting a facelift instead of a teardown."

"I've never lived in a new house," Harold commented. "I always wondered what it would be like to live someplace that's brand new."

"It has its benefits," Kingsley said. "But there's something nice about living somewhere with history." He glanced at me. "I heard you talking back in the store. Are you involved in the Harvest Party?"

"Ash has one of the businesses being highlighted," Harold said. "She's one of the Heavys."

"I don't understand that." Kingsley sighted down the trim piece, checking it for warpage.

"Every year, a local charity is tapped to come to the Harvesting the Future Charity Costume Ball and showcase their work. The categories are Homeless, Environment, Animal, Vets, Youth, and Seniors." Harold ticked off the names on his fingers. "See? H.E.A.V.Y.S. This year it's Ash's turn to get support for FTE."

"Do you alternate with other charities? Surely there aren't so many in this area."

"We were highlighted about eight years ago," I said, shifting the bale to sit more comfortably. "Us charity folks sort of take turns."

"Thanks for giving me the background. I was asked to serve on the judging committee, but I didn't get a lot of details." Aden smiled faintly. "I didn't realize it was such a major event. I'm having a pre-party at my house. Did you get my invitation?" He set down the piece of wood and lifted another one. "I assume the secretary in the office had a list of people to invite. I've been so busy I didn't check."

"Invitation? No, I didn't." I edged toward the door. The bale was getting heavy. "Frank brings in the mail. Maybe he put it aside."

"Frank?"

"My father-in-law. He lives at the farm with me."

"Pre-party?" Harold asked. "What's that?"

"It's for those charities being highlighted and the people representing them. It's in a week, on the Friday before the event. The judges will be there. It gives us a chance to chat with people in a more relaxed setting. And I wanted an excuse to show off what I'm doing at my house, too."

"You should go, Ash. Size up the competition." Harold grinned at me.

"What kind of party? Not a costume one, is it?" I couldn't come up with another costume on such short notice.

"No, just a casual get-together. Nothing formal. Cocktails and appetizers between five thirty and seven. Drop in any time."

"I'll have to check my schedule. Thanks for the invite."

"You should have gotten an invitation. Please let me know if you didn't." Kingsley picked up another piece of wood. "By the way, I have your boots in my car. Do you need them?" His eyes flickered to my rubber boots.

"You can toss 'em in the back of my truck. Thanks." I headed for the door.

"Why do you have Ash's boots?" I heard Harold ask behind me.

"It's a long story," Kingsley said, his voice thick with laughter.

I heaved the bale of wire into the truck, but my hair

got caught on the spikey edging. I ended up bent awkwardly stretched into the truck, trying to untangle myself without ripping out a big chunk of my ponytail.

"Here, let me help." I heard Kingsley behind me. My boots landed somewhere ahead of me in the truck bed then he clambered up on the tailgate and moved close to me where I was sprawled, half-in and half-out of the truck bed. "You're tangled pretty good. Hang on."

"I should know better than to handle netting without braiding my hair." I gritted my teeth when he tugged on a strand. "Seems like I'm always getting stuck." I glimpsed him nearby, his knees inches from my face and his body over mine. I caught a whiff of musky fragrance when his arms shifted. "Thanks for the help."

"Don't thank me yet. You're not undone. There." He leaned back to rest on his heels, peering down at me while I straightened up. "You're free."

I pulled my hair out of the ponytail since it was half-out anyway and dug my fingers in, pushing it back. "I might have put a big dent in my hair if you hadn't come along." I parted my hair and began loosely braiding it.

"That would be a pity. You have beautiful hair." He twisted to jump from the truck, landing next to me on the pavement.

"Thanks for the help and the invite to the party. I'll ask Frank if we got an invitation. Although it's possible somebody took it from the mailbox." I scowled, remembering other times mail had gone missing. "Probably those construction assholes again."

"That's a federal crime if they're messing with your mail. You need to report them."

"I don't have any proof who's doing it or setting off fireworks or calling at three in the morning and waking me up." I went to the truck cab and opened the door. "Maybe they'll get bored with trying to scare me and give up."

Kingsley went with me, watching me haul myself up into the seat by the strap. "I get the feeling you don't scare easily."

I laughed. "You can't handle wildlife and be scared. I'm cautious, but you can't let the critters know you're scared. If you do, you're in trouble."

"If you have disturbances tonight, I'd like to know about it. If any of our crews are involved, I want to be informed." He appeared serious about it.

"I'll give you a call." I tapped my shirt pocket. "I got your card, remember?"

His gaze rested on my pocket. And my breast. "Good. Call me if you need anything."

"Will do." I closed the door knowing damn well I wouldn't. He was just spewing the company line. I pulled out onto the street and peeked in the rear-view mirror. Kingsley watched me for a minute before going back into the lumber yard.

I told Frank about both encounters when I got to the farm. "And he's a retired cop." I watched Frank while he fed Pollyanna, the possum with the broken leg. We named our patients, not to claim them but to tell everybody apart. One possum pretty much looked like the next but naming them helped us keep them straight.

"Ex-cop? He might be useful to have around." Frank shook out pellets into the tin dish already holding a few strawberries, shards of carrots, and peas. Polly wobbled to him, waiting patiently until he set the pan down. As soon as he did, she picked up a strawberry and proceeded to nibble like you or I would eat an ear of corn, spinning it in her tiny paws.

"I doubt he'll be around much," I said. "He's working in the front office of Kingsley Construction. That kind of guy doesn't get his feet dirty."

"Sounds like he got 'em dirty today." Frank backed away from the stall and went to the ancient rocking chair, settling down and picking up his guitar. "I can't believe you tossed your boot at Parsons. Too bad you didn't knock him out. Maybe he'd drown in the mud."

"At least I got the boots back." I hefted the shopping bag I carried. "I got a bunch of syringes, some bandages, and the antibiotic we need. Plus food and supplements." I traded my skill as a vet tech with the local vets and animal hospitals for supplies we always needed.

"Was it bad?" His shrewd dark eyes were fixed on me.

"No worse than usual. No euthanasia cases, at least." I put the medication in the cooler and the rest of the supplies in the cupboard.

"That's a blessing." Frank rested the guitar on his knee and strummed a chord, his balding head hidden by the misshapen old knit hat he often wore. He had a worn and creased face, bushy white beard, and the kind of twinkling dark brown eyes I associated with Santa Claus.

He was also a gifted musician and often soothed ruffled fur and feathers with his folk songs. Frank had busked in New York City back in the day when folksingers were respected and got by on the money they managed to scrape up. That's how he met Bryan's mother, Grace, a musician and singer in a band at a nightclub. One thing led to another and before you knew it, they were traveling across the country, singing at clubs and living out of a minivan. When Bryan was born they decided to settle down on Grace's family farm in Iowa. They made a decent living through selling produce to farmer's markets, a few singing gigs, and a small inheritance Frank got from his parents.

Now Frank lived in a tiny house he insisted on building after Bryan died. "I won't stand in your way if you want to find love again," he said. "So you have your house, and I'll have mine. And we'll help each other when we need it if that's okay with you."

I watched him rock in the old chair, softly singing "Goodnight, Irene." Like Pete Seeger, one of his heroes, Frank was a "split tenor," singing somewhere between tenor and countertenor. His voice could soothe or incite anger, depending on whether he was singing a lullaby or a protest song.

I walked through the barn, checking our occupants, his gentle voice accompanying me. The two new possums were in the far stall, one that didn't have enough insulation. I'd have to work on that tomorrow but for tonight they were cozy in their donated blankets, tucked into an open-sided cardboard box giving them a feeling of safety. They wouldn't be with us long. They'd been poisoned, and the local vet I worked with had pumped their stomachs. They needed recovery time before I took them to the secluded spot in the southeast woodland portion of our property, near the stream.

I checked Rocky, the raccoon with the busted paw. He wobbled around, eyeing me balefully from the far end of his stall. Most of the animals tolerated us, but a few were hard to win over. I think they sensed we were trying to help and this was temporary. I liked to think that, at least. It made my job a bit easier.

Four baby squirrels were in their little nest in the

half stall, yawning and cuddling together. Their mother was killed by a car, and the nest was brought to us. After days and nights of syringe feeding every few hours, they were moving on to primate biscuits with fruits and veggies mixed in. So far, they were handling the diet well. I began introducing nesting materials in the hopes they would learn that essential part of survival training. We'd move them to the play cage soon where they'd learn to climb and jump. It would be weeks before we dared try to introduce them back to the wild.

I peeked in on our other occupants: two juvenile woodchucks recovering from shotgun pellets, an orphaned red fox kit, and a rabbit with a mangled front paw, caught in a trap. I wasn't sure what we'd do with her if the paw didn't heal at least somewhat. I couldn't release her if she couldn't run. Take it a day at a time, I reminded myself.

I joined Frank back at the sitting area at the end of the barn. "I thought I'd have leftover chili. Want to join me?"

Frank looked up from his guitar. "I had a big lunch. I'll hang out here for a time."

"Okay. Don't stay up all night again." I rested my hand on his bony shoulder and gave him an affectionate squeeze.

"Oh, we'll see."

I knew what that meant. He'd be out here in the early hours, checking on our patients.

I went to my house, the motion light outside Frank's tiny house lighting my way. I pushed through the windbreak of evergreens and the motion light at my garage kicked on. I paused by my truck and tossed my Last-Ditch Boots into the toolbox.

My barn boots were mud encrusted, so I left them in the truck bed. I'd clean them in the morning. I scampered to the house in my monkey sock feet, my porch light coming on to show me the rest of the way to my cozy little home. Four rooms downstairs, four rooms upstairs, and exactly what I needed.

I came in through the kitchen and shed my coat, then sorted through the mail I got from the box on the road. I had just put the chili in the microwave when the doorbell rang. I flicked on the outside porch light and saw a hunter in blaze orange. I sighed. I'd been through this more times than I could count. I opened the door and before he spoke, I said, "No. I won't let you hunt here."

His eager smile faded. "But there's deer trail all the way through here. I'm a licensed bow hunter. Don't you want—"

"No. My land is posted. Respect that."

"But I have the training." The guy kept an ingratiating expression on his face, but it was strained.

"I don't want any strangers hunting on my land. It's posted. If you hunt off my land and an injured deer comes here, I have to deal with it."

"No, not at all. I'll handle it."

"No, I'll handle it because I don't want any strangers on my land. Period."

"But I've seen a deer trail."

"No hunting. If you do, I'll call the sheriff." I closed the door firmly.

I listened to his footsteps stomp away, then I saw the shine of headlights swinging through my drive. I went back to the kitchen where my chili awaited me. I nuked it and sat at the kitchen table with the bowl of chili, a beer, and crackers.

The doorbell rang again. "Damn it." I jerked open the door. "Listen, I told you no hunting, and I mean no hunting."

Aden Kingsley stepped back. "I believe you."

Chapter Three

"Sorry. I thought you were a hunter. It's that time of year."

"I suppose it is. I saw deer on the road coming here." Kingsley had changed clothes and now wore faded denims, a heavy canvas jacket and a black plaid flannel shirt. "I saw your land was posted."

"I do allow some hunting. They're people I know, they're humane, and they know what they're doing." I wasn't sure why I was explaining myself to him and it peeved me. "I don't mind hunting. I mind having strangers around me with weapons."

"That makes sense. I hope you don't mind I stopped by. I'm still trying to get the lay of the land around here. I wanted to see how close you were to the construction site."

"The best time to see it is during the day," I pointed out. "When it's light."

"I also wanted to see how easy it would be to drive by your house and toss out a firecracker or two."

"Why?"

"Because if anybody associated with Kingsley Development is doing it I want to know. My crews don't do crap like that."

I glimpsed the motion light at Frank's house flicking on. Damn it. "We're fine. No need to worry about us." I longed to close the door in his face like I had with the hunter, but I knew it would be rude. Not that I cared, but the guy was one of the judges at the Saturday competition. I needed to stay on his good side, if he had one.

"Everything okay, Ash?" Frank strode into sight through the circle of light when the motion sensors kicked on at my garage.

"Yeah, no problems." I waited until Frank was nearer, then said, "This is Aden Kingsley. He's in charge of the development on Mara and Emily's land. Mr. Kingsley, this is Frank Goddard."

Frank sprang up the porch steps and stuck out his hand. "Well, it's good to know who the enemy is." He smiled when he said it but there was a shrewd expression in his rheumy old eyes.

"Please, call me Aden. I don't like to stand on formality." Kingsley shook Frank's hand. "Mr. Kingsley sounds like my father."

"God forbid," I muttered.

Frank frowned at me, but Kingsley ignored my comment. "I don't think we need to be enemies, Mr. Goddard. My company is in charge of the development. There is still a question about what type of structure will go there. It's possible the way the land is used might fit in with what you're doing here." Kingsley looked past Frank to the barn and outbuildings.

"Don't you think that's a little optimistic? Especially since you don't know what we do here." I crossed my arms and leaned in the doorway. His smooth-talking line of bullshit grated on my nerves, which were already frayed.

"I look forward to learning more about your work next weekend at the event."

"Next weekend?" Frank's gaze shifted between me and Kingsley. "Are you going to the party next Saturday?"

"He's one of the judges. Did we get an invitation from him to his house for next Friday? Supposedly they were sent out. All the charities at the party were invited and the judges. A chance to mix and mingle." I strove to keep my voice neutral, but inwardly I was groaning. I hated socializing and hated shilling for money, but it was essential. *It's just a few hours every few years,* I reminded myself. *Suck it up.*

"They were sent out," Kingsley said. "And I checked. One was sent to you."

"I put your mail on your desk. If it's not there, it never got here," Frank said.

"I wonder why someone would bother snatching an invitation to a party." I shook my head. "I'm glad I do my banking online. Otherwise, Lord knows what might get stolen from my mailbox."

"That reminds me," Frank said. "Our Internet is out. It's nothing to do with the solar panels because we still have electricity."

I blew out an angry sigh. "You think for what we pay we'd at least have somewhat reliable service. How long's it been out?"

"Just now. I was using my iPad to search for an alternative salve to use for Polly. I don't think she likes the one we're using. I remember reading about an herbal poultice. I wanted to doublecheck my notes, but I couldn't get online." Frank smiled apologetically at Kingsley. "I'm sorry, you probably didn't come out here to hear about our problems with technology. Is there something I can help you with?"

"He's worried guys on his crew might be the assholes who are tossing firecrackers at the house and scaring us," I said. "Let me check the WiFi. Maybe I need to reboot the router. Come in." I didn't wait to see if Kingsley followed or not. I went inside and down the hallway to the living room and picked up the TV remote. I got the "no signal" message.

"No TV, so no Internet. Doesn't matter. All we'd get is cooking shows and Christmas movies. You think they'd wait until Halloween was past to start inundating us with Santa. Oh, well. I guess we'll go old-school tonight."

"Can we use your phone as a hot thing?" Frank asked.

Aden shot me a quizzical look. I pulled down a book from the built-in shelves. "No, we can't use it as a hotspot. I'm getting low on data for the month. I think I read something in here about a salve. It worked for Opie and it might work for Polly."

"Opie?" Aden asked.

"A possum we helped once," Frank said. "Yeah, I remember something about warm poultices with sage. Check the herbal remedy book. I can't use your phone as a hot spot?"

Aden pulled out his phone. "Use mine. I have unlimited."

I regarded the shiny iPhone suspiciously. "Seriously?"

"Sure." Aden went to the pictures on the wall. "Is this you and your husband?"

I looked up from the bulky medical book I held. "Yeah."

"It seems like a hippy wedding." He studied the

picture of Bryan and me, barefoot and grinning in the back yard under the arbor.

"Nah. You want to see a hippy wedding, you should see my wedding picture with Grace." Frank went to the china cabinet, which was used to hold photographs and memorabilia, not china.

"Does it happen often? Losing your Internet and your TV?" Aden asked.

"They're connected. We can't get cable out here, so we have satellite Internet and TV. If the TV's out, the Internet's out. And no, it's been surprisingly reliable. Except during bad weather when the signal gets blocked. Usually it's fine."

"Where's your satellite dish?"

I lowered the book. "Why?"

"Let's check, shall we?"

"Why?"

Kingsley lifted one shoulder. "I'm a naturally suspicious person."

"That's right. You were a cop," Frank said, pulling a picture from the cabinet and joining Kingsley. "Here's me and Grace. Now that was hippy wedding."

Aden studied the photograph. I knew which one it was. Frank and Grace stood near their green VW minibus which was painted with New Age hieroglyphs and peace signs. Frank had a dark brown shaggy beard and wild, curly hair. Grace wore a loose, flowing skirt matching the blouse embroidered with flowers and symbols. Her blonde hair was long and tumbled down her back. They were young, carefree, and in love.

"How'd you know I was with the police?" Kingsley handed the picture back to Frank.

"Mara. She who knows all. If you live in a small

town, there are no secrets." Kingsley still held his phone. "Thanks for the offer of a hotspot, but I doubt you want to hang out here and provide Internet service for us."

He tucked the phone back in his shirt pocket. "Let's check your satellite dish. Maybe it's fixable."

The guy was like a bulldog. He got hold of an idea and wouldn't let go. "Sure. Come on." I went out of the living room, turning right and going through the back door. I paused to flip on the lights and to slip into a pair of red classic Crocs before stepping onto the back porch. "It's out here on the side of the porch. It's easy to adjust if we need to. At first they wanted to put it on the house roof, but I said no way."

"No boots?" Kingsley asked, glancing at my footwear. "Those ones you threw appeared well broken in."

"That's one word for it. They're ancient. But good boots cost money. I need to spend my money on more important things, like animal food and bedding and medicine." I went to the left, dodging porch furniture now wrapped in their cocoons for winter storage. "It's here, up on the roof of the porch."

A bright beam shone above my head. Frank brandished the flashlight he held. "Figured it might come in handy."

"Thanks." I led the way to the end of the porch and peered up. "There it is."

Kingsley moved past me and sat on the railing to swing out, his phone in hand. He shone it upward. "It's been moved." He gestured to me and I climbed up on the rail next to him. I clung to the roof post and leaned back.

"It should be pointing south. That's pointing east." I was surprised by my proximity to Kingsley. I was so close I saw the tiny little whiskers starting to sprout on his cheeks.

"Somebody messed with it." He wiggled the phone and I followed the beam, finally seeing the streak of brighter metal on the flat gray metal of the dish.

"I'll have to have the service guys come out and recalibrate it. Damn."

"I wonder if this is the problem." Frank had gone into the yard and he raised something. Kingsley moved the light to illuminate him.

Frank held an arrow.

"Those rat bastards." I pitched forward, catapulting off the railing. Kingsley made a grab for me. I caught his arm, pulling him with me before he teetered backwards. He landed with a thump next to me and for a second we were tangled up, arms around each other. I broke free and went to Frank, who was at the railing from the yard, watching us. "That damn hunter took a swipe at my dish."

Frank handed Kingsley the arrow. "That's a pricy piece of equipment. Those kinds of arrows cost ten, fifteen bucks each."

"And the hunter threw it away. It must be nice to have disposable income," I griped.

Kingsley examined the arrow. "Carbon shaft. What kind of gear did the hunter have?"

"Huh?"

"Did he have a quiver, a sight, an arm guard?"

I shrugged. "I don't know. He had a bow and something with a strap on his back. He didn't hang around long enough for me to interview him."

"Anybody can buy expensive equipment so it's hard to tell if he's experienced. It's pretty easy to take a potshot at a non-moving object, but it means he came into your yard to do it."

"I heard him leaving. I saw car lights out the kitchen window. It was a few minutes before you got here." I went to the mailbox fixed to the stair's newel post and pulled out the launcher pistol I kept there, to scare away skunks. "If I knew he was out here, I'd scream him."

"Scream him?"

"Scare cartridges," I explained. "They shoot 15mm scare cartridges." I tucked it back into the mailbox.

"That wouldn't be much good against an arrow." Kingsley stepped off the porch, his phone shining into the yard.

Frank joined him and added his flashlight to the illumination. "What has you worried?"

Kingsley stared into the darkness, his head swiveling back and forth. "This is an isolated spot."

"All farms are isolated," I snapped. He was starting to spook me. "It's the nature of the beast. There's big tracts of land and a house here and there."

"Not all farming has to be like that." He spoke absently, like he was talking out loud. "I've seen developments where farms are integrated into the community."

"Not in Iowa. This is the land of the industrial farmer with only a few small farms like us here and there."

"It's not so bad around here," Frank protested. "There's still family farms."

"They're getting fewer and fewer. It's too expensive."

Kingsley took one last look at the back yard then moved to the porch door. "You know, I'm surprised you don't have a big dog. A dog might keep the hunters away."

I stopped in midstep, a stab of grief shooting through me and leaving me gasping. I turned so he wouldn't see my tears.

"We had a dog," Frank said softly behind me. "He was poisoned a week ago."

"Oh, damn. I'm sorry."

"You didn't know," Frank said.

Someone touched my shoulder. I flinched and pulled away.

"I'm sorry," Kingsley said from close behind me.

"Yeah. So am I." I scrubbed my face before turning to face him. His eyes were soft with sympathy. "I reported it to the sheriff but, you know. They said it's just a dog."

Kingsley's face underwent an amazing transformation. It somehow tightened, and his mouth set into a grim line. He's a cop, I thought. That's what cops look like. "I've heard that before. Anytime we had a suspect who said it was just a dog, we knew that suspect would say the same thing about anyone who's vulnerable, like a kid or a woman or an elderly person. Those are the ones you have to be careful about."

I could almost see the memories swirling around him. I suppose he saw those kinds of horrors when he had a job like that.

"We'll get another dog," Frank said, going into the house. "We're dog people."

"Tell that to the two barn cats we have." I gestured and Kingsley went ahead of me.

He paused by the door to the dining room. "What's that?"

"This doubles as a nursery or operating room, depending on what we need." The dining room table was pushed against one wall and in its place was a large heavy-duty plastic table with drop cloths underneath. Small cages were off to one side, lined up against the wall. "I suppose my house does double duty."

"I thought you had a place where you cared for the wildlife that comes in." He followed Frank to the front of the house.

"I can't do surgery in a barn and not all animals can tolerate an outdoor environment if they're injured or just born."

"You do surgery?"

"I can, in a pinch. I'm a trained vet tech. I planned to do it as a retirement career. When I was working as a software programmer, I took classes on the side to get my degree. But Bryan died and a few years later, when I was laid off, I kind of fell into wildlife rehabilitation."

"How do you pay for it all?"

"Ash pays," Frank said. "It's costly."

This was one of Frank's sore points. He hated that he couldn't earn "real money" as he put it, to help with expenses. "I do volunteer work for several area vets," I explained. "In exchange they give me medication and other supplies. The vets volunteer to help me with surgery and exam work."

"How much do you work?"

"As much as I can. We need the help. I can always get shifts on the weekends and evenings."

"Evenings?"

"At the emergency clinics. Some vet offices also like to have a tech come in at least once a night to check on the animals boarding there. I'm working this weekend and part of each day next week. I think my next day off is a week from Sunday."

"The clinics like to have Ash work for them," Frank said. "She has a good touch with animals. She knows her stuff."

"That's a lot of shifts, plus taking care of the animals here." Kingsley took a look into my office, opposite the kitchen at the front of the house. "Not much time for anything else."

"There's a real need for the kind of work we do. It's in the report I put together for the judging committee."

"I know. I read it. But it's useful to see it in real life."

"Come out during the day," Frank said. "Most of our patients are sleeping now. They're usually nocturnal, but what with being injured, their schedules are kind of crazy."

"Thanks. I will. I plan to visit the charities up for the prize."

I snorted. "It's not actually a competition, you know. We have a chance to convince donors to give us money, but there's not a grand prize."

"Yes, there is," Frank said. "The winner gets to lead off the dancing."

I grinned. "Not much of a prize." I opened the front door.

"Do you have your costume ready?" Kingsley lingered, his hand on the screen door handle.

"Frank is doing it for me." I glanced at Frank but sighed when I saw his confused look. "Frank, you promised. You said you'd work with Mark and Columbine to get me a costume."

Frank's eyes widened then he nodded vigorously. "Yeah, yeah, we did. We got the perfect costume.

Columbine is putting a few touches on it. That's Columbine White," he explained to Kingsley, moving with him out to the front stoop. "She's a seamstress. Her husband has a car dealership. Mark Byrd's his name. They live in town."

"I'm glad they're handling it. Dress-up is not my thing." I walked with Frank and Kingsley to the sports car sitting next to my muddy truck. "I originally thought I'd write *This is my costume* on a T-shirt and go as me, but Frank talked me out of it."

"You have to show them the kind of work we do here," Frank said.

"Well, short of having people come out here, suit up with rubber gloves and help clean up after a coon poops his stall, I doubt they'll know what we do. Coons carry serious parasites. Well, most wild animals do, but coons in particular carry roundworm and they're deadly. So yeah, I wear a mask and gloves when I clean out the stalls."

"That's not what I mean," Frank scolded. "I got you a costume to show people who you really are. What a kind and generous person you are."

I laughed. "Does that mean I'm going as a red Salvation Army kettle? Now that's a good costume, Frank. Put a slot in the back and people can drop their donations in directly."

"It might be a little hard to socialize in a kettle." Kingsley had a faint smile as though visualizing me waltzing around the room wearing a red kettle.

"It would be perfect since I'm not much for socializing anyway. I can stand in the corner and appear forlorn. I bet we'll rake in the donations."

"You wait," Frank warned. "Everybody will be

surprised when they see you come into the ballroom with your costume on."

"Ballroom? It's the auditorium at the high school, Frank. It's not a palace."

"I heard the high school kids are decorating it nice. They had a contest and the winning theme is Happily Ever After." Frank beamed at me. "It's going to be special. You wait and see."

"Well, they have a week to work their magic. They'll need a fairy godmother to turn a gym into a fairy land."

"You'd be surprised what people can do when they put their minds to it."

"You could use a load of gravel on your driveway," Kingsley commented. "You've got a few big ruts. And there's wash-out on the road leading here."

"I could use a new roof on the barn and a load of straw around the back of the barn and new boots and—the list goes on. I'll add gravel to it, probably near the bottom."

"Put it closer to the top," Frank said. "It's getting bad."

"The county's responsible for the road coming to our house, but since we're the only ones out here, we're not at the top of their priorities. Yeah, I need to get gravel in. Someday."

"Will you report that to the sheriff?" Kingsley asked, eyes on the arrow Frank still held.

"I will," Frank said. "I'll take it into town tomorrow."

"And they'll say the same thing they say every year," I commented. "We're not within the city limits so hunters can shoot where they want, no matter how close to a home they get."

"That doesn't sound right." Kingsley paused, his car door open.

"They can do it if they have my permission, which I don't give. I have all my land posted, and they'll just ignore it. I can guarantee I'll go hiking in the woods at least once during hunting season and find a carcass or a blood trail." I scowled at the darkness around us. "I don't mind a good hunter, but these weekend wannabes do more harm than good."

"Well, take care. And if you're disturbed tonight by fireworks, please call me. I meant what I said. Our crews do not stoop to terror tactics."

I thought of Sammy, my black Lab, lying dead with white flecks around his muzzle. "Somebody stoops to it." My eyes filled with tears, and I blinked fast.

Kingsley slid into his car. "If it's the men hired to work on my crew, they'll be fired. You have my word on that." He slowly backed down my drive, making his way to the county road.

"He seems like a good fella," Frank said, tapping the arrow against his thigh.

"I don't trust him."

"You don't trust anybody."

"Nope. So why make an exception for him?" I went back to the house, my rumbling stomach reminding me about my abandoned meal.

"Because he might be worth trusting."

"Yeah, sure." I went up the steps to the door. "Don't stay up all night, Frank."

"We'll see." He ambled away, singing softly. I tilted my head to catch the tune. "Harvest Moon," one of Neil Young's songs. I went inside.

After dinner I called Columbine to verify we truly were on target for the party. "Frank ordered it online, and I'm adding a few embellishments," she assured me. "It's a marvelous costume. It's adjustable so we won't need a fitting, although it would be nice if you could try it on."

"You know she can't try it on," Mark yelled in the background. I imagined him in his lumpy recliner, newspaper on his knees. Mark and Bryan were friends in high school. We four used to picnic and party together. After Bryan's death, they remained companions, unlike so many people who weren't sure what to do with a thirty-four-year-old widow.

"Why can't I try the costume on?" I asked.

"Because it's a secret, and I'm still working on it, and we know you'll love it." Columbine was a breathless sort of person at the best of times. She was almost incoherent now. "Frank picked out the perfect, um, perfect character for you."

"What am I, the Wicked Witch of the West?" I joked.

"Oh, no. It's a beautiful costume. You'll feel like the belle of the ball." Columbine laughed. "You will."

"Okay, as long as it's ready next Friday."

"Saturday. It'll be ready for Saturday."

I rubbed my head. "I'm getting my parties mixed up."

"You're going to another party on Friday? Where?"

"Aden Kingsley. He's new in town. He's having a party for the judges and the people in the Heavys categories."

"Oh, I heard about him. He's handsome. And rich. I think he's rich."

I thought of Kingsley's expensive car and clothing.

"Yeah, he looks it."

"You met him?"

"It's a long story. Do you want me to come to the shop next Saturday and get the costume? Or are you coming out here?"

"I can come out there with the costume if—"

I heard Mark yell in the background, "She should come here. I'll have a car ready for her. She needs to go to the party in something besides a truck."

"I don't need a car," I protested half-heartedly. I was secretly pleased that I wouldn't have to drive my truck or Frank's truck, which was almost as old as mine.

"Oh, of course you do. And Mark will drive you, like a proper chauffeur. You need to make an impression."

"Chauffeur?" The last time I went to the Heavys party, I dressed like a cowboy so my truck was perfect. Since I had no idea what my costume was, I decided to rely on her opinion about my mode of transportation.

"You know. A driver." She giggled. "Too bad we don't have a carriage. Maybe he can dress up as one of your animals. Like a raccoon or a wolf or something. Better yet, are you bringing any of them to the party so people can see them?"

"Good Lord, no. They're injured critters, Binny. I can't schlep them around the county for people to see."

"Oh, that's too bad. If people saw those adorable little squirrel babies and that poor possum." There was a pause, then she said breathlessly, "I know. You need to make a video. That's it, you need a video. We'll show the video. I'll have Marky Mark come out and make a movie. He and his friends are always doing that kind of stuff."

Marky Mark was their teenaged son, a senior in high school. "I doubt if he'll want to come out here and shoot video of injured wildlife. He probably wants to do zombie stuff."

"He'll do it," Mark yelled in the background. "It's about damn time he did something useful with that fancy phone I bought him."

"I'll talk to him," Columbine said. "I'm sure he and his friends have ideas on how to make a video to highlight the work you do. When are you working this weekend?"

"I have a split shift tomorrow in Iowa City, and Sunday I'm doing the emergency clinic from five in the afternoon to midnight. Thanks for handling the costume."

"I love doing this kind of thing. Mark and I are going as Morticia and Gomez Addams."

I laughed. "You'll be perfect." And they would be. Columbine was tall and thin with long black hair and Mark had dark hair and a mustache. All it would take would be a bit of makeup and the right clothing and they'd own the part. "I'm sure you'll win the Townsman Trophy."

"Maybe. I heard that Mara is going as Maleficent. She has a gorgeous black gown and wings and a headdress."

"That's a part that was made for her." I easily imagined Mara as a glowering dark witch.

"Her gown is beautiful. It's got crystals and beads and lace."

"Yours is prettier, Ash," Mark called out. "Hers is too slinky."

"Gown?" I demanded. "What gown?"

"Oh, you know, it's a dress. Not a gown." I heard Columbine whisper, *Shut up, Mark, it's a secret.* She came back on the line. "Emily wanted to go as Cinderella, but I talked her out of it."

"Good Lord, I'm glad you did." I envisioned Emily in a gauzy gown, prancing around with a wand. It was not a pretty image. "What's her costume?"

"It's somebody from *Star Wars*. Not the girl with the buns, but the new one. She's wearing a tunic thing with leggings."

"Sounds comfortable, at least. I hope mine is comfortable," I warned. "I told Frank I wouldn't do anything fancy. He promised it was perfect for me."

"It is. Trust me. I'll see you next Saturday. Come here at five o'clock, and we'll get you dressed in your finery."

"Five? The party doesn't start until six thirty."

"Trust me. We need time. I'll have Marky Mark call you. See you then!"

I ended my cell phone call, frowning. What did we need time for? Oh, well. Five or six, what did it matter? I lit a fire in the fireplace and flopped down on the couch with a glass of wine and my herbal medicine book. I usually used TV for background noise, so tonight I played tunes on my iPod, which I had charging in my office next door. The ancient Bluetooth speakers were crappy, but it was classic rock so it didn't matter. I knew it by heart.

Aden Kingsley. His face popped into my mental viewscreen. Rich, handsome, and apparently eligible. Attractive? Well, maybe. I was in a weird menopause phase where my hormones were insane, and I lusted after men right and left. Or I was oblivious to them, depending on the day.

It's not him, I decided. It's hormones. He was exactly the kind of man Mara would set her sights on. She was thrice divorced, each of her marriages ending with her receiving a hefty settlement. As Frank said, she married well and divorced better.

I couldn't visualize Kingsley with Mara. Somehow the two images didn't go together. I didn't trust most people, but I had the feeling Aden Kingsley might be different.

I jotted notes while I read before taking a break at ten and going to the barn. I used the flashlight to pick out the pathway, although I knew it so well I could walk it with my eyes closed. We had a radio connecting the house to the barn and to Frank's house, but I didn't like to use it at night in case Frank was dozing.

All was quiet at the hospital, although the fox was restless, pawing at his bedding with muted whimpers. He was separated from his mother and cared for at a local vet's office in the first few weeks of life. Now we were preparing him for the next phase. I sat outside his cage for a time and talked, mostly nonsense words in a monotone. It always seemed to soothe the lonely ones.

I went back past Frank's house, peeking inside to see him stretched out on his daybed, snoring softly. He'd be up in a few hours to do the midnight feedings and bandage changes. He usually slept well for a few hours before tossing and turning, various aches and pains making a full night's sleep impossible. I tried to get him to take a sleep aid, but he insisted he didn't mind so I didn't push it.

As I walked back to my house, I wondered how much longer we could keep up this pace. We averaged a dozen or more animals at our makeshift hospital. But now a new, "official" wildlife rehab center was in the works at the university, twenty miles away. I'd spoken to the people in charge of setting it up. They asked me to consult and work there once they were up and running.

What would Frank do? I paused at the windbreak and looked back at the barn. This farm was his life for most of his life. His work with the wildlife orphans had been front and center for decades. If it was taken away from him, what would remain?

Well, I didn't have to worry about it. The new rehab center was still in fund-raising mode. It would be a few years before we'd be phased out. I had to focus on raising enough money to tide us over until I applied for grants next year.

I went inside and upstairs, missing the sound of Sammy's nails clicking on my hard wood floors. This was the first time in my adult life I didn't have a dog. I was unaccustomed to the loneliness. I fell into bed, wondering how the hell I'd find the time to train a new dog in between doing multiple shifts of vet work. Frank would help, of course, but if it was to be my dog I had to do most of the training. I set the alarm for five o'clock and prayed for a good night's sleep uninterrupted by idiots with firecrackers.

It wasn't firecrackers, though, that jerked me out of sleep in the morning.

It was gunfire.

Chapter Four

The gunfire was loud but in the distance. Sound carried through the cold night air. It was hard to tell how far away it was.

My alarm beeped at me. Five o'clock. We hadn't gone to Daylight Savings Time yet, so it was only faintly light, more a thinning of the darkness than sunrise. Hunters were allowed a half-hour grace period before sunrise and after sunset, but this was stretching it.

However, today was October 24 and shotgun season didn't start until December. The early muzzleloader season ended on October 20 and wouldn't resume until December. The other firearms hunts were limited to early November, at least a week away. I had the dates memorized because those were the times I needed to watch for blaze orange.

Two more shots fired in rapid succession. Not a shotgun, which had a distinctive sound. This sounded more like a rifle or maybe a handgun. A gun club was located south of us. I had heard enough practice rounds being fired to have a good idea of what was being shot.

I swung out of bed and pulled on my bathrobe over my sleep T-shirt before padding to my window. My room was in the northwest corner of the house facing the garage and the lane to our farm. The pasture was in the distance, faintly illuminated by the yard light on the side of the garage. I didn't see any movement, nothing to indicate a hunter might be out there in the dark.

I went down the hall to the bathroom. I showered quickly and dressed in my *It's all fun and games until somebody winds up in the cone* scrubs with dog paw prints running up and down the legs of the pants. I put my jeans and a flannel shirt in my duffel bag to change into later, grabbed the lunch I made the night before, and dashed to the barn to check on patients. I doled out medication while Frank dished out food, then I was off for a split shift day, the morning at the emergency clinic and the afternoon at a local vet's office.

I had a tough morning at the clinic with a cat with renal failure and a dog with a broken leg. The patients themselves weren't hard to deal with, but the owners were a handful. I finished my shift and changed clothes, experience telling me if I tried to eat lunch wearing my scrubs I'd end up giving free advice to anyone who saw me.

I was settling down to a peanut butter and jelly sandwich when my sister-in-law Emily headed my way. I was seated at a picnic bench in Clear Creek Park across the street from Dasdorf City Hall. It was an overcast, chilly day. I had the place to myself, at least until Emily bustled over to join me.

I watched her cross Clear Creek Road, her beige cape floating around her like the sails of a ship. Emily was big-boned and tall, a large lady with short wispy brown hair, pale green eyes, and a round face. She had a tendency to dress in long tunics, tights, and knee-high boots accenting her heavy legs. Emily was a hunting enthusiast and a prepper, convinced the apocalypse was nearing and by God, she would be ready for it. She chopped her own firewood, hunted and dressed her own kills, and taught other women basic survival skills in her Survival Sally classes.

Emily was also an astute businesswoman who'd parlayed her paranoia into a successful career. She had never married and lived on the outskirts of town on two acres of heavily wooded and secluded land. Kids in town called it the Witch's House because any time anybody got close to her, she came out and scared them away.

"What's up, Emily?" I asked as soon as she got closer.

She picked her way through the leaves to where I sat in a small spot of sunshine. "Mara spoke with Aden Kingsley yesterday," she said, struggling to settle her faux Coach handbag on her arm. It tangled with the voluminous sleeves of her cape instead. "He's the developer in charge of the parcel of land we inherited from our mother."

"I know." I polished off my sandwich and jammed its wax paper covering into my brown paper lunch bag. I would reuse both tomorrow.

Emily confronted me, uncomfortably near. She had a small mouth and eyes slightly too close together. It gave her a pinched, old lady appearance even though she was five years younger than me and Mara. "Do you really think you can stand in the way of progress? This town will never forgive you if you don't allow the construction to go forward."

I crossed my legs, deliberately nudging her booted shin with my Crocs to make her step back. "Nobody's mentioned it to me."

"They're talking about it behind your back."

I spied Jacob William crossing the street not far from where I sat. "Hey, Jacob," I called.

He meandered toward us, shoulders hunched in his denim jacket. Jacob farmed south of Dasdorf on land that had been in his family for generations. He was a year younger than me, but he always seemed like an Old Soul.

"Hello, ladies," he said, joining us. "It's a beautiful day, isn't it?"

"You bet. Listen, Jacob. Emily tells me people in town are pissed off at me because I'm blocking access to the parcel of land she and Mara own. How do you feel about it?"

He pursed his lips, head tilted to one side. "Some folks might be feeling that. Others, well, we figure what happens, it happens. Not our business."

"There, you see." I dusted crumbs off my jeans and stood.

"Although the mayor, well, I think she'd like to see a big development go in. You know, one of those retail things." Jacob frowned. "I saw her and that Kingsley feller having lunch the other day. They sure seemed chummy. And she's talked it up at local meetings. Says it would be good for the town."

"Really?" Our mayor, Charlene Parralt, had moved to town a decade earlier and promptly entered the local political arena. She had served on several county committees, which brought her within the purview of the larger political world of the university. "I wonder if he was bribing her," I speculated.

"Maybe she was bribing him." Jacob pulled off his cap emblazoned with *Pioneer Seeds* and ruffled his thinning brown hair. "That's how it seemed to me, anyway."

Movement made me turn to Emily. She was shell shocked, her mouth sagging open and her beady eyes wide.

"I don't believe it," she whispered. "I was told no decision was made about what would go in."

"Well, you know how those businessmen are," I said cheerfully. "Say one thing and mean another." I didn't believe it for a minute. Kingsley had struck me as being a straightforward kind of guy, but I couldn't resist the chance to dig at Emily.

She swung around, her expensive handbag almost knocking Jacob off his feet. "We'll see about that. I need to talk to Mara. She's been in negotiations with Kingsley. She'll know." Emily glared at me as though I was the cause of her distress. "I would think you'd be more worried about this. After all, it might affect the cabin. I'm sure you don't want to see that torn down."

"The cabin" was the home Bryan and I had when we were first married, a one-room log house smack in the middle of the land I refused to sell. "I am worried," I pointed out. "I filed an injunction to stop construction. You can't get too much more worried than that."

"True enough," Jacob agreed.

"I need to talk to Mara and see what's going on." Emily stomped off, her cape billowing behind her like bat wings.

Jacob watched her, frowning. "I always thought she was excitable," he murmured. "I wonder about Emily sometimes."

"Emily? It's Mara you need to worry about." I headed toward downtown.

Jacob fell into step with me. "Nah. Mara is what she seems. Mean and underhanded." He settled his cap back on his head, hair sticking out the sides. "Emily, though, she's volatile."

"That's a good word for her." I nodded.

Jacob shook his head. "Emily doesn't like to lose. That's what I've heard anyway. My wife and her are in the same card club, and Emily is a bad loser. Well, you have a good day there, Ash. Say hi to Frank for me."

"Will do, Jacob." I swung up into the truck and started the engine, thinking about what he said. I hadn't articulated it before, but Jacob was right. Mara was transparent with her ill intentions, one of those people who would come at you with her weapons drawn. But Emily was a schemer, somebody who would figure out a way to balance a can on the doorway so it would knock you in the head. Of the two kinds of enemies, I infinitely preferred Mara.

I drove through town, slowing when I passed the Kingsley field office, located kitty-corner from the City Hall. The building had a big picture window. I glimpsed desks inside and people moving around. I wondered if Aden Kingsley was there, maybe glancing out to check if Mayor Parralt was going past. They would make a good couple, I decided. She was in her forties, tall and athletic with short brown hair always tidily swept back from her face and a wide, perfect smile. A politician's smile that didn't reach her blue eyes.

A perfect couple, I decided. Both of them focused on business. Both of them anxious to make people believe them. Both of them probably considering a personal future that had little to do with the good of the town. A match made in heaven.

I drove to nearby Kalona and the vet's office there. This was an easy shift, two hours of soothing animals who were boarded there for the short term. I took the dogs for walks in the park and spent quality time with two kitties whose owners were away for the weekend. By four o'clock I was headed home, ready to relax for the evening.

But when I drove down our lane, I saw Billy Grimm, one of Dasdorf's four part-time police officers, standing near my garage, talking to Frank.

"Hey, Billy. What's going on?" I swung down from the truck and joined them. Just as I reached them, Aden Kingsley came around the side of my house. "What are you doing here?"

"I'm with him." Kingsley gestured to Billy. "I'd like to see your satellite dish in the daylight."

"I called the dish people," Frank said to me. "They sent somebody out to move it around. I gave 'em hell. Told 'em we had to have Internet service, and they listened to me. And I gave Billy the arrow."

"I suppose you'll dust it for fingerprints and run them through your database," I said. I noticed Kingsley's raised eyebrow at this offhand comment. Billy had been the local law enforcement as long as I'd lived in Dasdorf, splitting up the duties with the other three officers in rotating shifts. There wasn't much crime in town, mainly nuisance stuff like loud parties and an occasional drunk. "Is there something going on I can help you with? For once we had a quiet night last night. No firecrackers or hunters, at least none I saw or heard."

"It wasn't quiet at the construction site." Billy stuck his fingers in his belt, which had an impressive array of gadgets hanging off it. "Somebody shot up the equipment and jammed a tire iron into the axle of a couple of machines. Slashed a few tires."

"I'll bet that's pricy," I said to Kingsley.

"It's insured. It's more inconvenient than anything."

He was in businessman clothes today, creased and crisp-looking jeans and a sports coat with a pale blue shirt.

"Don't you have security on site?"

"Most of this equipment was kept at the far end of the area. We keep lights on at night, but whoever did this apparently wasn't worried about being seen."

"For good reason," Frank said. "Because apparently they weren't seen, were they?"

"We do regular patrols past there," Billy said quickly. "Either someone was lucky in their timing, or they were tracking us and got in at the right time."

I glanced at Kingsley and found him staring at me. "Do you think I had something to do with it?"

"I wondered if you might have heard or seen something," Billy said.

"Nope. I did hear gunfire this morning when I got up."

"What time was that?" Kingsley asked.

"Five."

"You get up early."

"I had an early shift at the emergency clinic and chores to do before I go there." I finally met Kingsley's stare. "Feel free to search. I have a shotgun in the garage. I also have a Winchester and a Smith & Wesson pistol in the barn."

"You have guns?" he asked.

His incredulous question irked me. "I do. And I'm licensed to use them, and I know how to use them."

"Ash and Frank are humane dispatch officers," Billy said.

"Humane—what?"

"When a deer or other animal is hit by a car or a hunter and is abandoned, we—" Frank raised his hands.

"You know. We shoot them."

"You don't take them in and work with them, try to help them?"

I jammed my hands in the pockets of my jeans. "Some can't be saved. The best we can do is a quick death."

Kingsley considered that. "That's tough."

"Yeah. It is. So Billy, do you want to search or not?"

"Nah. I figured you might have seen something, though."

"Like I said. I heard gunshots. Since it's not firearm season, I figured it was something going on at the gun club." I looked away from Kingsley's intent dark brown eyes. Damn menopause. I got hot flashes at the worst possible moments. "Maybe it was your vandals doing their thing."

"If you hear or see anything in the future, give us a call," Billy said. "I realize you're not a big fan of the construction going on. I also know you're a good citizen, and you'd report anything you saw."

I was careful not to appear too innocent. "You bet, Billy. Good citizen here."

He and Frank strolled back to the sedan. I followed, Kingsley trailing along next to me. "Law enforcement is different here than what I'm used to," he commented.

"If you want to live here, I guess you'll need to adjust. I think you might say we have a pragmatic attitude about crime. I'm sure the police do what they can with what they have to work with, and that's not much, so—" I shrugged. "Arrows fly. Nobody investigates. Dogs die, and nobody can do anything about it."

He slowed, looking around the yard. "Do you feel safe out here alone?"

"I'm not alone. Frank's in his house. And I've got possums, and a fox, and assorted other animals in the barn to keep me company."

"I wasn't talking about loneliness. I was talking about security."

We reached Frank and Billy, standing next to the car. "That's my problem, not yours, Mr. Kingsley. You need to worry about your chippers and your bulldozers."

"Someone is shooting arrows at your satellite dish."

I wanted to tug on my braid, a habit I had when I got angry. But I knew if I did that, Frank would know how I felt and things might get weird. "You know, I live on a farm in the middle of an area where people like to hunt. I'm always on the lookout for bullets or arrows." Billy nodded his agreement. "If you live in the country, you're in danger. I'm used to it."

Kingsley seemed like he wanted to continue arguing, but Billy said, "Thanks for your time, Ash. If you hear anything, get in touch, okay?"

"Will do." I waited until they left, then I headed for the barn. Frank fell into step with me. "How did things go today?" I asked, ignoring the sedan when it drove off.

"I still say he seems like a sincere kind of guy."

"I'm sure he is. I talked to Emily today. She's convinced the town hates me because I'm opposed to the construction."

Frank sighed. "I never connected with those girls. They worshipped their father. When he and Miriam got divorced, I think they felt betrayed when Miriam married me."

I kept my poor opinion of Frank's second wife to myself. Miriam had latched onto poor Frank after Grace died and Frank was vulnerable. He was miserable for the entire ten years they were together. It would have been a blessing when she died except her death meant he was stuck with the evil stepsisters to care for.

"Emily's crazy, and Mara's a bitch," I said. "It's nothing to do with how they were raised. It's who they are." I put my arm through his and tugged him toward the barn. "Come on. We've got chores to do."

"And we need to practice your song." Frank went into the barn and took down his Martin acoustic guitar from the wall where it hung.

"It's hokey, Frank. Too hokey."

He strummed the first few bars of the song. "Come on, now. People will join in. It's for a good cause. You know you love singing for folks."

He was right, of course. That's how I met Bryan, in college. He had a small band, and they needed a female vocalist. I was a mezzo-soprano but could sing contralto when called on. We had great success in college and did a year of touring before the band broke up. That's when Bryan and I returned home and settled down.

"People will think it's stupid."

"People will be drinking and having fun. They'll want to sing. Come on." He fingered the opening bars of the song. I hummed along, finally picking up the words to "Imagine." I sang it through one time then Frank paused, guitar on his lap. "I just learned this one. Give it a try." He tapped the rickety wicker side table and I picked up the sheet music.

"Lady Gaga?" I knew the song, of course. Anybody who'd seen the movie knew it. The range was a stretch for me. I had to reach deep to hit the high notes of "Shallow" and keep it mellow so my singing didn't disturb the critters. We went through it then Frank switched to folk music. Soon I was doing barn chores and singing along to "The Reuben James," "Last Night I Had the Strangest Dream," and "Tom Dooley." I loved singing, and it made the chores go faster.

I finished as it was getting dark. While I could still see to do it, I pulled out the water testing kit and got a sample from the well. I fed the barn cats and went to the house to make a sandwich before putting my feet up for the night. This was a rare event for me, an entire evening to relax without going in for a shift at a clinic or office.

I didn't get a chance, though. I had no sooner flipped on the television when a car pulled into the drive. I peeked through the front curtain. Marky Mark and two other teenaged boys piled from the car, talking excitedly. I recognized the car. Anybody would. Mark was the one dealer around who gave teenagers a chance to own a car, but in exchange they had to do advertising for him. He usually sold kids older cars emblazoned with Mark's *Byrd's Best Buggies* logo. This car was a big old sedan, probably a retired Caddy. Mark's "bird" logo was plastered on the hood, the bird sitting in a buggy and flapping its wings at anyone nearby.

His son, Marky, was a tall, lanky kid with an engaging grin, long hair that got in his eyes, and feet the size of small boats. Columbine said it seemed he grew another size every month. His father was about six six, and Marky was well on his way to catching up to Mark.

"Hey, Ash," he called when I came out on the front stoop. "Mom said you needed some film work done, so I brought my crew." He swung out an arm, almost hitting one of the other boys. "That's Bart, and that's Gordy. We're taking a film class, so we're using this for our class project. Where's the hospital?"

"Hi, guys. Most of the patients are bedded down for the night."

"That's okay. This is a preliminary walkthrough so we can see what we have to work with." Marky sounded briskly professional. I had to hide my smile when he dug out a clipboard from the car and held it up. "Once we see the site, I'll set up a shooting and editing schedule and get the actors lined up."

"Actors?" I turned to the other boys. "You guys?"

"Nah. We do the production work behind the cameras." The boy—I think he was Gordy—had bright blue hair cut into a Mohawk and multiple piercings that made my ears hurt.

"Why don't we look the place over?" Marky suggested, walking toward the house. "We'll get the lay of the land and figure out the best way to handle the filming."

"Over there. Hang on." I grabbed a jacket before joining them, leading them along the path to the barn. I caught snippets of conversation as we walked.

"…good camera angle there if we get the sunlight coming in…"

"She's really pretty. We got to get pictures of her with the animals."

"…her costume. Mom is working on it. It's great. She'll win the Costume Award, hands down. You should see it. I don't…"

"The competition is fierce this year. The Youth guys are the tumbling team, and they've got a killer routine. I heard they're using a professional promo agency to do their stuff."

"Yeah, well, she has us, so it's in the bag."

I grinned at their enthusiasm. There truly were no

"winners" in the Heavys contest, but town pride was at stake, not only for the charities but for townspeople in their costumes. I wondered what kind of costume Columbine was crafting for me. As long as I could move in it, I didn't care. Thank God somebody was taking care of it.

When we got to the barn, I raised a hand. "Hang on. I'll let Frank know you're here." I slipped inside and found Frank, as I expected, reading a magazine and listening to music. It played softly on speakers, relayed through the barn from the old CD player in the office, a partitioned off space where we stored medical supplies and bedding.

I explained about the film crew outside, and he got to his feet. "I'm glad Binny thought about that. We need something to explain what we do. Those posters and things we used the last time won't cut it. Times change, and we got to change with it." He went to the door and ushered the boys inside. "Come on in. Let me introduce you to our guests."

The kids dutifully followed him down the length of the barn, Marky making frantic notes on his clipboard. Frank gave them a brief overview of each of our occupants while the guys asked intelligent questions about safety, disease, and care. If that kind of information came through in the film, I'd be satisfied.

They spent a half hour or so in the barn, prowling around and checking it out before Frank shooed us away. "Critters got to get their rest," he said. "Our goal is to get them healthy enough so they can go back where they belong."

"That's good," Marky said, jotting another note among the sheaf of papers on his clipboard. "We can use that."

I escorted them back to the house. "You know, a film is good, but where do we play it? We're using those long display tables along the side of the gym. I thought I'd take pictures and do posters or something."

"No, that's too old school," Bart said. He was a big, lumbering kid, probably a linebacker on the football team. He'd been snapping pictures with a digital camera the whole time, *making visual notes*, he told me with a knowing nod. I suspected the idea came from his teacher. "No, video is it. Hey, I know. My little sister has these stuffed animals. We set up the animals on the table to play the video on their iPads."

"iPads?" I held up my hand. "I can't buy iPads."

"Nah, we'll get 'em," Gordy said. "No worries. Yeah, we'll do a whole diorama thing like in school. Set up the animals, and they'll tell the story of how they got into the hospital and how they're being taken care of." His spikey head bobbed enthusiastically.

"We'll get Molly and Tiff to help," Bart said with a grin.

Gordy dug his hands in the pockets of his saggy jeans. "They won't do it," he muttered. "They're too stuck-up."

"Yeah, they will. These are injured baby animals. This is a Disney movie come to life. They'll be standing in line to help." He slapped Gordy on the back, sending the smaller boy into the path. "This is babe-magnet stuff. You wait and see."

Marky was at the car, resting against it and jotting notes. "We'll have voiceovers. We'll ask the girls to audition." He scribbled furiously, long hair flopping in his eyes. "Yeah, good. I like it."

73

"We need somebody to write the scripts," Bart said.

"Scripts?" I looked from one to the other.

"How about Brittany? She's on the newspaper staff. She can write scripts."

"Danny can help, too. He's good at the kind of shit." Gordy shuffled. "That kind of stuff."

Good heavens. It was a tidal wave of creativity. "Thanks, guys. I appreciate the help. I wasn't sure what to do."

"Hey, if we can sell the public on those ugly possums, we can do anything." They piled back into the car. The last I heard was someone shouting, "This will be awesome!"

I laughed and went back inside. The water sample was sitting on the counter, reminding me to do the test. I pulled out the kit and went through the routine of dipping test strips in the water and sitting them next to the proofing paper.

I went upstairs and changed into my sleep T-shirt and bathrobe, then shuffled back downstairs in my slippers. The test strips awaited me. I took them to the kitchen table to examine. Damn. There were elevated levels of copper, heavy metals, and nitrates. Any of them might be caused by groundwater contamination or run-off. I jotted down the levels in the log we kept, comparing them to last month's test. They were high. And they'd been getting higher consistently over time.

I would need to talk to the folks at the water treatment plant in town to see if their numbers were high as well. The town drew water from the same aquifer we drew from. The treatment plant's testing methods were far more accurate than mine. I would need to compare notes with them.

I wasn't too worried, at least not for now. We had a water filtration system set up for our drinking water. It would handle all but the higher levels of contaminants. But we didn't have it for the barn. I hated to think I was spending my time helping wounded animals only to kill them with toxic water.

Nothing to do about it now, so I consigned the worry to my DIL list. I went back to the living room to flop on the couch and watch inane television shows until I dozed off at midnight. I went to the kitchen and prepared the coffee for the morning, blessing whoever it was who invented automatic coffeemakers with timers. I stumbled upstairs and considered calling down to the barn. But the lights were off at Frank's tiny house, so I decided not to wake him.

I dove into bed and huddled under the covers, shivering until my body heat got the warmth going. This time of year was a lonely time for me because it was in November Bryan died, succumbing to his battle with bone cancer. We were married for fourteen years and now he was gone for twenty, going on twenty-one. The time with him was a blur, a memory of a person I once was, a person who laughed and loved and once considered a future far different than the life I had now.

No regrets, I reminded myself. There were many points in my life where I might have taken a different path. I might have stayed in a high-tech field. I might have pursued music more seriously. Or maybe found a permanent job as a vet tech somewhere instead of this piecemeal career I had now.

I yawned and tugged my blankets higher, smiling when I remembered the enthusiasm of high school boys as they planned ways to entice high school girls into joining them. If they had their way, we'd have an awesome video to show for my work here. That was fine by me. I fell asleep with visions of stuffed animals holding iPads in my head.

Less awesome was the pounding on my door at five thirty the next morning. I tumbled out of bed, flicked on the porch light, and found Billy Grimm on my front stoop. "What's up, Billy?" I pushed my sleep braid over my shoulder and shivered in the cold morning air.

"We found Mara."

"Was she missing?" I yawned and tugged my bathrobe tighter against the chill.

"She was lying in the road at the end of your lane. She's dead."

Chapter Five

I stared stupidly at him. "Dead? How? When?"

"Not sure exactly when. It looks like she bled to death." He was dressed for the cold morning in a leather jacket and a sweater, jeans, and a hat with *DPD* on it.

I wasn't dressed for frost, though. "Come in." I stepped to one side. "Where was she? When did she die?"

He came into the hallway and followed me into the kitchen. I turned on the lights and went to the coffeepot near the sink. "You want coffee?" I asked.

"No, thanks." He pulled out one of the bar stools at the kitchen island and sat. "You don't seem too shocked."

"I'm still asleep. Give me a minute to consider it." I poured myself a mug of coffee and leaned against the sink, Billy watching me from where he sat. "Who found her?"

"Ginny Basile. She was delivering the newspaper to the folks in the subdivision down the road. She thought she saw something so she drove up to the intersection to check."

I winced. Ginny was a middle-aged lady with a tendency to drink heavily and gossip freely. The news was probably already spreading throughout the county.

"She called it in about a half hour ago. That's one advantage to having a mobile phone." Billy regarded me calmly, his face impassive. "I don't suppose you heard or saw anything."

I sipped my coffee. "Where was she? Mara?"

"Like I said. At the end of your road."

"She was on Hazel Lane?" The road that ended at our farm intersected with Hazel Lane, a poorly maintained road leading to town. "Well, since that's about a half mile away, no, I didn't see or hear anything. You said she bled to death?"

"Looks that way."

"An accident? Was her car there?"

His expression didn't change, but something about him did, a tightening around his eyes or maybe it was tenseness in his posture. "No, it wasn't."

My fogged brain cranked into full speed. "What's that mean? Did somebody put her there? Did she walk there?'

"She couldn't have done that."

"How come?"

He was quiet for a long few seconds. "She's missing a big chunk of her right leg."

I almost dropped my coffee mug. "What?"

He dipped his head. "Nasty wound. Like maybe from a saw or axe."

"Holy crapola," I murmured. "If it was a thigh wound, it might have hit the femoral artery and she'd bleed out in minutes. There's no treating a wound like that." Billy gaped at me. "Hey, I'm sorry. I'm a trained medical professional."

"Yeah, for animals, not humans," he said, his eyes narrowing suspiciously.

"It's not much different between animals and humans. Whoever created mammals didn't do a whole lot of design work. It's basically the same. You hit a deer in that spot, and it'll bleed out within a hundred yards. Humans are the same." I took another swallow of coffee. "Is there a significant amount of blood there?"

"I can't discuss it with you. It's a crime scene."

He sounded so pompous I wanted to smile. I stopped myself in time when suddenly the import of what we were discussing hit me. Mara was dead. "Who the hell wanted to kill Mara?" Then I heard what I said. "Who the hell didn't want to kill her?"

"That's brutal. She wasn't that bad."

I eyed Billy over my mug. "You've known her about as long as I have. Be honest."

He pursed his lips. "Murder is a big step for somebody to take."

"No shit. Hey, what about the bowhunter who came by the other night? Is it an arrow wound? Maybe she got shot by mistake. It can happen, especially with new hunters. That guy struck me as an eager, wannabe hunter. An arrow in a leg would cause a bunch of damage, especially if somebody pulled it out. Hunting arrows are barbed."

He slowly shook his head. "You know too damn much about how to kill things, Ash."

"You gotta know what kills a creature in order to stop it from dying. Don't blame me because I'm good at what I do."

"Where's Frank? Maybe he heard something. I know he's up at night taking care of the animals." Billy slid off the stool. "Is he out at the barn?"

"Probably. I'll get dressed and come with you." I put down my coffee mug and headed for the doorway.

"No need to do that. I know my way." Billy went to

the front door, but I stepped in front of him.

"I want to go with you." I was accustomed to staring down people who were taller than me, and Billy wasn't too much taller. "Wait here for me."

"Like I said. No need. I know my way."

I knotted the tie on my bathrobe and jammed my feet into my Crocs. "Okay. Lead on."

Billy sighed theatrically. "At least put on pants, would you?"

I leveled a finger at him. "You wait here."

"Okay."

I raced upstairs, dragged on a sweatshirt and jeans, then ran back downstairs. "Let's go." I grabbed my heavy denim coat from the rack and opened the front door, going left to Frank's house. "We don't have any patients in the exterior pens," I explained as we walked along the path. "The big pens are for the larger mammals, but we haven't had any brought in lately. All the animals we're treating are in the barn. So Frank wasn't outside much last night." I pulled my jacket tighter around me against the frosty morning air. The ground was white, and leaves crunched underfoot.

I poked my head into Frank's tiny house when we passed, but he wasn't there. We continued on to the barn. I opened the side door quietly, easing inside. The lights were on low, casting long shadows on the aisle between the two sides of stalls.

Frank lay in the middle, stretched out on his back. My heart stopped. This was my nightmare come true. Frank, who had a heart attack and died while I was somewhere else. Then I saw the pillow under his neck and the inflatable pad underneath him, the blankets kicked off to one side. I breathed again.

"What the hell?" Billy hurried forward.

"Hold on." We went to Frank, and I knelt next to him. "Come on, old man, wake up."

His eyes fluttered open. "Hello, honey. You're a sweet sight to wake up to. What time is it? Did I oversleep?"

"Billy's here, and he needs to ask you a couple of questions." I hooked a hand under Frank's arm and tugged. Billy got on the other side and between the two of us, we got Frank on his feet, disheveled and sleepy.

He patted down his unruly hair. "What's going on, Billy? Twice in two days. That's a record."

I busied myself with morning chores while listening to Billy quiz Frank, my mind churning. Who would kill Mara? Murder was so extreme. I didn't know anyone capable of murder, did I? Was it a stranger?

I checked our residents, making notes about weight gains, food, and poop, the typical logs I kept. Next I pulled on my leather gloves and with Frank's help, I sedated Rocky to check his bandage and did the same for Roberta, the rabbit. I let out a sigh of relief when I saw her paw didn't appear infected. Maybe there was hope for her after all. I kept an eye on each of them until I was sure they were moving around okay before I began dishing out the day's rations of food.

"Whoever did that to Mara has a pretty damn messy pickup truck," Frank commented while mashing up grain with warm water. "If that's what killed her, that is."

"There's an image I won't erase from my head for a long time," I muttered.

"Yeah, we'll be trying to backtrack a blood trail." Billy watched us work. "I already called in to Iowa City PD to help us. They've got the forensics unit who can narrow down what it was that killed her."

"What about Aden Kingsley? He was a cop, wasn't he?" I spoke with Billy while I pitchforked out the soiled straw in the possum stall. They were tidy little animals and kept their latrine in one corner, bless their hearts. They muttered worriedly while they peeked out at me from their cardboard home.

"Yeah, but he was involved with Mara and Emily on the development deal, so it might be a conflict of interest." Billy headed for the door. "If you folks think of anything odd or out of place, give me a call. And maybe lock your door, Ash. You're isolated out here. Like you said, there are hunters out and around."

A locked door wouldn't help me if somebody wanted in my house, but I didn't voice my opinion. "Will do, Billy."

I didn't have too much time to worry about Mara. Marky Mark and his crew descended on us an hour later, three carloads of kids sweeping me up in a tide of teenage energy.

"Why aren't you in school?" I demanded.

"Teacher education day or something. What happened out at the junction?" Marky asked, arms full of cameras and tripods.

"I'm not sure," I lied. "Must have been an accident out there."

"Lots of yellow tape and stuff," Gordy said in passing. "Can I set up in the barn?"

I went with him to direct traffic and make sure none of the girls got into any of the animal pens. "Look at the baby squirrels," one of the girls cooed. "Aren't they adorbs? You just want to cuddle them, don't you?"

"Nope," I said firmly. "We release them back into

the wild. I don't want them to get used to humans. No cuddling."

The kids asked a bunch of questions, pelting Frank and me for details about handling and care. "Most of what we do is feeding and getting them strong enough to be released. For the ones with injuries, I have a low-level sedative we use when we have to change bandages."

I noticed each pen was assigned a different girl, who sat outside and watched the animals, taking notes in a spiral notepad. The girls had papers sticking from their pads and when I asked to peek at one, I found pictures of the animal and Wikipedia information about them. "Who did this?" I asked Marky.

"Gordy. He got online last night and printed out the pictures and stuff about what the animals eat and all kinds of junk. Tiff and Danny are working on scripts for the girls."

One of the girls, a skinny child with bright pink hair worked into tiny braids, raised her arm. As she did, she displayed an amazing wealth of henna tattooing along its length. "I'm Tiff. I may need to call you to get data."

"Sure," I murmured.

"We wanted our voice-over artists to see the animals so they can visualize the right voice." She surveyed the other girls lined up outside the stalls.

Voice-over artist? The right voice? I decided not to ask.

Three hours later, they jumped back into their cars, Marky Mark and Gordy brandishing their cameras. "We got it on film," Marky said. "Now we'll do the voiceovers and editing and get it ready. I have a stage crew who will get the diorama ready and we have all the stuffed animals and iPads we need."

"Except for a possum," one of the girls said. "I can't find a possum."

"We'll figure out something," Gordy assured her. "I have an idea."

"Do I get to review the final product?" I asked.

"Yeah, sure." He wedged himself into one of the cars already full of teenage bodies. "I'll be in touch!"

I watched them drive off. If only I could bottle that energy, I thought. I fixed lunch and worked on house chores until midafternoon when I went to Frank's house. "I'm going in for work," I said. "Will you be okay out here alone? I admit, I am worried about that."

He was restoring an old Fender Dreadnought 12-string guitar, a labor of love he'd been working on for months. "I'll be fine," he assured me as he painstakingly cleaned the fretboard with a Q-tip. "Don't worry about it. Whoever hurt Mara was out to hurt Mara, not you or me."

"Yeah, but…" I looked over my shoulder. "But she was there."

"You want me to ride into town with you?" He set down the guitar. "I can do that. I'll drive you in and pick you up."

"No, you won't. I don't get off shift until ten. I'll be fine." I went to the door. "And don't forget to eat dinner. Don't only feed the patients, Frank."

"I'll remember." He winked at me and returned to his inspection of the inlaid wood on the fret. I knew he probably wouldn't eat until he saw my car lights come in the lane that night.

Oh, well. It worked for him, so I wouldn't complain. I drove down the road and stopped at the junction with Hazel Lane. Yellow crime scene tape fluttered around the northeast corner, opposite where I stopped. I debated getting out to get a closer look but decided I didn't want to know. I drove to the Emergency Clinic.

We had our usual influx of patients for a Monday evening, animals whose regular vets were closed. We were the stopgap measure until vet offices opened tomorrow. A couple of cats who had opened their stitches from neutering, a dog who swallowed a bone, and a urinary tract infection in a cat requiring an I.V.

It was quieting down at about nine o'clock when the front receptionist came into the exam room. "We've got an injured dog," she said. "Maybe hit by a car."

"Bring him in," I said. "I'll do the prelim exam." I finished wiping down the exam table when the door opened and Aden Kingsley came in carrying an injured dog lying on a board. The dog was small, a terrier/Sheltie mix, mostly gray and black with short curly fur.

"Put him here." I tapped the metal exam table. "What happened?"

Charlene Parralt came in behind Kingsley. They were both dressed up, or what I thought of as dressed up, her in low heels and a skirt and him in a suit and tie. "We were driving back from dinner, and Aden saw him on the side of the road."

Kingsley set the board with the dog on the exam table. "I wasn't sure if he was alive or not. When I saw he was moving, I decided to bring him here. He doesn't have a collar, so I'm not sure if he belongs to anyone."

I noticed the board the animal rested on. It was thin and somewhat flexible. "Paneling?" I tapped the board.

"Yeah, I had it in my trunk. I thought it was better than trying to lift him. I wasn't sure if there were broken ribs. I sort of slid him onto it."

I examined the dog. He was alert but quiet, his eyes fixed on me while I gently touched his body, running my hands on his ribs and hindquarters. When I got to his front leg, he growled.

"There's a problem with the leg," I murmured. "It doesn't appear broken, so maybe it's a sprain. I'm not sure about internal injuries, though. I need to turn him and check the other side." I went to the drawer under the sink and got out the leather gloves I kept there. "You'll want to step back."

"Can I help?" Kingsley reached for the dog.

"No, you can't." I opened the door to the clinic's back rooms and gestured for another tech to join me. He came in and between the two of us we managed to lift the dog, who, as I expected, tried to bite us when pain startled him. I took the bite on my glove and gently pried the dog's jaws loose. He let go with a chagrined expression in his soulful eyes.

The doctor came in and finished the exam before running the scanner to check for a microchip. I glanced at Kingsley and the mayor. She seemed anxious to leave, glancing at her wrist gadget with obvious exasperation. He ignored her, his eyes fixed on the vet while he completed his exam.

"It's a BPA in the front leg that should be stabilized. Otherwise, he got off lucky. A couple of bruised ribs and he needs dental work. He's been neglected. Dehydrated and underweight. He might have been out on his own for a while."

"BPA?" Kingsley asked.

"It's essentially a sprained paw. We'll wrap it and give him anti-inflammatory drugs." The vet stepped back from the table and regarded the dog. "It might be one of

Marian Cox's dogs. She lives west of town. I've seen her dogs before."

"I've heard about her," I murmured. "Not good."

"I suppose we'll need to inform her the dog is here so she can get him," Mayor Parralt said briskly. "It's her responsibility."

"She's not a responsible pet owner," the vet said. "A responsible pet owner would have the animal microchipped, and if one went missing, we'd be informed. I hesitate to turn this dog over to her. She doesn't spend much money on care for her animals."

I kept my mouth shut, but it was an effort. I had opinions about backyard dog breeders and none of them were good.

"I suppose we need to have the dog taken to the Humane Society. That's their purpose, isn't it? To find homes for animals." The mayor kept her attention on the vet, soliciting his agreement.

She didn't get it. "An injured animal isn't likely to find a home," the vet pointed out.

"I'll pay for his care," Kingsley said quietly.

"That's generous of you, but we're a temporary solution here. Animals come here when their regular vets are closed. Do you have a vet in town who can care for the dog?"

I knew the answer before Kingsley spoke. "No, I'm new to this area."

"Well, it's sad, but not all animals can find happy homes." The mayor smiled forlornly. Or maybe it was supposed to be forlorn. It seemed strained to me.

Kingsley met my gaze across the exam table. "Will you take care of him until I can find him a new home?" I began to protest but he hurried on. "I'll pay for his care and any medical requirements for him."

"Why?" I rested a hand on the dog's head. He studied me with the same question I knew I had in my eyes. *Why me?*

"You can do it, can't you?" Kingsley asked. "You have the space for him?"

Damn him. Why did I let him in my house last night? Well, if he was paying, I'd make sure to get his money's worth. "We'll need x-rays and have blood work done. I want to make sure he doesn't have heartworm or distemper."

"We'll do full labs." The vet checked the wall clock. "You're due to go off shift soon, so we'll keep him here until morning. You can come back, and we'll have the results."

I evaluated the dog, mentally measuring him to see if he'd fit in the front seat of my truck.

"I'll pick you up and help you get him settled," Kingsley said.

"He won't fit in your sports car," I snapped. "I'll manage."

"I have an SUV. What time?" Kingsley asked the vet.

"We discharge patients at eight in the morning."

"I'll pick you up at seven," Kingsley told me. He went to the door so quickly the mayor fell over herself to keep up with him. "I'll take care of the billing before I leave." The last I saw of him, he was heading for the reception desk.

The vet and the tech regarded me. "I think you got a dog," the vet said.

"Temporary only," I warned. I ran my hand over the dog's fur. "Give him a bath, too, okay? God knows what kinds of vermin he might have picked up at Cox's place."

"We'll take care of him," the tech said with a grin. "You got yourself a hot early morning date."

I snorted. "I think he has a hot date tonight."

"I'm surprised the mayor is out and about so soon after her divorce," the vet commented. "The ink's barely dry on the papers. But I suppose he's hard to resist." He regarded me with one quirked eyebrow.

"Don't look at me. I don't play in his league."

"Don't be so sure about that." The vet touched the dog's head and the animal's stubby tail thumped the table. "Let's get you taken care of, guy."

The tech went out and got a gurney, and we transferred the dog. He was wheeled away to the back room and I went out front to the reception desk. "All paid for," I was told. "He left a credit card on file. Said to do whatever was necessary." The receptionist nodded knowingly. "The mayor was hanging on him like he was a lifeline and she was drowning. She's out to land him hook, line, and sinker."

"She just got divorced," I muttered. "You'd think she might want to enjoy the single life for a while before settling down again."

"He's a catch, or so I've heard. I suppose she doesn't want to let him get away."

I considered that as I drove home after my shift. I never thought much about marriage again after Bryan died. For one thing, I was too busy trying to stay afloat financially because his illness took a big chunk out of our savings. Plus I was in the I.T. field and that's not exactly a ripe marriage mart. Oh, I had friends, and I dated, and I even had a brief affair a few years ago with a guy I met at a charity fundraiser. But somehow things never happened at the right time with the right person.

I drove through a dark night, clouds passing over the full moon and casting shadows on the road. I turned at the corner where Mara's body was found. The tape was still there, fluttering in the breeze, looking ghostly when my headlights shone on it. I drove down our lane, automatically avoiding the rutted areas. When I got to our driveway, I spied the glint of something ahead. It was light reflecting off something. Eyes? Deer? Or something metal? I slowed, but the glint didn't come again.

I went past my drive and made the left turn to the rutted driveway between Frank's house and the barn. He emerged when I pulled in, peering into the truck when I rolled down my window.

"Everything quiet?" I asked.

"Yep, we're tucked in for the night. Roberta was fussy, but I got her quieted down with lettuce."

"Good. I'm bringing a dog home tomorrow," I said. "Kingsley found one on the road, and it was hurt. He's paying me to care for it until we can find it a home."

"Is it hurt?"

"Not bad. I'll find out for sure when we go pick him up tomorrow."

"We?" Frank tapped his chest. "You and me?"

"No, me and Kingsley. He's coming by to pick me up."

Frank began to smile. "Maybe you'd better get breakfast ready for him. You know. Invite him in."

"It's not a date, Frank. We're picking up the dog."

"He doesn't need to pick you up to pick up the dog." Frank pushed away from the car and waggled a finger at me. "You mark my words, girl."

Rather than argue, I backed up, ignoring the big grin he flashed me before he went into his house. I drove the few yards to my drive and went into the house, belatedly reminding myself that I should have locked it when I left.

I went inside, poured myself a glass of wine to take upstairs. It was midnight, and I was beat. My day began with me being wakened with a dead body on my doorstep followed by hours of teenagers and hours on my feet at the clinic. I brushed out my hair, re-braided it loosely, and pulled on my sleep T-shirt. I turned out the light and went to the window to look outside while I sipped my wine.

Someone moved under the illumination from the yard light at the end of the drive.

I glimpsed a blaze orange jacket before the figure vanished into the darkness of the field across the road. My first impulse was to get dressed and go out and confront whoever was out there. Damn hunters. My fields were posted.

Common sense prevailed. I put down my glass and crept downstairs, verifying I had indeed locked the front and the back door. I peeked out the kitchen window but saw nothing. I didn't feel safe going back upstairs. If somebody were to break in, I'd be trapped there. I flopped on the couch, dragging an old afghan on me. Rain began sometime after that, a gentle snapping sound against the windows that lulled me into a doze.

I tossed and turned until dawn, haunted by dreams of hunters and Mara, mixed up together. I woke groggy and went upstairs to shower, then put my hair into double Dutch loose braids, or what Frank called my "hippy child look." I pulled on jeans and a flannel shirt, scooping up my scrubs and tossing them in the laundry. I didn't have any clinic work today, only a stint later at a vet's office, filling in for a receptionist at the front desk.

Then I remembered Kingsley was due in about twenty minutes. "Shit," I muttered. There went my leisurely day. To top it off, I'd forgotten to get the coffee set up the night before too. "Double shit."

I remembered the hunter I saw. I went out to the garage and got my shotgun, loading it and cracking it over my arm before walking out toward the road where I saw the person the night before. The ground was hard and rutted with tire tracks from my truck or Frank's. The field opposite the house held soybeans during the summer but it was harvested. Now only runty stalks remained.

If a hunter was out here, there was no place to hide. A hunter might hide in a cornfield before it's harvested, but soybeans? No way. I examined the field, empty except for a hawk circling high overhead, scouting for mice. If a hunter was out here, where did he go? I'd have seen any lights outside from a car. I turned to survey the house, the windbreak, Frank's house, and the barn. Maybe behind the barn?

I started down the road but stopped when I heard a car behind me. I turned. A dark blue SUV was coming, the driver deftly avoiding the bigger potholes. The vehicle pulled to a stop near me. It had a small Kingsley logo on the driver's side door.

"When you said you have an SUV, I didn't think you meant you had a tank," I said to Aden Kingsley, who looked down at me from the height of the SUV. He'd changed his suit and tie for a sports coat and flannel shirt. His curly hair was mussed with one curl hanging on his forehead.

"It comes in handy sometimes." He eyed my gun. "Are you aiming for anything in particular or out for a stroll?"

His cheerful question made my sour mood even sourer. "Just strolling. I'll be ready in a minute." I went to the garage and stowed the gun before returning to the SUV, idling in the driveway. I went around to the passenger side and pulled open the door. As I did, an automatic running board slid out from under the car. I hopped up and into the car. When I turned to find my seatbelt, I saw Frank peeking out from behind the evergreens, grinning. I shook my head at him.

Kingsley drove in silence to the corner. "I heard what happened to your sister-in-law."

"Yeah."

"Pretty shocking."

"Yeah." I glared at the road ahead, not sure why I was pissed off.

He was silent for another minute or two. "What did your late husband do? What was his profession?"

"I hate it when people say 'late,' " I muttered.

"What?"

"My late husband. It makes it sound like he'll drive in at any moment." I stared out my window at the windswept fields. "He's dead. He's not coming back."

"You still miss him." Kingsley stated it as a matter of fact.

I wanted to disagree but stopped when I considered it. "No. I don't miss him. It's been years. It's—" I tried to find the words. "I hate to explain him, I guess. I'm sorry. I shouldn't take my pissy mood out on you."

"Problems with one of your patients?"

"No. I saw a hunter outside last night, and it spooked

me. I didn't sleep much."

"That's why you were out there with a shotgun? Would you shoot someone?"

"Probably not. But whoever is watching me doesn't know that."

We drove in silence for another half mile. "Your last name is different than your father-in-law's."

"Yeah. I didn't change my name when Bryan and I got married."

"Why not?"

"Why should I?"

He smiled, small dimples popping up at the corners of his mouth. "That's what I thought."

"What?" I demanded.

"Nothing." He hummed a song and it took a second for me to decipher what it was. "Hard Headed Woman," a song by Cat Stevens. Funny. I didn't take him for a Cat Stevens fan.

We got to town and passed the City Hall. I itched to ask him about the mayor but wasn't sure how to work it into a conversation.

"The mayor is concerned about your opposition to the project," he commented.

"She's never said anything to me about it." I waved to a couple of people I knew. They gaped at me, driving by in such a princely and pricy car. "She seemed concerned last night about staying on schedule."

"We were coming back from a meeting. I suppose she was anxious to get home." He turned to regard me when we stopped at the one stop light, waiting for it to change. "I like your hair that way. It's pretty."

"It's comfortable."

He let the car move forward through the green light.

"You don't take compliments, do you?"

"What do you mean?"

"The other day I said you had beautiful hair. And now, I said I like your hair."

I touched one of my braids. "I do have beautiful hair. It's a fact. Good genetics."

"See? You can't take a compliment. Just like you don't like to ask for help."

I considered it. "I hate owing anybody."

"I noticed."

I simmered in silence for a few seconds then blurted, "My parents bounced around, unlike Frank and Grace, who settled down when they had their son. My parents relied on others to bail them out. I had to borrow money to pay for their nursing home care and funerals. I hate being obligated to anyone."

"I get that. But accepting help doesn't mean you're obligated. It means someone might want to help you because they want to."

"Why?"

He drove into the parking lot at the emergency clinic. "Maybe because they like you."

I backed away from the intent expression in his dark eyes, a familiar flush of warmth flooding me. "Whew," I murmured. "I'm flashing." I fanned my face.

"What?"

"Menopause." He appeared so shocked I laughed. "It's a normal thing for women."

"No, I mean you don't seem old enough for that."

"I'm fifty-five. Prime of life and all that jazz." I reached for my door handle.

He put his hand on my arm. "Prime is right." He winked at me, opened his door, and stepped out.

Chapter Six

Good heavens. Now I *was* flashing. My face got so hot I was sure it was steaming. I struggled with the big door, trying to get it open. Kingsley came around the vehicle, pulled it open—

And I fell out, into his arms. It was so stupid, so perfect, I began to laugh, looking up into his dark eyes. "I couldn't have planned that better if I thought about it with both hands for a week," I gasped.

He grinned. "So you admit it? You are trying to seduce me?"

I disentangled myself from his arms. "I wouldn't know how to do it if I tried. I'm long out of practice with the romantic arts." I led the way to the front door of the emergency clinic.

He followed, pulling the door open for me and ushering me ahead of him. "After you, Princess." The door closed behind us, and for a second we were in the foyer, alone. "I don't think you're out of practice at all," he whispered, his lips brushing my ear. He strode to the front desk.

I followed more slowly. Flirting hadn't been on my radar for many years. Oh, well. He was probably kidding me. The receptionist called the back room, telling them we were here. She handed me the printout from a folder in the upright stacker on the desk.

"He checks out okay," she said. "He's about a year

old, relatively healthy except he's underweight. He was neutered, which is a miracle if he's one of Cox's, considering how she manages her animals. He's a schnoodle."

"What?" Kingsley asked.

"A cross between a poodle and a schnauzer." I scanned the facts on the sheet. "Did you give him his shots? He's current?"

"Yep. We bandaged the leg with a tension wrap. Try to keep him quiet for a few days. Keep an eye on the leg to make sure there isn't any tendon inflammation."

The door to the back offices opened, and the dog sauntered out. Now that he was upright, I got a better sense of his size. He was maybe forty pounds and about fifteen or sixteen inches tall with a round face, droopy Schnauzer beard, and floppy gray ears. When he caught sight of Kingsley, the stubby tail began a furious wagging. He tugged at the lead held by the overnight vet tech. His right foreleg was covered with a bright red bandage decorated with fairy tale creatures like Cinderella, Pinocchio, and Aladdin.

"I think he likes you," I commented.

Kingsley knelt on one knee, and the dog swarmed up to him, limping slightly. Instead of knocking into the man, though, the dog paused, then sat, head tilted to one side as though asking permission to approach.

"He's polite, too." I held out my hand for the lead. The dog regarded me, brown eyes curious and unafraid.

"You should check with Cox," the tech said. "I heard she's been breeding schnoodles. She might want him back."

"Like the vet said last night, a responsible pet owner would have posted he's missing. Nobody's done that, so

I think he's a stray." Kingsley reached out his hand to let the dog sniff him. I applauded his common sense. Too many people assumed friendliness on the part of animals and often regretted it.

"If Marian Cox wants to try to claim this dog, she can talk to me." I gave the leash a small tug. The dog stood and pressed against my leg.

"I know what you'll say, too," the tech said with a grin.

"Nothing you can print in the newspaper, I'll bet." Kingsley took the folder I still held. "Let's get Cinders out of here."

"Cinders?" I moved forward. After a slight hesitation, the dog followed me.

"Yeah, it's a real Cinderella story, isn't it? Dog saved from a bad home by the handsome prince?" He held the door open for us.

"That's conceited, isn't it?"

"What, that I'm handsome? That's what my name means. Aden." He got to the SUV and opened the back door. "I think he would have fit in my car."

I bent to lift the dog. Kingsley bent at the same moment. I barely avoided hitting him and instead ending up facing him, his lips an inch from mine. His dark brown eyes were alight with mischief. "Let me do it," he said. "Come on. Let me help you."

"Okay," I said softly. "Help me." I backed up while he lifted the dog, settling him in the back seat on a blanket already spread out there.

"See? That wasn't so hard, was it?" Kingsley turned to look at me. "Give it a try."

"Give what a try?"

"My name." He smoothed the blanket while the dog

peered above his head. "Give it a try."

"Aden." It had a nice ring to it, I had to admit. I smiled prettily at him. "Mr. Kingsley."

He reached for me, and I laughed, scrambling up into the front seat. He closed my door and came around to the driver's side. I had turned to watch the dog.

Aden turned to look, too. Our eyes met. I didn't know what to say when I saw the speculation in his gaze. I hurriedly faced forward again, wiggling the folder I held. "You've got a hefty vet bill here."

"And I'll have a boarding bill, too. How much will you charge me?" He fastened his seatbelt and started the car.

"Standard rates." I clipped my seatbelt. "Seventy-five dollars a day." I peeked sideways at him. He didn't seem surprised by the price. Maybe I should have charged more. "Plus his food and treatment, of course. That's extra."

"What kind of treatment?"

"We'll set up exercises to make sure the leg doesn't stiffen. But they have to be specialized, so he doesn't strain the leg any further. Either Frank or I will need to watch him." I used my thinking about the dog's care as a means to avoid thinking about Aden Kingsley's proximity to me.

"You and Frank are quite a team," he said. "You never told me what your husband did. Notice I didn't say 'late husband.' "

"Bryan was a foreman on a landscaping crew during the summer months. He had a degree in landscape design, so during the winter months he taught at the community college. We also had a small vegetable farm. We sold produce at the farmers' markets on the weekend.

I worked as a programmer for Lerner Software."

"A programmer? How'd you end up doing wildlife rehabilitation?"

"Somebody brought Bryan a hurt raccoon, and one thing led to another. I always wanted to be a vet tech, so I took classes in the evening while I was hacking code."

"Sounds like you were busy."

"We were. It was fun, though. We were doing what we wanted to do."

He was quiet for a few minutes. "Are you continuing to do it to honor your husband's memory?"

I shook my head. "No, of course not. Yes, he cared a great deal about the environment and wildlife, but it's not a legacy, if that's what you mean."

"Are you sure you're doing this for you, not him?"

I considered his words. "Have you ever been married? Ever shared your hopes and goals with someone? After a time, those hopes and goals become yours, too. It's hard to separate the two, I think."

"I'm divorced," he said. "So no, I guess I didn't share my hopes and goals." He glanced at me. "You never had children?"

"No, we didn't think we were parent material. And we both felt strongly about the environment. The world doesn't need more people."

"Do you regret it? Regret not having a part of him still with you?"

"A child isn't a duplicate. Besides, he is still with me." I raised my hands. "With the farm. What about you?"

"We weren't married long enough to consider kids. My former job was a tough one to ask anyone to share."

"How so?"

"I was a police officer in a high-pressure job. It was a tough environment to live in." His gaze went to the farm fields around us. "It's a far cry from this life."

"But it appears big city crime found us," I pointed out.

"Yeah. You didn't answer my question. Surely you can do something else than these piecemeal jobs, scraping by to support your work."

I should have been offended, but I wasn't. I saw his point of view. "I could, and I might. I have a chance to do consulting at a new rehab center that's going to open at the university."

"Wow. That's a great opportunity."

"Yeah, but I'll be gone three days a week. They want me onsite to advise and assist."

"Is that a problem?"

"I'm worried about Frank. Like you said, we are a team. We'll have to shut down our little hospital if I take the job."

"Why?"

"He can't do it alone. I handle the medical stuff. We can't afford to get anyone else to come in."

"So talk to him about it," Aden said. "Maybe he was ideas about how to handle it."

I stared at the cold fall morning. The sun was low in the sky at this time of year, throwing everything into sharp relief. "Yeah, maybe." I finally faced Aden. "Thanks for letting me talk about it. Keep it private, okay?"

"Sure. But discuss it with him. Frank may surprise you." He turned into our lane, carefully navigating the ruts and bumps. "Where do you want Cinders? At your house or at the barn?"

"Let's start at the barn, but I won't let him go inside. But he may as well get used to the area since he'll be out and about here."

Aden drove past my driveway and turned onto the drive leading to the barn. Frank poked his head out when he heard the car, his guitar in hand. "Is this our new dog?" he called.

"It's his dog." I gestured to Aden.

He gave my hand a squeeze. "It's our dog. At least for now."

I looked at our hands, resting on the console of the car. "Sure," I said. "It's ours."

Frank ambled over to the SUV. I quickly released Aden's hand before slipping from the SUV. "Is that the Fender? You finished it?"

Frank held up the guitar. The light shone off the rich walnut of the sides, the spruce top pearl-like in comparison. "I'm giving her a try today. Come on." He moved to the path leading to his house, guitar in hand.

The dog stood, wobbling on the uneven seat. I reached in for him, but Aden got there first, nudging me to one side and wrapping the dog in his arms. I held my breath, ready to intervene in case Cinders got snappish. But the animal was quiescent, only struggling slightly when Aden set him on the ground.

I took the lead and let the dog get a good sniff of the ground, casting about to get the scent of the grass and gravel of the path. I led him to the barn door and let him sniff there. Aden moved past me to open it, but I put my hand on his arm.

"I don't let dogs in here," I said. "I'm not worried about controlling them, but I don't want the patients to feel comfortable around a dog. A dog's a predator, and they can't forget that."

Aden backed away. "I never thought of that, I guess."

"Yeah, we have to remember. They're wild animals, and everything is a possible predator." I tugged on the lead. Cinders reluctantly moved away from the intriguing odors at the barn and loped ahead of me, limping. I would need to check his bandage and make sure to massage the leg tonight.

Frank waited for us in the doorway to his tiny home. "Interesting looking dog," he commented, eyeing Cinders doubtfully. "Schnauzer?"

"Poodle and schnauzer, we think," Aden said. "I found him by the side of the road. The vet said it might be a runaway."

"One of Cox's," I said.

Frank stretched out his hand to give the dog a sniff. "You were a smart one if you ran away from her," he said, rubbing the dog's ears.

Cinders remained at a standstill, then inched forward, his muzzle quivering at the odors in Frank's home. Frank moved to the back of the long rectangular space, taking a seat on his couch which doubled as bed. Cinders followed, sniffing eagerly at the furniture and the rug, which probably smelled strongly of Barn.

I sank down next to Frank on the bed, and the dog roamed around the five hundred square feet before stretching out on the floor at my feet, his gaze bouncing around the small house. Aden took Frank's Martin from its spot on the wall and strummed a chord.

"Do you play?" Frank settled back with the Fender. He gestured to the wall and the fold-up chair there.

"A bit." Aden sat, head bent above the guitar. "I

used to sing, too." He touched his throat.

"What happened?"

"A guy hit me in the throat. That's why my voice is screwed up."

So that explained it. "That's tough," I said.

"Nah. The other guy with me was beaten to death. I figure I came out on the winning side."

I sucked in a hard breath at the calm way he said it. What kinds of atrocities had he seen? I noticed Frank seemed unsurprised by such a comment. Then I remembered. Frank was a Vietnam vet and had seen more than his share of horrors. I know he still had nightmares sometimes.

Frank shook his head sympathetically. "You had a hard job."

"Yeah, but I liked doing it. I knew I was doing something good with my life." Aden ran his fingers over the guitar strings. "I wasn't in an office or a board meeting."

Another revelation, I realized. I had assumed he enjoyed being in a position of relative power. What a shock it must have been to go from being an on-the-street cop to sitting in endless meetings with a bunch of strangers.

Frank nudged the stack of sheet music on his kitchen table with his Fender. "I've been tuning this guitar most of the morning. Let's see how it sounds. Find us something to play, Ash."

I shook my thoughts away and leafed through the stack of music. "How about John Denver or John Prine?"

Aden strummed the opening chords to "Rocky Mountain High." Frank chuckled and picked up the melody, changing the range to something more suited for my reach. I waited until Aden had adjusted before I began to sing, the twelve-string guitar taking my words and making them sound fuller somehow in the tiny room.

Then Frank began "Angel from Montgomery" and to my surprise, Aden joined in on the singing, his raspy voice a startling contrast to Frank's countertenor and my soprano. That led us to "Big Yellow Taxi" followed by "Hey, That's No Way to Say Good-bye." Aden and Frank did some fancy finger work on "Here Comes the Sun," then Aden sang a chilling version of "After the Gold Rush," which was perfect for his voice. My accompaniment was background to his haunting whispered lyrics.

"That's a fine guitar," Aden said, resting the Martin on his knees. "Thanks for letting me give it a run."

"You come out any time and sit in," Frank said. "I've got work to do to get this Fender sounding the way I want. I can use another ear to help me."

"You've got a beautiful voice," Aden said to me. "Have you sung professionally?"

"Here and there. Now I sing to possums and coons." I reached down and touched Cinders' head. He waited patiently nearby, watching us while we played and sang. "And to dogs."

"I need to get back to town. Thanks for taking care of him. I'll see what I can do to find him a permanent home. I feel responsible for him since I found him." Aden stood and replaced the Martin on its hook. "Thanks again."

"Any time. I mean that. Your voice might not be what it was, but it's still got power to it." Frank went with us to the door, and we walked into the chilly morning. "Feels like winter is coming on. I'll take the pup to the house, Ash." He took the lead from me and went left, going along the path, the dog pausing to sniff avidly every few steps and piddle here and there.

I went with Aden to his SUV. "You might want to be careful looking for an owner for the dog," I warned. "If it's one of Cox's, she might try to claim him."

"Let her try," Aden said. He pulled one of my braids over my shoulder, his hand sliding down its length. "It is as soft as it looks," he murmured.

I shivered at his touch. "Like I said. Good genetics."

"Yeah." He opened the SUV door. "I'll call later on and see how Cinders is doing."

"No need to do that. He'll be fine. I'll let you know if—"

"I'll call." For a second I thought he might move even closer and kiss me, but instead he swung up into the SUV. "Thanks, Ash."

I waved a hand in acknowledgement and stepped away while he backed down the drive to the road. I went to the barn to check on the patients, happy to see Roberta attempting to move with the injured paw. Rocky appeared to be resting comfortably, the groundhogs were racing around their pen, and the possums ventured out to eat. And the squirrels had made a half-ass nest. Messy, but it was a start. A good morning.

I went to the house where Frank was in the kitchen, mixing up a bowl of cereal while Cinders watched hopefully. Frank watched me when I went to the bin in the corner and dished up dog kibble. "He seems nice," he commented.

"Very well behaved," I agreed. "He won't be a problem at all."

"I meant the man, not the dog."

I grinned. "I know you did. Yeah, he seems nice."

"Seems? What does it take to convince you? He rescued a dog and he's paying for the animal's care. That's pretty darn nice." Frank sat at the kitchen island.

I set a dog bowl in the corner. Cinders limped to me to check it out. "We'll need to set up a therapy schedule for him," I said. "Bandage on for four hours, off for one with massage. You know the drill."

"Yeah, I know. It doesn't seem like it pains him much." Frank regarded the dog, both of them munching with the same rhythm.

"He was lucky."

"Yeah, lucky Aden Kingsley found him. Lucky you were there to help out. Lucky all around, I'd say."

The dog regarded us, bits of kibble dribbling off his beard. He inspected the water bowl, lapped a few gulps, then came back to me and sat, eyes on my face.

"I think he's in love," Frank said around a mouthful of flakes.

"He knows I'm the giver of food." I gave Cinders a good head rub. He rumbled with pleasure.

"Wasn't talking about the dog."

"Oh, for heaven's sake, Frank. Grow up. Come on, Cinders." I left the room and Frank's chuckling behind and went to the once-dining room now-clinic room. I slipped a body harness on the dog. That made Cinders nervous when I clipped it to the ring embedded in the floor. I soothed him for a minute or two with back rubs and petting, before I cautiously removed the bandage, letting him walk about in a small radius so I could check his gait.

He favored the leg, but it wasn't extreme. It was probably stiff from the bandage. I massaged the leg and removed the harness, letting him off the lead for the first time. He hesitated, not sure where to go, but he trotted after me when I went to the back of the house.

I opened the porch door. He hesitantly followed me, staring at the expanse of back yard and the fence in the distance. "It's all yours," I said. He looked up at me then at the grassy yard, liberally coated with leaves. "Go on. Explore."

He left the porch, one cautious step at a time, nose up and questing in the breeze. He got to the grassy patch near the step and sniffed it. "Go," I said with an outflung gesture. "But not too much running."

He trotted out to the middle of the grass and turned in a slow circle. Then he suddenly leapt in the air and raced to the far end of the yard, wheeled around, and raced back to me. He limped, but it wasn't slowing him down any.

"I'll bet that's the first time he's been allowed to run," Frank commented behind me. "I heard Cox keeps her dogs cooped up in kennels all the time."

"I hope she comes out here and tries to claim him." I sat on the step and smiled at the dog, who was rolling the grass, paws waving in the air. "I'll let her know what I think of her."

"You and me both, honey. I'm going to town for supplies. Don't let him run too long."

"I won't." I leaned back on my hands, letting sunshine warm my face and make little patterns on my closed eyes. It was so good to relax like this, to let the weight of the day slide off me and to simply enjoy the moment like the dog, snuffling in the grass and finding new and exciting things.

I heard Frank's truck in the distance, the crunching

of gravel under tires. The world was silent again, or as silent as it can be in the country. Birds sang, squirrels and whatever crunched through leaves, and the breeze ruffled the stalks of dry grass and leftover flowers in the beds near the porch.

I don't know how long I sat in mindless bliss, simply communing with the world. Then I heard Cinders growl. I shot upright, my eyes snapping open.

Emily stood at the gate leading to the backyard, watching the dog. She was so still, so intent, at first I didn't even realize she was there. It was as if she was a piece of the landscape, blending in even though she wore unrelieved black: pants, jacket, sweater, and boots.

Her gaze shifted from the dog to me. She stared at me as though I was an oddity she'd never seen before. I was scrutinized and studied, evaluated. This is what she does when she hunts, I thought. She studies her prey. The idea made me shiver.

Cinders kept his gaze on her, his body stiff and his muzzle extended as though calculating the distance to her from his spot near me. "Hey, pup," I said softly.

He shook himself and trotted to me. That seemed to break Emily's concentration. "Hey, Ash. Do you have a minute to chat?"

"Sure. I didn't hear you drive in."

"I parked down the road. I wanted to see where Mara…" She put a hand on the gate. "What about him?" Her eyes were fixed on Cinders.

"He's new. And nervous. Move slowly." I got up to meet her at the bottom near the mailbox affixed to the newel post.

She opened the gate and stepped in the yard. Her dark appearance was like a cloud moving over the colorful fall leaves underfoot.

"The police told me about Mara. I'm sorry for your loss," I said when she got closer.

"It's your loss, too." She stopped several yards away from Cinders and me. "Mara was related to you, too."

Related to Bryan. Oh, well. "I wasn't as close to her as you were." I tapped the mailbox nervously. Something about Emily seemed different today, but I couldn't figure out what it was.

"What's that?" she asked, looking at my tapping fingers. "Your real mailbox is out on the lane, isn't it?"

"Oh, yeah. I used it to store a shock gun. I keep it to scare away skunks and other critters." I opened the mailbox to show her the bright orange plastic gun inside.

"Why don't you kill them?"

Because I don't like killing animals. Because they have as much right to be here as I do. Because this was their home before it was mine. None of those answers would satisfy her. "It's too messy."

"That's true. It can be messy." She gazed past me, her eyes unfocused. "I'm not sure I was close to Mara. She and I didn't have the same goals. I found that out lately."

It seemed to make her sad. Or mad. Cinders growled softly. "Well, we can't all have the same goals," I said inanely. "But we're still family."

"Of course. It's all about family. I owe everything I have to Bryan. And to you, too, of course. He's the one who gave me the confidence to start my own business." She flashed a smile so obviously fake I wondered why she bothered. "I came to tell you about the funeral. It's on Friday. Mara will be cremated. We'll have the memorial service at the cemetery in the afternoon. It's what she would have wanted."

Mara would have wanted a universal wailing by thousands and rending of clothing by the masses, I thought, not a low-key and brief service. "I'm sure it will be nice," I murmured.

"I hope you and Frank will attend. You're both family."

Oh, shit. I struggled to find a valid excuse to avoid such an unpleasant event. "We're prepping animals for release soon, and Frank is busy with that. But I'll talk to him." Maybe we could come up with an emergency. "I'm surprised you can have it so soon. Don't they have to run tests or something?"

"They know how she died. It was shock from blood loss." Emily stated this without any indication of grief or distaste. "They don't know what caused it." She eyed Cinders, who sat next to me, his eyes fixed on her. "It's a pretty dog. I heard your other dog died."

"I'm boarding him. He belongs to Aden Kingsley." I touched Cinders' shoulder and the dog relaxed.

"Kingsley? I didn't think you knew him so well."

"I don't have to know somebody well to board their dog."

"True enough. He and the mayor have been spending time together."

I felt a brief stab of something. Jealousy? Envy? Nothing easily identifiable. "I suppose that makes sense. They seem suited to each other."

"Do you think so? I think the mayor is artificial. He didn't strike me that way. Of course, I only spoke to him briefly. He and Mara had more interaction than I did."

Something about the way she said *interaction* made me take notice. "I thought they were only acquaintances."

"Oh, no. Mara and he have had several meetings." Emily pursed her lips, giving her the sour old lady look. "I was under the impression she and he had come to an understanding about the property."

"An understanding? That wouldn't matter much unless you were involved, would it?"

"I think she hoped she'd present me with a finished agreement, and I would go along with it." Emily ran a hand through her hair, making it fluff around her face. "Mara thought she had far more expertise in those kinds of things than I did."

"Well, I know I'm not supposed to speak ill of the dead, but the only thing Mara had expertise in was divorce settlements. You're a far better businesswoman than she ever was."

Emily straightened in surprise. "Why, thank you, Ash. I know some people think Survival Sally is a foolish waste of time and money. They think I'm duping the women who take my course, but I feel like I'm serving a useful purpose."

I remembered Aden and his comment about his former life as a cop. Once again, a revelation. Here I always thought Emily was just a paranoid prepper. Yet she thought she was serving a specific niche in the world.

"I've always wondered why you didn't try to change careers and do something more lucrative. You're the perfect role model for so many women, so small and pretty. When you prove you can be independent, it shows other women what they can accomplish. But this animal rehabilitation business makes you seem like another woman who's swayed by misguided compassion."

"What?" I wasn't sure if I'd been insulted or not.

Funny, Aden had said something similar but from him, it didn't sound like an insult.

"Your work with the abandoned animals. It's such a stereotype of the nurturing, sweet woman. Humans have precedence now. It's foolish to try to rescue possums and groundhogs. They're prey. Let them die."

"Humans are only another mammal on this planet, no better or worse than any others." I'd heard this argument so many times I could argue it in my sleep.

"Except we're at the top of the food chain."

"Only when you're holding a gun. Take the gun away and see who's on top."

She went still. For one crazy instant, I was sure she'd lunge at me. I felt the anger churning in her, her rage building. Cinders saw it, too. He moved closer to me, his gaze fixed on Emily.

"You've never hunted, have you? You don't know the first thing about what it takes to track and kill an animal. I remember when Bryan was teaching me and you'd sit in on our lessons. You always acted like it was so distasteful. Bryan understood, though. I think if you did, you'd have a much better appreciation for how ludicrous the work is that you're doing." She wheeled about and stalked across the yard.

"The difference between us is I've never needed to kill anything to feel alive," I said. "I don't need to kill things to prove anything."

She jerked open the gate and left, slamming it shut behind her. "Well, maybe we don't have to go to the funeral after all," I murmured to the dog.

He wagged his stumpy tail in reply. I turned to go into the house but stopped when I saw a flash of white at the end of the yard, near the fence. "Damn skunks," I muttered. I pulled out the scare pistol and took a few steps into the yard.

Whatever it was had left. I went into the house, Cinders following me. I moved to the kitchen window. Emily's big SUV was parked about halfway down the lane. She stomped to it, but when she neared the vehicle she slowed, pausing to stare at my house, as though assessing how the house sat in relation to the lane.

I kept hidden behind my curtain, watching until she slid into the SUV and pulled into my drive to turn around and leave. I raced upstairs and went to the front northeast room, which we used for storage or for an infirmary if we had patients who needed round-the-clock care. I peered out the window and saw her at the corner in the distance. The SUV pulled to a stop, and she got out to stare at the crime scene tape.

She looked up at the sky as though asking a question. When no answer was forthcoming, she got back in her SUV and drove off.

I moved away from the window. I realized I still held the launcher that I grabbed from the mailbox.

Chapter Seven

I put the gun back in its spot, shaking my head at my own idiocy. What was I thinking I'd do, launch a scare cartridge at Emily? Good heavens, I was getting as paranoid as she was.

I rebandaged the dog's leg before sitting down at my computer to get caught up on email and bills. Marky Mark had sent me a sample video file. *Tell me what you think. This is the kind of thing we'll do for all the patients.*

I smiled at his use of that word. I always referred to the wild creatures as patients because it allowed me a measure of separation from them, helping me keep what I did in perspective. These weren't pets, they were temporary.

I played the video which focused on the possums. The girl narrating it had an enthusiastic, perky kind of voice that actually matched the poky little possums quite well. She talked about their injuries, their care, their diet (along with admittedly adorable video moments of Polly eating her berries). I gave it my stamp of approval as long as the display they were planning was acceptable. *Don't do anything that would embarrass your mom or dad,* I warned in my email reply.

I was due for my stint at the vet's office at two, so I ate a quick lunch and took Cinders out for a short walk, giving him a chance to do his potty business in the roadside ditch rather than the back yard where I'd have to clean it up. Frank was back, so I left the dog with him and headed into town.

My first stop was the water treatment plant, where I chatted with the technician on duty. These guys were accustomed to me stopping by. Often they gave me a second opinion on my water samples, which I appreciated since official testing from the government was costly and time consuming.

I showed him my logbooks and he compared my notes to the detailed logs they kept on the desktop computer in the office. "We're getting a few contaminants, but nothing like those figures," he said. "It might be from runoff from the fields. It happens after a hard rain."

"I know, but it's spiked in the last couple of months, since they brought in the construction equipment. I'm worried something they're doing is getting into the aquifer."

"They have the necessary permits, and we had inspections out there, so I'm not sure we can blame it on them." He swiveled around from the computer. "Kingsley is gung-ho about getting permits and making sure they're compliant. If he wasn't such an asshole, I'd like him."

"Asshole? In what way?"

"Oh, he's put a bug up the mayor's butt about the parcel of land your stepsisters own. We never saw her before he came to town, but she's been out here twice in the last week, asking about the load our system can handle if more infrastructure is added. I told her that's in the report we put together for Kingsley Senior, but she tossed a bunch of new figures at us and wanted a report

A.S.A.P." He snorted. "That kind of stuff takes time, plus we need to get buy-in from people up and down the pipeline. It's not a matter of throwing together numbers and calling it done."

"What kind of figures did she toss?"

"A bunch of what-if things. What if a car dealership went in, what if a subdivision went in, what if a park, or a big box store went in. You know the kind of things."

"Not while I'm breathing," I muttered. "Why are you blaming him?"

"Because every time she's been in here, he's been with her, making suggestions and kind of prodding her. I think he's behind it all. I mean, it's his company that will make a killing depending on what kind of deal is made."

"What do you mean? They're a development company. It doesn't matter what goes in, does it?"

He shook his head. "They get a cut of the deal. If it's a big car dealership plus retail it would pay better than parceling it out into half-acre lots and selling those."

"I thought they were hired to tear stuff down and build it back up."

"No, his company has to submit the designs, draw up the figures for costs, do the environmental impact study. If it's a big project, they can charge more."

"You think he's deliberately puffing up the project so they'll make money?" I asked.

"Why wouldn't he? The mayor sure likes what he's saying. I'd feel better if we had someone working with him who wasn't in bed with him, too."

"What?"

"Oh, maybe not really. Although they sure do hang out together. No, what I meant was it would be good to have a disinterested third party guiding the mayor instead of somebody who'll profit off whatever she decides to support." He glanced at the wall clock. "Sorry, I have to make the rounds."

"And I'm almost late for work. Thanks for confirming my numbers."

"Keep an eye on them. If you want, I can test it for you in a couple of days."

"Thanks, I'd appreciate that. I'm never sure if these over-the-counter kits are reliable. I know you guys are."

"We try." He went with me to the office door, and I left, hurrying to my truck. It was a short drive to the vet's office where I was subbing. I drove past the Kingsley field office and saw Mike Parsons talking to someone on the sidewalk in front of the office. He seemed pissed off, an expression I was familiar with. As I passed he gestured to me and I slowed my truck.

"Listen, if you keep making trouble for us at the site, I'll report you to the police." He put his hand on the truck door, his tanned face splotchy with rage.

"Now what? You can't blame me for rainstorms and poor planning on your part."

He glared at the Kingsley office. "He doesn't know shit about field operations. Damn front office guy. It's not my fault we had to pay overtime to get the site stabilized."

"That's not what I heard. It sounded to me like Aden Kingsley knows exactly whose fault it is. Is it coming out of your paycheck?"

I thought he might hit me. Instead he pushed away from the truck, shaking one finger at me. "Your whole family acts like you can do anything you damn well please. You'd better be careful or someday an arrow might find its way close to you or one of those animals you're caring for." He stalked away, fists clenched.

Arrow? Did he have something to do with the one we found? He wasn't the hunter who came to the house. Was it one of his friends? A guy from the construction site? And what was his comment about my whole family? Did Frank piss him off?

I tucked the idea away to consider later. I went to the vet's office where I did an easy three-hour receptionist stint, checking in pets and helping owners understand the paperwork they got. It was six thirty when I left, darkness starting to soften the sky. I swung by the Gas-and-Go for a slice of pizza and drove through the town, which had a sleepy feeling to it since most of the stores were closed.

I spied Aden outside the Kingsley office. I considered slowing to give him an update on the dog. But I saw the mayor was with him. She wore a slinky dress and he wore a business suit again, this one more formal than the ones I'd seen previously. I made a quick turn before I got to the corner, almost spilling my pizza on the floor.

Okay, so what if he and the mayor were out on the town? It wasn't like he and I were dating or anything. I munched pizza, but it tasted stale. I ended up tossing it in the ditch on the way home.

Frank was in the barn when I arrived. We did our evening chores and I spent time with Roberta while she was mildly sedated, thoroughly cleaning her wound and testing the paw's flexibility. I rebandaged it and checked the two poisoned possums. They were doing much better. We decided we could release them in the morning.

I got Cinders at Frank's tiny house and made my

way to my house through the dark. The phone was ringing when I got there. I raced for the landline in the living room, falling on the couch like a football player making the winning catch. "Hello?" I asked breathlessly.

"Hi, I wanted to check on your new dog," Aden said. It was hard to hear him clearly because there were voices in the background.

"He's not mine, he's yours." I snapped my fingers and Cinders wandered over to sniff at me. "He's doing pretty good. I let him out in the yard today, and he had a run. I don't think there'll be any permanent damage."

"That's good. I appreciate you helping me out like this. I was wondering if maybe we can get coffee sometime. I know you're always working odd shifts, but maybe you can give me a call and we can meet."

"It's hard to hear you," I said. "That's quite a crowd with you."

"I had to give a presentation, and this is the post-question-and-answer crowd."

"Where at?" The way he was dressed and the way the mayor was dressed, I guessed where he was. There were only three or four swanky restaurants within a thirty-mile radius where a group of people could gather.

"The Golden Slipper. It's a nice place. Have you ever been here?"

"No, that's not in my price league."

"We should come here sometime. They have the best steaks. Oh, wait. Are you a vegetarian or vegan?"

I sighed. "No."

"Oh, good. I mean, I thought because of the animals, well, you know."

"I struggle with it."

"I'm sure you do." His voice was laced with humor.

"Well, I'm sorry. But—bacon!"

"And hamburgers."

"Yep."

"Good. It's a date. We'll come here sometime."

"Sure, that sounds good." I had no clothing suitable for such a high-class establishment, but I'd worry about it if and when the time came. I heard someone call his name in the background.

"I have to go," he said. "Thanks again. I enjoyed today, playing guitar and relaxing."

"Well, like Frank said, come out and sit in anytime."

"Okay. Thanks, Ash. Hey, maybe we can have coffee tomorrow afternoon."

I laughed. "Sure. Give me a call. I'm on duty at the emergency clinic starting at midnight, so I'll need the caffeine."

"Okay. I'll call you."

He hung up, and I leaned back, grinning. Then I remembered he was with the mayor, who was in a slinky dress, and my spirits plummeted. Oh, well.

I worked on my small speech for Saturday's party before taking the dog to Frank's for one last stretch of his legs and potty break. "I had a good time today with Aden, playing guitar," Frank said overly casually. He was bent over the Fender, adjusting the strings.

"Yeah, I didn't know he played. And played pretty darn good."

"I wouldn't be surprised if he stopped out here again." Frank shot a covert peek at me. "You know, to check on the dog and maybe play some guitar."

"Hmm."

"It would sure be fine if you can find someone to sort of go out with now and again."

"Hmm."

"He seems like a nice fella."

"Hmm."

Frank set down the guitar. "Is that all you got to say for yourself?"

I laughed. "Quit trying to play matchmaker." I pushed up off the daybed and went to the door.

"You know I won't mind, don't you? I know how much you loved Bryan, but he's gone. I want you to be happy." He put down the guitar and joined me, pulling me into his arms. "You're my daughter, honey, not just a daughter-in-law."

I hugged him, tears making my eyes smart. "I know that, Frank." My mobile phone thumped in my back pocket. "Saved by the buzzer," I murmured. I checked the display and sighed. "Hi, what's up?"

"I know this is short notice, but one of our techs called in sick. Is there any way you can come in and help us out for a few hours tonight?"

"Sure. I can get there in an hour or so, how's that?"

"Great, thanks. I know you're on for tomorrow night, too. We'll look at the schedule and see if we can adjust it."

"Okay. See you soon." I ended the call. "The Emergency Clinic is down a tech and want me to come in. I'll be gone until morning."

Frank shook his head. "You need to get yourself a regular job where you can have regular hours." He grinned at me. "It's hard to manage a romance when your feller doesn't know if you're home or not."

I slapped him on the arm. "I'll leave the dog with you tonight, okay? I don't want him alone in the house."

"Sure, sure. Me and the pup will have a beer and

watch TV."

"Don't let him in the barn," I warned.

"I know the rules. You go on." Frank smiled at the dog, who had curled up on the rug near the fridge. "It's boy's night out."

I went back to the house, changed clothes, and was checking in for my shift an hour later. We were busy through the night with the usual sprained paws, ingested chocolate and stomach pumping, and a first—an iguana with a minor burn on his belly. One sad patient was an elderly beagle with an equally elderly human, both of whom were tottery. The beagle was on insulin, but I suspected the owner had given him the wrong dosage. Blood work showed the dog's levels were dangerously high, so we put him on fluids to flush his system.

Things began to quiet at six in the morning and the office would close at eight, so I left, knowing I would be reporting back in at midnight. I drove to the gas station and got a cup of coffee then, on a whim, I drove to the construction site, which was somewhat on my way home.

Dense fog covered the road. The site didn't come into view until I was at the front gate. Equipment was lumbering around like giant insects blundering here and there. To one side was a pile of trees with a big picker-upper lifting the trunks and dropping them in a machine making a horrible noise of chewing and spitting out bits.

It was too depressing to watch. I easily visualized the enormous store with the wide glass doors welcoming people into their idea of a shopping mecca. Birds would get trapped inside or die crashing into the walls, deer were displaced and homeless, and countless other small mammals had already been chased away or killed. If this was progress, I wanted nothing to do with it.

I drove home on the county road and came to town, driving past Aden's house on Nightingale. It was dark. Apparently he wasn't an early riser. I stayed on Nightingale, which was a pleasant, tree-lined street. It ended at Maple, where I had to go right to go south and pick up old Creek Road and head for home.

The mayor's house was on Maple, her backyard backing onto a cornfield. Her driveway was at the side of the house and when I passed I saw a blue sedan.

Aden's sedan.

At six thirty in the morning.

I slowed. Yes, it was his. A low-slung BMW 340i in dark royal blue. There couldn't be two of those in a town our size.

I drove off, not sure which pissed me off more: he did flirty crap with me the night before or that he was sleeping with the mayor, who was as superficial as they come. I gave a croaking laugh when I remembered the water treatment plant tech's comment about him sleeping with the mayor. I guess it wasn't metaphorical after all.

I got to the farm and dumped my scrubs in the laundry bin and changed into my usual sweatshirt over a T-shirt and my patched jeans. I brushed out my hair, thankfully releasing it from the tight braid I needed at work. I redid it into four loose braids which I braided together so it would still stay tidy but was more breathable than my usual work style.

I opened the barn door just as Frank was starting the daily chores. "You look beat," he commented.

"Only because I am beat. How'd the dog act last night?"

"He stuck close to the bed. I don't know if he's been around humans too much. Every time I got up to pee, he had to follow me. I left him in the backyard to get some sunlight."

I rubbed my forehead. "He'll have to adapt wherever he goes."

"I thought Aden was keeping him?"

"I don't know what he's doing. I'll do rounds, but I need to sleep. I have a midnight shift again tonight, and I have to work on my damn presentation for the stupid party on Saturday."

"Is something wrong? Something I can help with?"

"No, I just need rest." I pushed past Frank and went into the barn, my pissy mood made even crappier by Rocky, who tried to hide from me, Roberta, who had chewed off her bandage, and the two possums who refused to peek out of their hidey hole. "I give up," I said to Frank. "I can barely see straight. I'll come back and do rounds later. We'll release the possums this afternoon."

"You get a nap. I can handle things this morning. What's that?" He went to the barn door and peeked out. "Did you order gravel?"

"What?" I pushed past him to our lane. A full dump truck was trundling toward me. I met the driver before he got too far. "You must be lost," I said. "I didn't order a load of gravel."

The dusty-looking driver shrugged. "Guy in town said they ordered too much. The guys at the quarry said you could use it so he said to come out here and spread it."

"Hold on." I peeked at the back of the truck. "That's a full truck. Who donated it?"

"I don't know. Call the quarry. Maybe they can tell you. Where do you want it?"

I jerked a thumb over my shoulder at my rutted lane. "Straight ahead. You'll see the potholes."

"You got it." The truck belched away, shuddering and shaking.

Frank joined me at the lane. "Well, look at that. If that's not a sign of true love, I don't know what is."

I shot him an angry glare. "He's worried about his fancy fucking car, that's all." The car that's sitting at the mayor's house, I fumed.

"Whoa. What's got into you?"

"I need sleep." I had to shout to be heard above the dump truck. I stalked to the house, the dust from the gravel adding to my grievances. I was a lackluster housekeeper, but I'd recently given the downstairs a good going-over. Now I'd have to redo everything because of the damned road.

I muddled around in the house for a time, knowing I wouldn't be able to nap because I was so angry. I went out back and Cinders loped to me, still limping but not as bad. I undid the bandage and massaged the foreleg, then left the bandage off to see how he did.

The truck was gone outside, so I finally lay down on the couch to nap, getting an hour of sleep that did nothing to improve my mood. I fed the dog and myself and went to the barn to pick up where I left off, leaving Cinders attached to the tie-out we had outside the barn.

Frank had tried redoing Roberta's bandage, but he did a half-assed job of it, so I ended up sedating her again to get it done correctly. When he came in with the old shop broom and started sweeping, I snapped, "Don't use that broom, Frank. It stirs up the dust, it doesn't move it from place A to place B."

"Well, excuse me, Princess. I didn't realize you were such an expert on brooms." He tossed the broom into the corner. "What has your undies in a bunch? You've been snipping and sniping at me all day."

I went into Polly's stall. "I'm pissed off at Kingsley."

"Why? Because he bought us a load of gravel?"

"No, because he acted flirty with me, but he stayed overnight at the mayor's house."

"What?"

I stabbed the pitchfork into the straw. Polly chattered angrily at me. "Oh, hell," I muttered. I was in no frame of mind to be working with the animals. I left the stall.

"There must be some kind of explanation," Frank said. "Are you sure it was his car?"

"It's a pretty distinctive car. The explanation is he's sleeping with the mayor and making nice with me. And with Mara," I added. "That's what Emily told me."

"Oh, I do not believe that. He has better taste than that. The mayor, maybe. But Mara? No way."

"You see? Him and the mayor—it makes sense. It makes more sense than him and me."

"I didn't say that." Frank crossed his arms and gave me his *I'm the grown-up talking* look. "Ask him."

"What? I can't ask him. What am I supposed to say? Hey, Aden, are you screwing the mayor, because if you are, I don't want to have anything to do with you."

"Well, maybe not in those words, but something like it." Frank frowned at me. "You want me to ask him? I can ask him what his intentions are."

"Oh, for heaven's sake, Frank."

"I'm serious, honey. I can find out if he—"

"Don't you dare," I threatened.

"You need to talk to him. I think he might have ideas you'd like to hear."

"What?" I tugged on my braid, trying to jumpstart my beleaguered brain. "What are you yattering about?"

"He and I talked yesterday, while you were at work." Frank evaded my angry gaze, instead going to the supply closet and getting out the barn broom. He made a great show of focusing on sweeping the floor with brusque little dabs.

"Huh? Yesterday afternoon? He didn't mention it to me when he called last night." I frowned at Frank. "What are you doing behind my back?"

"I'm not doing anything behind your back. He came to talk to me because I know you so well and, well, I don't want to say anything. It's for him to explain. Just keep an open mind, that's all. I know he's been working on something big. He needs to get buy-in from a bunch of folks to make it happen."

"What can he say that would make any difference to me?"

"He has good ideas, and you should hear him out. And I don't believe anything about the mayor. He's sweet on you."

"Bullshit."

"I know my way around a romance, and that man is sweet on you. Give him a chance to explain."

I heard Cinders barking outside the barn. I went to the door and peeked out. "Speak of the devil," I muttered when I saw the Kingsley SUV pull in.

"Okay, that's my cue to stay the hell out of your way," Frank said. "You talk to him. I'll get the possums ready for transport and maybe take 'em to the woodland for release."

"Frank, I don't need to talk to Kingsley."

"You go on and talk to him. I can handle two possums. Go on. Quiet your dog, and hear what the man has to say." Frank turned his back on me and went to the storage room where our transport cages were stored.

Cinders barked again. I heard a car door slam. "Damn it." I left the barn and went to Cinders, who was stretched against the thirty-foot lead toward Kingsley, who walked to me. He seemed relaxed. I couldn't figure out why until I decided every other time I saw him, he looked like a man who was at work. Today he seemed at ease, as though a burden had lifted off. His casual clothing—faded jeans and jeans jacket and a flannel shirt—emphasized it.

"Just the person I wanted to see. I have a proposal for you." He paused by Cinders and touched the dog's head.

"I doubt whether anything you propose would interest me." I considered going back inside, but I didn't want any drama playing out in front of Frank.

"Why don't you decide once I tell you. Maybe we can get the coffee I talked about? Or go inside and sit down?"

"I'm busy." I crossed my arms and leaned against the door to block it.

"Okay." I think he finally caught my less-than-pleased attitude because he stiffened. "I didn't want to tell you about it until I was sure I had the backers. We're planning a co-housing site for the parcel of land owned by your stepsister."

"A what?"

"It's a deliberate community of people who want to live together in a neighborhood. Like a planned suburb. We'll have a large common house with a community kitchen and where dining can take place. There will be some apartments, duplexes, and houses with the residents sharing resources. Not everyone needs a chain saw, for example, so we'll have a central spot where folks can check out equipment they might need."

I tried to envision what he was talking about. "A commune?"

"Kind of like, but with individual living spaces so people can either gather if they want or be private when they want. We'll be building to LEED certification so it's environmentally sound and the whole site will be solar ready." He smiled tentatively at me, his gaze fixed on my face. "We'd like your farm to be part of it. A big part of co-housing living is having a farm-to-table component. Your farm can supply most of the produce to the people living there. In exchange, they'd help you out here."

"You got Mara and Emily to agree to this?" I couldn't believe it.

"I was working on it. I was under the impression Emily would agree. She mentioned a couple of times she hoped for something other than retail there. Did you know Emily borrowed money from Mara and used her part of the land ownership as collateral?"

"What? I thought they were co-owners."

He shook his head. "Emily needed cash to get her business off the ground. Mara lent her the money on the stipulation the land be used as collateral. Apparently Emily was having trouble keeping up with payments. At least, that's what Mara said."

"But Mara's dead. Will her heirs have something to

say about it?" I had no idea who they were, but it was probably Emily. Mara had no children, and she was between husbands when she died.

"I'm sure they will. We'll find out when her will is probated. I thought you'd be pleased with this. I wanted to tell you before, but I needed to get the support I needed from the community."

"The mayor?" I asked, struggling to keep my voice disinterested.

"Her and others."

I considered the site in my mind, trying to visualize what he was talking about. "What about my parcel? What about those acres on the eastern side, where the road is needed?"

"We'd like to incorporate it into what we're doing, but we won't need your land to make this work. It would be great, though, if we had your farm working with us. Don't you see? It might be the answer you need. Frank would be a part of a community. He'd do farming, maybe some teaching."

"I'm not sure that's what he wants."

"He's tired, Ash. He told me. He's supported you all these years, but he wants to quit. He doesn't want to disappoint you." Aden moved closer to me. I felt pinned to the barn door by his intense stare.

"How would you know?"

"We talked yesterday. I wanted to lay out the details to him so he knew what kind of opportunities would be there for him and you."

My anger began to bubble up again. "I don't believe this. You're trying to convince him behind my back. You're sneaking around trying to talk Frank into giving up this property."

"No, it's not that. Frank will do anything to make you happy." Aden touched my arm, but I shook him off and he stepped back, almost treading on Cinders, who watched us with a puzzled expression. "Frank loves you, and he wants what you want. Remember when you asked me about sharing hopes and dreams? That's what he's doing."

"How would you know? You barely know him. You met him and me a week ago. You don't know jack-shit about us."

"I know how he feels," Aden said, his voice so low I had to strain to hear him. "You're a person—a woman—a man wants to be happy. He'll do everything he can to make it happen." A low buzzing tone came from his jacket. He reached in and checked his phone display, then jammed the phone back in the pocket.

"That's bullshit. I don't need you or your fancy suburb to be happy." As soon as I said, I wanted to take the words back. It sounded so harsh. It wasn't what I meant to say.

He stared at me for a long moment. "No, I'm sure you don't. I think you've forgotten how to be happy."

"You don't know anything about me." I was so angry I could hardly talk. A small little voice in my head said *he's right.* I used my anger to drown it out.

He turned away. "I'm sorry, Ash. I think this project is the best thing for the town and its future. I'm sorry you can't agree. If you want to isolate yourself, go ahead. But don't condemn Frank to your lifestyle choices."

My mobile phone thumped in my pocket. I pulled it out and checked the display. "I have a call I need to take."

Aden shook his head. "Yeah, I'm sure you do."

I put the phone to my ear. "Hi, Billy. What's going on?" I watched Aden get into the SUV and drive off, the dusty gravel road laying a fine coat of white on the dark exterior.

"I'm trying to track down Aden Kingsley. His office said he was driving out to talk to you."

"You just missed him. He's going back to town, I think. Why not call him on his mobile phone?"

"I did, but it went to voice mail."

"He'll probably check it when he gets back to his office. Did you find out who vandalized the equipment?"

"No, this is something else. I suppose I can tell you. It'll be all over town by the end of the day. Mike Parsons is dead. Somebody beat him to death."

Chapter Eight

"What? When? Where?" I paced outside the barn, phone to my ear.

"We found what's left of his body at the construction site. He was run through the chipper they have there."

"Oh, my God. That kind of thing only happens in movies, doesn't it? How do you know it's him? I mean, the chipper is a real grinder. No. Wait. You said he was beaten to death. How would you tell if he was put through a chipper?" My brain was spinning in a million directions.

"It's a crime scene, Ash. I can't tell you details. We're sure he was beaten around the head with a blunt object and at least part of him was fed into the machine."

I staggered to an old bench we had near the windbreak and sank down, unmindful of pine needles and dirt. "That's awful. Who would do that?"

"We're working on it." He sounded grim, which I suppose, in a terrible way, was appropriate given his name. "I called to tell Kingsley, but now I'll warn you and Frank. I think folks who are associated with the construction site are in danger. First it was Mara, and now it's Parsons. The site has been in contention for a long time. Maybe somebody is getting tired of the fight. A couple of folks mentioned they saw you and Parsons arguing yesterday."

"What? Are you thinking I might have done something like this? You're crazy, Billy. I could no more beat a man to death than—"

"Relax. I already checked your alibi."

"My what?"

"Time of death was in the early morning hours. I called the Emergency Clinic where I know you work. They confirmed you were there. That's another reason I need to talk to Kingsley. I'm not sure if he has an alibi."

"I think he was with the mayor last night," I said. "I saw his car at her house this morning when I got done with my shift."

"Okay," he said slowly. "I'll give the mayor a call maybe. You make sure to tell Frank about this, Ash. And for God's sake, lock your damn doors."

"I will. Thanks for calling, Billy." I ended the call and sat for a minute, trying to absorb it. Mike Parsons was an asshole, but heavens, nobody deserved to die like that. Fed into a chipper? I shivered.

The sobering call had somehow dampened my anger at Kingsley. Maybe it was a matter of perspective, I decided. After all, you hear about somebody dying a horrible death and suddenly the romantic entanglements of a possible suitor seemed insignificant.

I unleashed Cinders and took him to the house with me. As I suspected, a fine layer of dust covered most of the furniture, so I let the dog out to the back and tackled the cleaning. It was three in the afternoon by the time I finished. Common sense said I needed to take another nap because I was due at the Emergency Clinic in seven hours.

I went to the back yard and played with Cinders, tossing a hard rubber toy for him. It took a while for him to figure out if he brought it back to me, I'd toss it again. That and his lack of leash etiquette told me how much socialization he had. He seemed anxious to please, though, and that counted when it came to training a dog. If Kingsley found him the right owner, he'd be a good companion.

We played for twenty minutes or so, then we went into the house. I had just stretched out on the couch when I heard the crunch of tires in the driveway. I got up and saw Kingsley's SUV pull in at the barn. I considered letting him find out I wasn't there, but I didn't want him and Frank in cahoots, so I put a lead on the dog and went outside.

I met Kingsley near Frank's house. "Is everything okay?" he asked as soon as he saw us. "I was worried. I talked to Officer Grimm. He told me what happened to Parsons."

Cinders tugged on the lead, his head up while he scented the breeze. "I'm fine," I said. "All quiet here."

"Where's Frank? You shouldn't be out here alone."

Cinders pulled me forward. "I've got your dog to keep me company. Frank was doing a release out in the woods. He'll be back soon." Cinders pulled harder at the lead. "Hang on, dog. You need to learn the rules." I pulled back, and he strained forward, eyes on something in the distance. A rabbit, or maybe a squirrel. Lord knows there were enough of them in the woods behind the barn.

"The police seem to think Parsons was killed early in the morning. If you worked one of those night shifts, you might have been driving home when it happened."

"I did work a night shift last night. I was called in because they were short-handed, so I have an alibi," I said with a shrug. "Otherwise I suppose I'd be a suspect."

"Yeah, I have one, too. I have to admit, it's weird being on the other side of a police investigation. I haven't been out of the business too long. I still feel like I should be interviewing people and reviewing evidence."

"You have an alibi for the night?" I asked, trying to sound casual. "I drove through town after my shift yesterday. Everything sure seemed quiet." I tried for a chuckle. "You know, not like there was a murder a mile or two north of your place."

"I wasn't home. Listen, I honestly hoped you'd be pleased about the co-housing deal. I wasn't trying to go behind your back or anything. I apologize if it offends you. I thought, well, I thought you and I were getting along okay. I don't want this development project to, well, to cause problems."

I barely heard him. The son of a bitch was admitting to being away last night. What kind of idiot did he think I was? I was working up to something scathing to say but he continued.

"I came out because I was worried, that's all. Two murders in a small town means there's someone out there with a grudge."

"I don't hold grudges, so I guess it's not me."

"You don't? Does that mean you forgive me for talking to Frank without you being there?" He smiled at me.

I ignored it, focusing on Cinders, who was pulling me toward the barn in small increments. "No, I don't forgive you. I still think you went behind my back. Damn it, dog, would you quit it?"

Kingsley held out his hand. "Let me hold him."

"I can handle a damn dog."

"Is there a reason you won't accept any help from me?" Now he sounded peeved, something that gladdened my heart.

"I don't need your help or your apologies. Leave us the hell alone." I stumbled on the uneven footing when Cinders lunged toward the barn door.

Kingsley grabbed for the lead. It slipped through his fingers and Cinders was off and running, racing past the barn.

"Damn it!" I ran after the dog, skirting the holding pens south of the barn, spying the dog running into the woods. "Shit!" I slowed when he disappeared into the underbrush. I turned on Kingsley, who was beside me. "I told you I didn't need your help and look what happens."

"It looks like you needed help after all," he shot back.

"I wouldn't have lost him if you hadn't interfered." I tossed up my hands and stalked to the tree line. This small stand of "forest" was mainly deciduous trees, oaks, maples, basswood, and a few poplars that came from God knows where. Most of the leaves were down, so I had a clear line of sight into the distance, although it was somewhat hilly.

I started into the trees, searching for any sign of a bright red leash line among the brown and discarded leaves. I heard Kingsley behind me. "You'll get your boots dirty," I tossed over my shoulder.

"You need to worry about keeping your Crocs on your feet. If you're not careful, you'll lose a shoe again."

I stopped, and he ran into me. I turned on him. "I don't need your interference here." He was so close I saw his chest moving up and down, his flannel shirt inches from my nose.

"Listen, I don't know what I did to piss you off, but would you get over it? I apologized for the only offense I know about, although I don't consider it objectionable." He pushed past me, bumping me so I had to hop to keep my balance. "I can talk to your father-in-law without you being present. He's not a child you have to care for."

Cinders barked frantically ahead of us. I followed Kingsley, glaring at his back. "Just great. I'll bet he found a skunk or a coon." I kicked a downed branch out of my way, ducking under a sapling that snapped back when Kingsley moved it. "Watch it!"

"Sorry." He stepped aside. "You lead. Go on."

I sprang ahead and pushed through the undergrowth, watching where I went because the ground was wet from the rains and spongy in spots.

"I told you I'd pay for his care. If a skunk sprays him, I'll pay for you to bathe him."

"It's not the money." Good Lord, didn't this guy have an ounce of sense? "It's him getting bit by a coon or maybe biting one. That's a hell of a lot more serious than stink." I paused, listening for Cinders, then struck out to the right, following the sound. "If he gets in a fight with a coon or a possum, he may have to be put down. They can carry rabies, and it doesn't matter if a dog is vaccinated. That's serious shit."

I stopped, not sure what I was seeing ahead. Kingsley bumped into me, pushing me forward. Something was on the ground ahead of me. Cinders was jumping around, tail wagging furiously, as he circled the pile of clothing.

Oh, crap. It was Frank. He was lying face down in the leaves, body sort of scrunched up, like he pitched forward. His white hair was covered by his dark knit cap.

He wore his dark brown jacket and dark blue jeans, so he blended in with the leaves and debris.

Cinders danced to me, whining anxiously. "Frank?" I hurried forward. The transport carrier was near his outflung left hand, the door open and the cage empty. Did he fall? Hit his head? I stumbled to where he lay, a branch tripping me so I fell on all fours near him. "Frank?" I leaned above him, trying to get a glimpse of his face. "Come on, Frank. You're scaring me."

"Move back, Ash. Let me check him." Aden pulled me away, gently but firmly. "Get the dog. He's getting in the way."

I pushed Cinders back and snatched the lead, tying him to a small sapling nearby. "Good dog," I said inanely before going back to Frank. I dropped to my knees next to him. "Frank, are you okay? Frank?" I tried to pull him into my arms. "Come on, Frank. What happened?"

Aden knelt opposite me, his fingers on Frank's throat. "There's a pulse." He ran his hands over Frank's back and sat back. "Give me your sweatshirt."

"What?"

"He's been shot. We need to stop the bleeding." He sat back on his heels, phone in hand. "Do it, Ash."

Frank was so pale, so still. I tugged my sweatshirt off, my braid swinging down and brushing Frank's face. His eyelids fluttered and he tried to speak. "It's okay, Frank." I fumbled with my bunched-up sweatshirt. "I don't see where it is."

Aden pointed to the upper left quadrant on Frank's back. That's when I saw it was darker colored. I touched it hesitantly and my hand came away wet. I pressed the shirt against the wound, one hand holding the shirt in place and the other around his back so I held on to him to talk. "It'll be okay, Frank. We're here. We'll get help."

"Where are we, Ash?" Aden shook me gently. "Come on, Ash. I need to tell dispatch."

"South of the barn, about a half mile into the woods. We're not far from Little Creek, near where it comes out by County 96."

Aden spoke into the phone. "It might be a through-and-through. I can't tell. Probably small caliber or he'd be dead. There's blood loss, though. I don't think it hit the artery."

Oh, God. The subclavian artery ran through the shoulder and it was one of the main arteries in the body. And the brachial plexus was there, too. It controlled the arm's function. If he was hit in the plexus, he might lose the arm.

"Frank, it's okay," I murmured, once against pressing against him.

"We can't bring him out," Aden said. "We don't have transport nearby. You'll have to come in and carry him out." He watched me from the other side of Frank's body. "We'll be with him and do what we can. I'll leave my phone on. Triangulate against my signal. It's an iPhone, so use the app." He listened, his face taut. "Damn it, figure it out." He tapped an icon or two on the screen and set the phone on the ground. "Somebody needs to teach your police department about twenty-first century technology."

Frank stirred, moving away from the shirt I had pressed into him. The fabric was turning red under my hands. "He's bleeding too much," I whispered. "Who knows how long he's been here?"

Aden moved around to crouch by Frank's head. He peered under Frank, gently touching Frank's cheek.

"He's doing okay," he murmured. "He's still warm and there's pupil dilation."

"I'm the medical professional," I said, my voice so shaky the words came out slurred. "I should be doing the assessing."

"I have experience with gunshot wounds, some of it first-hand. Let's keep him quiet and stable until help arrives. This town does have EMTs, doesn't it?"

"Yes. They're volunteers, but we have a good group. I trained with them. I wanted to take a volunteer shift or two, but my schedule bounces around too much for me to commit."

"That's one thing we need to change. We need paid professionals. We need professional police, fire, and ambulance."

"We?" I asked.

"I'm part of this town. If it's going to grow, we need to make changes. We can't always rely on volunteers."

"You should run for office. Maybe city council." I lifted the fabric and peeked at the wound. The blood flow had slowed. I resumed pressing. "Was it a hunter? I told Frank he needed to wear his safety vest whenever he was out and about."

"Maybe. It's turkey and pheasant season, so I suppose it's possible. I doubt any hunter would be here, though. This isn't the kind of habitat for those birds."

"You know a lot about it for a city slicker who only recently moved here." I was getting cold, goose bumps popping up on my arms. My knees were getting wet, too, from kneeling in the damp leaves.

"I told you before. You're making assumptions based on my car and my clothing. I've hunted deer and duck. I also make it a point to know when people might be carrying guns, especially since I live on the outskirts of town and there's a cornfield not far away where hunters might be tempted to walk."

"Iowa's a concealed carry state. Anybody can have a gun. Hell, I was in the electronics department of one of those big blue box stores, and a guy came in with a gun strapped to his waist. Almost gave me heart failure." I was grateful for the talking. It somehow made this seem not as critical, not as scary.

"True enough. I got used to it when I was on the job. I guess I never got out of the habit of staying alert."

"On the job? Is that what they call it? Were you a detective? A beat cop?"

"I was a beat cop for a while, then I made detective. I was a hostage negotiator. I worked on special teams used to diffuse tense standoffs. I'd go in and assess, try to talk people down from whatever they were planning on."

"Sounds scary. And dangerous." I peeked under the cloth again. The bleeding had slowed, but there was still some coming from the ragged jacket hole.

"It was. But it was satisfying, too. In many cases, I was able to prevent bloodshed."

"Not in all cases?"

He stood. "No. Sometimes people didn't want to stand down. I hear them."

"What?"

"Listen."

I lifted my head. Cinders was huffing and making growl sounds. "Hush, dog," I murmured. I heard the sirens. "I hear it. They'll be here soon. The road is there." I pointed to my right. "We don't have any direct access to the county road from the farm. They'll come overland."

"That's one thing we need to change if the co-housing project goes through." Aden picked up his phone and moved back a few steps along the way we came. "It makes more sense to use an existing road than put in a new road through prime farmland. We'll have to put in a connector to link the farm to the road."

"Good luck with that. We've suggested it a couple of times and are always shot down."

"If you're part of a bigger development, the roads people will listen. I'm going out to meet them. Keep pressure on the wound."

"Aden."

He turned.

"Take the dog. He'll lead you back to us in case you lose the way."

I thought he'd argue, but he just untied Cinders, tugging the dog away from me and Frank. They soon disappeared from sight, the slight hills hiding them.

I kept my arms around Frank, pressing the shirt with my body. "Hang on, old man," I whispered. "They're coming." I began to hum, a mindless tune until my brain fixed on a melody. I began to sing "May the Circle Be Unbroken" but realized how grim the lyrics were. I switched to "Both Sides Now," a song Frank loved to hear me perform.

I finished it and moved on to "Amazing Grace" before I heard voices. Cinders burst through the leaves, dashing to me. A few seconds later, people surrounded me. Someone wrapped their arms around me and pulled me away from Frank. It was Billy.

"What happened, Ash?" Billy kept his hands on my shoulders, staring into my face. I tried to peek past him to see what they were doing with Frank, but he shook me. "They'll take care of Frank. You tell me what happened."

I babbled something about the dog being lost and running into the woods to find him. Billy kept his eyes on my face the whole time while I tried to peek around his body.

"When did you last see Frank?" He shook me again. "Come on, Ash. Think."

I stopped struggling and focused. "It was before you called me. Aden came out, and he and I talked. Frank was in the barn. He said he was going to release the possums."

"Okay. I need to get the timeline figured out." He released me, and I pushed past him. The medics had Frank on a stretcher, still face down. My sweatshirt lay near him. I felt faint when I saw how much blood it held. Aden stood off to the side, Cinders straining at the leash next to him.

The next few minutes passed by with agonizing slowness while they stabilized him on the stretcher. Then two of the four men lifted him. One of the others led the way and the other man brought up the rear, carrying their gear. I longed to question them, to suggest medical treatment, but I knew it would be stupid. Time was more important now. I followed, Aden behind me. Billy Grimm and a deputy stayed behind, probably looking for evidence.

It was silent except for an occasional comment by the lead man. "Watch out here. It slants." "Careful. It's soft ground here." "Almost there."

We left the trees and the ambulance was there, sitting on the strip of grass separating the barn and outbuildings from the woodland. "We owe you replacement turf," one of the EMTs said. "We tore it up when we came overland."

I saw the tire tracks sunk deep into the earth, leading from the road a quarter mile away. "Don't worry about it, guys. I'm glad you got here so fast."

"We're taking him directly to Iowa City, to the university's emergency room. It's a fifteen-minute drive. Billy assigned a deputy to clear the road for us with lights and sirens. You can meet us there."

I began to protest, but Aden took my arm. "They need to work on him in the ambulance." He pulled me toward the barn. "Come on. I'll drive you."

I hesitated but knew he was right. I tried to keep up with his longer strides, but I kept tripping on my own feet. When we got to the barn, I stopped. "I have to—" So much. Animals to care for. Work tonight. Frank hurt. "I need to do stuff. They need shots and food and—"

"I'll take care of it. Come on."

"What do you mean, you'll take care of it? You don't know how to."

"Let me handle it, Ash. Come on." He dragged me past the barn to his SUV. "Come on, Cinders." He opened the back door and the dog jumped in.

"We can't take a dog to the hospital."

"We won't." He opened the front door for me, then held out his arm to block me when I tried to get into the SUV. "You need to change your shirt." Aden stared at my chest.

I looked down. Blood splatter covered me from my neck to my waist, with a heavy splotch near my heart. My formerly pale blue "Dasdorf Titans" T-shirt was now red.

I was familiar with blood. Animal blood. But this was human blood. It was Frank's. I began to tremble, shaking so hard I thought my spine would snap. Aden pulled me into his arms, hugging me tightly. "He'll be okay."

"Blood," I stammered. "It'll stain your coat." Tears poured down my face.

"I don't care."

"I can't go on without him. Frank does so much. He's always been there." I pulled away from Aden to wipe at my tears.

"I know." He put his hand on the back of my head and pressed me to him, cradling me. "Don't worry. We'll figure it out."

"We?" I mumbled into his coat.

"Yes. We." Aden's breath was warm on my face. "I'm with you, Ash." He pulled away, his lips brushing mine. "Now take off your shirt."

"What?"

"Take it off." He peeled off his coat and unbuttoned his flannel shirt, revealing a black T-shirt underneath. "Take mine."

I didn't hesitate. I shucked off the horrible T-shirt and tossed it to one side before taking the flannel shirt from him. It was way too big, of course, but it was warm and dry. I buttoned it and tied the tails around my waist. Otherwise it would have hung to my knees.

"Let's go." He helped me up into the SUV and hurried around to the other side, slipping into the driver's seat. "While I drive, you call the vets you work for. Ask them to sub for you here, at the barn. Call the Emergency Clinic and tell them you can't come in. Ask them if we can drop off Cinders for them to take tonight." He backed out of the drive, turned, and headed down our lane toward town. "It sure would be nice if your lane went through to the county road," he muttered. "This is a roundabout way to get there."

"Believe me, I know. A couple of times, we needed to have an emergency surgery, and those few minutes make all the difference in the world." I dug my phone from my pants pocket and tried to find the contact list. Before I could, the phone rang. I didn't recognize the number but it was local, so I answered.

"Ash, this is Harold. I heard what happened to Frank. How can I help? I got folks here asking if you need anything."

I sagged back on the seat. "Thanks, Harold. They're taking him to the emergency room at the university. I'm on my way there. I need somebody to organize help out here at my hospital. Can you call the vet's office and see if they have somebody who can come out and fill in?"

"They already called and volunteered. I'll send 'em out there."

"Oh, and call Binny. Her son made videos of the animals for our party on Saturday. There's a bunch of details about their treatments and stuff."

"That's a good idea. I'll get Marky Mark out there as soon as I can track him down. Anything else you need?"

I heard Cinders in the back seat. "I need somebody to take care of our dog. We'll be at the hospital. I didn't want to leave him alone at the house because he's new."

"You swing by here and drop him off. I'll take him home with me. My Sheltie will love to have a playmate for the night. The church ladies will get the food organized and ready to go, so you and Frank won't have to worry about a thing once he comes home from the hospital."

"It's bad, Harold." I could barely talk, my voice hoarse. "I don't know—"

"He's coming home from the hospital," Harold said firmly. "You can count on that. They'll patch him up as good as new. You have somebody to be with you at the hospital? Do you want me to send out Emily or somebody?"

"Good God, no. I'm with Aden Kingsley. He'll drop me at the hospital. I may need a ride home at some point."

"I'll stay with you," Aden said. "Don't worry about that."

"I heard that. He's good people, Ash. I'm glad he's with you. Now get over here and drop off your dog so you can get to the hospital."

"Thanks, Harold." I lowered the phone and took a deep breath for the first time in what seemed like hours. "The small-town emergency crew is at work."

"I heard. You're lucky to have them. And they're lucky to have you. Frank and you are a big part of this town. They're proud of the work you do."

"I think a few think I'm crazy." I closed my eyes but when I did, a memory of Frank lying still on the ground swam into my internal view. I couldn't bear that.

"That's why the party on Saturday is important. It gives you a chance to tell them what you do and why you do it. Although I think most of them know why."

"Yeah? I wonder why I do it myself sometimes."

"You do it because you care about the world and you don't like to see any creature suffer. That's who you are, Ash."

"And people think that's crazy," I muttered. "Did someone shoot Frank on purpose?"

Aden didn't answer immediately. We were almost to town when he did. "Who else knew you were doing a release today?"

"I don't know. I may have mentioned it in passing to people, you know, when they ask how things are going. Why?"

"I was trying to figure out if somebody was waiting for him or watching him. I think watching him makes more sense."

"What?" Nothing made sense to me.

"There's not a set time for you to release an animal back to the wild, is there?" He glanced at me before turning onto the main road into town. I shook my head. "Okay, so no one would have waited for him. I'll bet someone was watching."

"From where?

"The county road. Anybody can sit out there and see your barn, see you go in and out. If they saw Frank come out with a carrier, they'd know he'd go to the woods, wouldn't they?"

"Maybe." I started to tug on my braid, but I realized my hands were grimy with blood and dirt.

Aden pointed at the glove box. "I have wipes in there."

"You do?" I opened the compartment and pulled out the box.

"It gets messy on construction sites. If I have to go from a site to board meeting, I usually don't have time to stop and clean up. There's Harold."

I hurriedly cleaned my hands and was ready to leap from the car when Aden slowed. I opened the back door and tugged on the leash. Cinders reluctantly hopped out and I handed him to Harold. "Thanks," I said, stepping up on the running board.

"I'll take care of him. You folks take care of Frank." Harold moved back and within a minute we were on our way again.

I heard the ambulance ahead of us, the whoop-whoop siren combined with the scream of a police siren in the distance. Aden took my hand. "It'll be okay, Ash."

I stared out my window, tears dribbling down my cheeks. I didn't believe him.

Chapter Nine

Thank God it was a weekday and not a weekend so we didn't have university football traffic to contend with. We navigated the intricate maze of the hospital complex, finding the emergency room entrance after going through a roundabout twice.

"Frank Goddard," I told the woman at the desk.

"Sign in." She gestured to the clipboard next to the ledge in front of the window protecting her from the public. "We're expecting you." She slid two laminated badges through the little slot in front of her. "Wear these at all times. He's being examined now. The doctor will consult with you in Room 30 when he's ready. Through the door, go right, then go left."

"But I need to be there."

Aden pulled me toward the door. "They won't let you in the examining room. They'll do triage and determine next steps. You'll need to sign consent papers." He steered me through the corridor, past rooms with patients in various stages of dress or illness, and past a big nurse's station full of monitors and computers. "I've been through this."

"Have you been shot?" I went into the minuscule room, which was barely big enough for three chairs and a tiny table that had seen better days.

"Twice. The second one was the one convincing me to retire. It missed my heart by about an inch. Too close for comfort."

I dropped into the armchair. So many questions, so many worries, were buzzing in my head. I didn't want to think about them. Didn't want to consider what might happen if Frank—"Did you always want to be in the police?"

He sat next to me and leaned forward, his hands clasped between his legs. "I worked construction for my father for a few years and thought about doing that. But there were some burglaries and I saw how the police handled it. I was impressed. So I went to community college to get a degree in criminal justice. I applied to the academy and was accepted. I worked nights on getting a bachelor's degree so I could move up in the ranks."

I stood and paced nervously to the door and back, just a few steps. What was taking so long? Maybe we should have gone to the other city hospital. This hospital, affiliated with the university, was always so damn busy. "Emily should have been a cop. She has unresolved aggression issues."

"You think cops have aggression problems?"

"Maybe. I can't figure out why anybody would volunteer to be a cop." I peeked out the door, but the scene outside hadn't changed much.

"Maybe they want to help people."

"There are lots of ways to help people that don't involve carrying a gun," I pointed out.

"True enough." He straightened. "I hate waiting rooms."

"I'm usually on the other side of it. I'm the one who comes in and talks to the family. I have a good idea what's going on. It doesn't make it any easier." I looked at the white walls, the inane paintings, the cheerful magazines on the table. "I spend too much time in emergency rooms."

"If you take a consulting job, then you won't need to, will you?"

"I don't know." I stood, full of nervous energy. I eyed myself in the reflection from one of the pictures. My hair was a real mess, so I quickly undid the braids and pulled a scrunchie from my pocket. I bent over, pulling my hair into a ponytail. I braided it loosely then straightened. I checked my reflection and nodded with satisfaction.

"You do that so easily."

I turned. Aden was staring at me, his eyes wide.

"I've had years of practice." I peeked out the door. It was the familiar hustle and bustle of an emergency room, a sense of controlled chaos under a layer of calmness. "It's easier for me to care for long hair than short hair. I should get it cut now it's going gray. Few women can carry off long gray hair."

"I think you're one of them." He cleared his throat. "If the co-housing project goes through, you'll be able to take the consulting job. Frank will be around people, and you won't have to worry about him."

I went back to the picture and studied myself, more to avoid looking at Aden than to check my appearance. "What about Fairy Tale Endings, though? I don't want to give it up."

"But you won't have to give it up. You can still have animals there, maybe the ones transferred from the university's rehab clinic. Maybe you can be sort of a halfway house or something that's not as much effort."

"Maybe." I turned away and went back to the door. If Frank had been seen immediately, he was in triage for about twenty minutes. How much time did they need?

"Have you discussed it with the university people?"

"They're still in the fund-raising stage. They're not ready to talk details." I went to the picture, then back to the door. As I did, it opened and a young Asian man in blue scrubs stepped inside, closing the door behind him.

"You're Frank Goddard's family?" He took the seat across from Aden. "I'm Dr. Cam. I'm treating him."

"Yes, I am." I sank down in the remaining chair. "How is he? He lost a lot of blood."

"That's one concern we have. His age is another. Luckily he's healthy. We need to do surgery, though, and there's always a risk with that."

"What kind?" I visualized the area of the gunshot wound. "I was afraid the bullet might have hit an artery."

"I don't think it did, but we won't know for sure until we get him into surgery. We're prepping him now." He stood. "I'll go over the details of the surgery with you in a few minutes. I'll be assisting our surgical specialist who will handle extracting the bullet. For now, I want you to know we're doing everything we can for him. He's unconscious but stable, his heart is strong, and his vital signs are good."

"What caliber bullet was it?" Aden asked.

The doctor paused at the door. "Are you with the police?"

Aden glanced at me. "I'm a friend of the family and an ex-police officer. It wasn't a handgun, was it?"

"I doubt it. I've seen enough hunting wounds to think it's a 30-30 or something like that."

"What's a 30-30?" I asked.

"A rifle," Aden said. "If they can extract the bullet and it's intact, they'll be able to match it to a specific rifle."

"One of our administrative staff will be back to discuss the surgery with you and have you sign the forms. We'll report our results to the police. They'll be the ones who will update you on what we find." Dr. Cam turned to Aden. "Including forensics results."

I moved forward. "Can I see him before he goes in for surgery?"

"No, that's not possible. He's in good hands. Don't worry."

I longed to ask more questions, but I knew there weren't many answers. "Sure, thanks," I mumbled. The man left and I turned to Aden. "Somebody shot him on purpose?"

"I think so. Everybody connected to the damn construction site is getting hurt." He stared at me, his eyes haunted. "You're the only one who hasn't been hurt."

"Well, you can't blame me. I have an alibi, remember?"

Someone knocked on the door, and a brisk woman came in with a clipboard. We spent the next few minutes going through insurance details, hospital forms, and more hospital forms. "We'll keep you posted on how the surgery is going. Go to this room and sign in." She handed me a slip of paper. "We'll assign you a pager and also take your phone number so we can text you during the surgery. Or you can wait there if you'd like."

"How long will this take?" I asked.

"It's hard to say. It depends what they find when they start surgery. I think you can count on at least two hours, though." She left, forms in hand.

"I meant to ask her about parking. I'm not sure we

can stay in the parking lot. It might only be for short-term parking." Aden hurried after the woman, catching her in the hall. They had a conversation, and he came back.

"I hope I didn't sign away the farm," I said.

"You'll find out in six months when the bills start coming in. Let's get you checked in and get some food."

I checked my watch. "Holy crap. It's seven o'clock. Where did the day go?" I followed him into the maze of corridors. We found the surgical waiting area. I took one look at the jammed room full of anxious family members and decided not to wait. I gave the receptionist my phone number and took the red-light-thumpy gadget. I handed it to Aden, who tucked it in his coat pocket. Then we wandered through the maze of buildings to the cafeteria.

While we were dining on chipped beef on biscuits, Binny called. "How's Frank doing? What happened?"

I filled her in on what I knew in between bites of food. "He's in surgery now. Lord knows when he'll be done."

"I'm sure he'll be fine. Frank is one tough old guy. He'll pull through this with flying colors. I called to tell you Marky Mark is at the farm. I gave him the spare set of keys to your house. He and some of the kids volunteered to stay out there tonight. They're chaperoned, so you don't have to worry about finding empty beer cans everywhere. Mark is there, and so are a couple of other parents. The kids are helping the volunteers from town care for the animals."

I had visions of teenagers getting bit or sprayed and sighed. "I'll try to get home tonight and help get things organized."

Aden shook his head. "Not going to happen."

I ate my cooling food and ignored him. "Make sure

to thank everyone for their help. I appreciate it."

"I hope this doesn't mean you have to cancel the party on Saturday. I mean, I know Frank would want you to go."

"We'll see how he's doing." There was no way in hell I would go to a party if Frank was languishing in a hospital, but I wouldn't tell her that.

"Okay, well, listen, you focus on Frank. Everything's under control here. Harold said your dog is fitting in fine at his place, and Marky is having the time of his life. I think he'll get an A on his class project because he's shown how his documentaries are saving lives." She laughed. "I know he didn't plan on that, but it's working."

"Thanks again, Binny. I'll be in touch as soon as I know how Frank is doing." I ended the call and ate a few more bites. "Everybody is pitching in. But I should go home and make sure things are being done correctly."

"You should be here with Frank. Your patients will manage without you for a time." Aden sat back on the metal chair, smiling at me. "This isn't the date I thought we'd have when I suggested we go out for dinner sometime."

I peered around the bright cafeteria. "It does sort of lack atmosphere." I pushed my tray to one side and rested my hands on the table. "Thanks for the help."

He grinned. "See? That didn't hurt, did it? You were able to accept help and it didn't incapacitate you, did it?"

"No, it didn't hurt," I admitted. "Seriously. Thank you. I don't know what I would have done without you."

"I like helping you," he said in his low, husky voice. "Let me do it more often."

I shied away from what I heard. "I'll bet you say that

to all the girls."

He pitched forward and covered my hands with his. "You refuse to believe me. Why?"

I wiggled my fingers free. "I barely know you. Why would I believe you? You waltz into our town and claim to offer up a plan to help everyone. What are you getting out of it?"

"What do you mean?"

"It's good for your company, isn't it?"

"Of course it is. Not as good, maybe, as a retail development but still profitable. I'm in the business to make a profit, you know." His phone chimed in his coat pocket. He pulled it out and checked the screen. "Excuse me. I need to take this call." He stood and moved a foot or two away, phone to his ear. "Hi, Charlene. Yes, I'm with Ash. Frank was hurt." He listened intently. "I'm sorry, but I won't be able to be there. I need to stay here with her."

"You can go," I said. "Please. I know you have things to do."

He shook his head, still listening on the phone. He chuckled, and I think his voice got even huskier. "No, I can't. You'll manage without me. I know you'll be fine." He grinned at whatever she said. "Charlene, please, I need a night off."

Good heavens, he was simpering or—I couldn't think of the word. Pleading? Teasing? Whatever word it was, it refueled my anger, making my gratefulness vanish. I took my tray and went to the service conveyor belt. I headed for the exit. Aden hurriedly finished his call, dropped off his tray, and dashed after me.

"Is everything okay? Did they call?" he asked.

"No, I have a feeling. I need to be there, waiting.

You can leave. I'll call Binny for a ride when I need it." I stalked through the hallways, trying to remember which corridor led where.

"I'm with you in this." Aden hurried to keep pace with me.

"You don't have to. I'm sure there are other things you'd rather be doing."

"Nope. Spending a night in the hospital is a high spot for me." He winked and took my arm. "This way."

Good Lord, how could I shake this guy? "I know you and the mayor are busy."

"Hey, it's thumping." Aden pulled the gadget from his coat pocket.

My phone pinged me. *Surgeon consult.* "Oh, crap. Is that bad? Good?"

He pulled my arm through his. "Let's find out." We found the elevator and soon were in the waiting area again. The receptionist took the gadget and led us to yet another small room, this one with a couch and two chairs.

I sank down on the couch. "It must be bad news. It's only been an hour-and-a-half."

He sat next to me, resting his head against the couch cushion. "Let's wait and see what they say." There were dark circles under his eyes. I got the sense he was exhausted.

Yeah, from entertaining the mayor all night, I fumed. "It's not your loved one who's in there. If I want to worry, let me, okay?" I sprang to my feet and paced the tiny room.

"You know better than most people that surgeries can be tricky."

His calmness was infuriating, but I knew it wouldn't help if I got angry out loud. He would deflect it the way he deflected everything I tossed at him. I paced and fumed, angry at whoever shot Frank, angry at Aden for being so helpful and calm, and angry at the white walls closing in.

Fifteen minutes later, the same doctor came in. He was in scrubs and not covered in blood, which I took to be a good sign. His face mask was down around his neck. Papers stuck out of his breast pocket, which meant he hadn't come directly from the surgery.

"The good news is he's doing very well in surgery," Dr. Cam said, taking the chair across from me. "The bad news is the surgery is complicated. There's been injury to the brachial plexus. And he may need follow-up surgery in the future. It depends on how well he recovers."

Brachial plexus. Oh, damn. "Will he lose the use of his arm? Frank's a musician, Dr. Cam. If he can't play guitar, I don't know—"

"We'll find him an instrument he can play," Aden interrupted. "You said it's more complicated. So you're not done?"

"We've finished our assessment. There's at least another hour, maybe two of surgery. Then he'll be in ICU and monitored for at least six hours because of his age and the type of injury he has. We want to keep him sedated to make sure he doesn't tear any stitches. You may as well go home because it will be early morning before you can see him."

I was shaking my head before he stopped speaking. "No, I want to stay here, in case something goes wrong, in case I'm needed."

"I thought you'd say that. He'll be transferred to a room once he leaves the ICU. You can wait there. It's a private room, so there's a couch and a chair for visitors. The couch can be made up into a bed if you want to stretch out. Stop at the desk, and they'll tell you where he'll be. We'll keep you updated on his progress via text messages."

"Private room?" Dollar signs danced across my vision.

"Thank you, Doctor." Aden stood and extended his hand. "We'll go to the room and wait there. We appreciate everything you're doing for Frank."

"It's a tricky wound. I hope you understand that…" Their voices faded when Aden left the room with the doctor.

Private room? Yikes, we couldn't afford that. I would need to check with someone about it. I didn't know the details of Frank's insurance, but I was pretty sure Medicare and his supplemental policy were bare bones when it came to hospital stuff.

Aden came back to the doorway. "I checked at the desk. They gave me the room number."

"I can't afford a private room. I need to talk to someone about getting it changed." I got to my feet and swayed when exhaustion hit me.

"Hey, are you okay?" He put his arm around me.

"I'm tired. I worked a long shift last night after a shift in the afternoon. I need to get this room thing straightened out before they move him." I headed for the door, slipping away from Aden's arm.

"They told me surgical recovery patients always have private rooms." Aden consulted the piece of paper in his hand. "Something about them needing more care than regular patients. She said the room is in the next building. We go down this hall, take the escalator down to the fourth floor, go to the next building. His room is upstairs, on the third floor. This place is a real maze, isn't it?"

"You don't have to come with me," I protested. "I'll find the room and wait for him. This isn't your problem."

"It's my job site, so I feel obligated. Besides, I like to help." He flashed me a smile. "Remember? Police? Wanting to help people?"

"That's ridiculous. Just because your company is managing the development, it's not your responsibility. Besides, we don't even know if this has anything to do with the site."

"Mara, Parsons, and now Frank. All of them were affiliated with the job site. It has something to do with it." He led the way out of the waiting area and down the hall. "I'll make sure you get to where you're going. Come on."

I was too tired to argue. We navigated yet another maze of corridors and escalators, finally arriving at a room in a hushed wing of the hospital. I introduced myself to one of the nurses at the nursing station. She assured me we could go in and make ourselves comfortable.

"How comfortable can it be?" I asked, pushing open the door. I stopped in surprise. We were in a spacious room with a large window framing a view of the Iowa City skyline. The bed was at an angle in the corner, and a long couch was against the wall near the door. A recliner-style chair was near the couch. The sink and other hospital equipment were tucked into a corner near the bed. "Wow, this is nicer than our house," I said. "Frank will feel spoiled here."

"Why don't you lie down? There are pillows here."

Aden poked around under the bed, where a drawer opened to reveal blankets, sheets, and two pillows. "You may as well catch a nap before he gets here."

A nap? That sounded like heaven on earth.

"I'm going to get water. You want a jug of water?"

I yawned. "Yeah, please." He left. I took one of the pillows and rested it against the couch arm, kicking off my Crocs and stretching out.

What a crazy, stupid day. I was at work, I saw Aden's car at the mayor's house, and I got home. Parsons was killed, and Frank wants to move to some kind of suburb and...

When I woke, the lights were dimmed in the room. The bed was still empty. I craned my neck and saw Aden, sleeping in the chair. He had one of the blankets on him, and one was over me. A peek at my watch said it was three in the morning.

I studied his face. He didn't look like the kind of guy who would sleep with one woman while flirting with another one. Was it flirting? Maybe he was sincere. Maybe he felt guilty because it was his job site. In a way, it would sure be easier if it was only guilt. I wasn't anxious to have a guy in my life. I yawned and punched the pillow. I'd worry about it later.

I slept again and woke to voices. Aden and a nurse were talking at the doorway near my feet. Aden saw me stir. "They're bringing him up now."

I sat up, groggy and feeling grimy from sleeping in my clothes. No, his clothes, I realized. Aden's shirt. "What time is it?"

"Eight in the morning. They kept him longer in ICU than they planned." Aden looked worried, fueling my worry.

"What's wrong? Is he okay?"

"He's recovering, but he didn't come out of the anesthesia as quickly as they hoped he would. We'll keep an eye on him closely today." The nurse moved into the hall. "One side, please."

Aden came to the couch and picked up the pillow and blanket, piling them on the chair with the ones he used. A few minutes later a gurney was wheeled in, several nurses surrounding it.

Frank seemed so old. That was the first thing I noticed. There were deep lines drawn in his face. His hair was fragile and wispy, curling around his forehead. I waited until the nurses had transferred him to the bed then I approached, picking my way around the tubes and wiring. I touched his hand, but there was no response.

"We'll keep him sedated for most of today." The nurse bustled around to adjust monitors and dials. "It's important he stay immobile for at least twelve hours."

I brushed a kiss against Frank's cheek. "I'm here, old man." I smoothed back his hair, letting a curl wrap around my finger.

"He's doing fine," the nurse said. "We'll keep a close eye on him. If you want to go home, this might be the time to do it. It might be the evening before he even knows you're here."

"I don't know. I feel I should be here."

"Why don't you go home, get a shower, pack a bag, and come back?" Aden suggested. "You can check in with the volunteers and make sure things are going the way they should. Then when you come back, you can relax."

"That's a good idea," the nurse said. "We have your phone number and if there's any change in his condition, we'll call you immediately."

I knew they were right, but a part of me wanted to stay there, to hold his hand. Frank was always there for me. I wanted to be there for him.

"Okay," I said reluctantly. I kissed him again, resting my cheek against his briefly. "I'll be back," I whispered. "Don't go anywhere without me, you hear?"

We left the hospital, Aden navigating me through the maze of corridors to the parking lot. I stared at the autumn morning while we drove along the Interstate. All these people, going to work or school or wherever. And Frank was back there, with a gunshot wound. "Why?" I murmured. "Why shoot Frank?"

Aden kept his gaze focused on the road. "The first motive a detective considers is money. If Frank dies, who gets his money?"

"What money?" I shook my head. "There's the farm, but it's not valuable. I'll inherit that. I've seen the will. Frank might have money tucked away that he's saved, but it's not much."

"What about the parcel that's in contention, the one you own? Who gets it if you die? Did you will it to Frank?"

"I wasn't the target. Frank was."

"If Frank was eliminated, you might become a target." Aden's hands flexed on the steering wheel. "What happens to the parcel?"

"Frank and I had an arrangement. If I died before him, he inherits the parcel. If he dies before me, I get the farm."

"And what happens to the parcel if both you and Frank are dead?"

"The lawyer in Des Moines asked me the same

166

question. It goes into a land trust and the Iowa Conservation Department decides what to do with it."

"Who knows about the provision in your will?"

"Frank does. My lawyer does." I ticked off people on my fingers. "And now you do. It doesn't make sense. No one would kill us for it. It's not valuable."

"It might be valuable to someone. Maybe not monetarily, but in some other way. What's special about that part of the property?"

"Special?"

"What makes it different than the other parts of the property? Why was it set aside and handled separately from the farm and the construction site?"

"It has sentimental value," I said. "Bryan and I built a cabin there and lived there when we were first married." I smiled, remembering the one-room log cabin with a wood stove and a pump in the kitchen. "It was more like camping than living, but we wanted a place of our own. Frank was renting the farm. He and his second wife had moved."

"Was it a special place to anyone else besides you?"

"It might have been to the girls, to Mara and Emily. We'd have them out to the cabin for picnics. We tried to be close to them, but Miriam, their mother, was so jealous of Bryan. I know it was a fun place for Emily. That's where she got her start, I suppose. She was ten or twelve, I think, when we moved there. Mara got the attention because she was the pretty one. Their mother didn't care much about Emily. She ended up spending time with us at the cabin. That's where she learned hunting and woodcraft. Bryan used to teach her. He enjoyed doing it. I never liked it, but he and Emily would talk for hours about hunting and guns."

"In your home? You'd listen?"

"It was such a tiny cabin I had to. It was so weird. I was in a high-tech job, and I remember thinking I was in the twenty-first century during the day and the nineteenth century at night, when he was teaching her." I remembered one awkward memory. "I think Emily had a crush on Bryan at one time."

"What? They're stepsiblings, aren't they? Or weren't they?"

"Yeah. Bryan was ten when Frank married Emily's mother. Emily was four years old, and she worshiped him. Frank didn't want to live on the farm without Grace, and Miriam wanted to live in town so they moved." I knew how much it pained Frank. He loved being in the country, but when Grace died, he was left with a small child to raise. I suppose that's why he married Miriam, who was a Bitch with a capital B.

"Bryan went to college, and he met me. We came back here and started a life together. We stayed at the cabin for a few years, but Frank insisted we take the farmhouse. After Miriam died, Frank moved out of town and built the tiny house. Then Bryan died and that's where we are now."

"Emily had a crush on him?"

"Not so much a crush but hero worship. She always admired him. He was so patient with her." I frowned, shaking my head. "Emily was such an ungainly child, so big-boned and plain. And Mara was a fashion plate even in high school. Bryan never liked Mara, but he and Emily were friends."

"You got along okay with them? With the stepsisters?" Aden took the exit for town and headed north to the farm.

"Yeah, we had our squabbles, but generally we get along. Their mother was a real control freak. She adored Mara, but Emily was always an afterthought. I was glad when Emily found her niche. Her mother and Mara thought it was awful, of course. So unladylike." I rolled my eyes. "At least Emily's making a living at what she does. Bryan's death hit Emily hard. He truly was a big brother to her."

We drove along the outskirts of town. I spied the mayor's house on the far side of the harvested cornfield separating her road, Maple Road, and my road, Hazel Lane.

"How did he die?"

I turned away to stare at the fields on my side of the car. "It was an accident. They were at a job site, clearing brush and debris to prepare it for landscaping. One of the workers' hoses got clogged on the canister of herbicide they were using. Bryan went to help, and the container exploded. He was doused, head to foot, in chemicals."

"That's horrible," Aden said softly.

"At first we hoped it would just be chemical burns. Just." I closed my eyes, remembering the puckered flesh on Bryan's arms and chest. "But it was cancer. It came on fast. He must have ingested some of the chemicals because his windpipe was burned."

I struggled past my long-ago pain, less terrible now but still sharp. "He died six months later." I cleared my throat, trying to clear away memories. "We got a settlement from the herbicide company and his landscape company, but how do you quantify someone's worth?"

Aden nodded. "I've seen it happen with police, when someone is killed. It's hard to put a dollar figure on a life."

I pushed aside the old memories. "I still don't see a motive to shoot Frank."

"That's because you don't think like a killer." His hands flexed again on the wheel. "You're too open and honest."

"Honesty is the best policy. It's easier than remembering what lies you've told."

"You refuse to take a compliment, don't you?" He shook his head. "If I leave a copy of the co-housing proposal with you, will you promise to read it when you get time? I gave Frank a copy, but I'd like your ideas, too."

"I'm not sure." I breathed a sigh of relief when my lane came into sight.

"Read it, would you? I know, I know, you're busy and Frank's hurt and there are animals to care for. But read it, please?" He pulled into the driveway where Marky Mark's car sat, the bird logo looking like it would take flight from the hood of the car.

"I don't know if that's the kind of community where I'd want to live."

"Think about it." Aden put the car into park and reached into the console and pulled out a sheaf of papers, stapled in the corner. "This is it. Please review it."

"If I get time, I will." I took the papers he pressed into my hands.

"I think you'd like it. You and Frank would fit in. I mean, I don't mean to tell you how to run your life—"

"Good. Because if you tried to that, it wouldn't go well for you." I smiled and batted my eyelashes at him.

Aden regarded me, his face still. Then he smiled, too, and I felt it all the way to my toes. "Yeah, I see that.

But if you need help, I'm willing to step up."

"Why?"

He blinked. "What?"

"Why help me?"

His cheeks darkened. "I want to."

I heard Frank's voice in my mind. *He's sweet on you, honey.*

Frank was right. I was out of practice with this romance stuff. "Okay, well, thanks," I said lamely. "For the help. For the gravel." It was so long since I could truly lean on someone. Frank was there, of course, but I tried to protect him as much as he tried to help me. What would it be like?

"I like helping you," he said softly.

Why? Why me? I threw a boot and almost hit him. So why me?

Why not?

These thoughts and more zipped through my brain in the time it took to blink. "Good to know," I managed. "Thanks. I'm saying that a lot lately."

"Get in the habit. I'll be around." He kissed me, then gently shoved me out the door.

Chapter Ten

I didn't have time to consider romance. I was immediately swept into a tide of worry and concern and pride. Worry for Frank, concern about me, and pride in what was accomplished while I was gone.

Marky Mark and his "assistant," a girl named Roxy, filled me in. "The patients are resting now. We've had rotating shifts of doctors come in from the offices around the county." Roxy consulted a clipboard with a checklist on it. Her hair was the brightest pink I'd ever seen. It was trimmed so one side was shaved close to her head and the other had hair flowing past her shoulders. "We had plenty of volunteers. They reviewed our film, so it was easy to make sure the proper care is given."

I went to the barn to check for myself and was relieved to see things appeared normal. The baby squirrels were actually playing and had built a respectable nest. "A milestone," Roxy said proudly.

I consulted with the vet on duty, reassured when I saw the logbooks documenting what was done during the day I was absent. Marky told me he had shifts of students on duty all day and night, monitoring what was done and making notes. He was so enthusiastic about his organizing skills, I didn't have the heart to tell him it might not be necessary.

It was noon before I got back to the farmhouse and was able to peel off my clothes and step into the shower.

It was invigorating to wash away the smell of blood and hospital and fear. I scrubbed my hair and my body and came out feeling like a new woman.

Clean jeans, a comfortable sweater, and sneakers completed the fresh start feeling. I bundled my hair into a towel for later drying. I got Aden's shirt from the floor where I dropped it, running it through my hands. It was soft and still had a faint aroma of Man. I reluctantly put it into the washing machine with the rest of the laundry.

I dug out an old knapsack from the storage closet, packing a spare shirt, underwear, sweatpants, and a T-shirt to sleep in. Then I found a portable hair kit of scrunchies, ties, and barrettes. I gathered up my phone charger and my tablet and its charger and stuffed them in the outside pocket.

I saw Aden's report, sitting on the hassock. I leafed through it, but it was too detailed for a casual skim. I needed to read it when I wasn't pressed for time. I tossed it on top of the knapsack to take to the hospital with me. I stepped outside to do my hair, toweling and brushing until it began to get dry. I put it into a double braid, one near my crown, pulling it back from my face and another at my neckline to trail down my back.

The phone rang while I was gulping down a bowl of warmed up soup. "How are things at the hospital?" Harold asked. "I've got folks in here wanting to know how Frank is doing."

I gave him an abbreviated summary of what was happening. He promised to relay it to those who wanted to know. "He'll come through this with flying colors," Harold said confidently. "We'll take care of things here, and you take care of yourself and Frank. Your dog is fitting in fine at my house, so I can keep him as long as you need me to."

"Thanks, Harold. It's great having friends like this who jump in and help."

"That's what a community is all about. We're here to help each other."

He hung up and I considered what he said. Community. Frank and I were part of this community. If the co-housing thing went through, we'd be part of another one. There were definite benefits to such a thing.

I called Binny and updated her. "Thanks for the loan of your son," I said. "He's been invaluable."

"Don't tell him that, it'll go to his head. I'm glad Frank's getting better. Do you need me to do anything? You were lucky Aden Kingsley was with you yesterday to help out. Mayor Parralt was in the shop today, and she said he was with you. I don't think she was happy about it. Apparently they were supposed to do something last night, but he blew her off."

"They're quite a couple, aren't they? I told him he didn't need to stay with me, but he insisted. I think he's worried about his job site."

"What? That's silly. He's worried about you."

"That's silly," I countered. "He and the mayor are in cahoots. He doesn't have time to worry about me. No, I think he's afraid somebody is out to sabotage his project."

"I did hear Billy Grimm said they had to halt work there until the police get to the bottom of these attacks. And of course they stopped anyway because of the crime scene." Her voice lowered. "Can you imagine? A chipper? I heard blood and bones were blown out all over the site. It's cursed now. They'll have to bring in a priest or a shaman to cleanse the site of toxic vibes before they can build anything there."

"I doubt Aden Kingsley is the kind of guy to bring in a priest to exorcise a construction site. But I'd pay good money to see it if he did," I admitted.

"Will Frank be home from the hospital by Saturday? I hope you don't have to miss the big party. Oh, and you have a party tomorrow night, too, at Kingsley's house. You have to tell me what it's like. I've heard he has the house restored and it's charming."

"I doubt if I'll go. I'm sure Frank will still be in the hospital. I don't know about Saturday. We'll have to take it one day at a time."

"Oh, I hope you can go. Your costume is perfect." Binny sighed. "Well, Frank is more important than a dress. But it's such a beautiful dress."

"I know you worked so hard on it. I hope I can go, too." I seriously doubted I would, but I wouldn't crush her hopes yet. "I have to go now. Frank might be waking up any time, and I want to be there."

"Okay. You give him our love, and don't worry about a thing here. We have it under control."

I pulled the laundry from the dryer and got it folded, wondering when I'd see Kingsley again to give him back his shirt. I checked my watch and called the hospital. Frank was still resting comfortably. They would be waking him in an hour or two to get him moving around. Well, that was my cue to get moving, too.

I grabbed my truck keys and left, but when I got outside I saw Emily's SUV pulling in the drive and parking behind my truck. I slung the knapsack on my shoulder and rolled up Kingsley's report, slapping it against my leg. "Hey, Emily," I called as soon as she opened her door. "I'm heading to the hospital. I don't have time to talk."

She met me at my truck. "I heard what happened to Frank." Today she wore hunting clothes: an olive T-shirt covered by a brown jacket with camo pants tucked into brown boots. One splotch of blaze orange on her back seemed fluorescent in the sun. "Why was Aden Kingsley with you when you found him?"

Of the questions she might have asked, that one hadn't occurred to me. "He came out to talk to me and our dog got loose. We followed him into the woods."

"Our dog? You mean you and Kingsley own the dog?" She frowned at me. "You said it was his dog."

"Yes, it is, but I'm caring for it, so I guess it's ours." This was stupid. Why was I explaining myself to her? "It was only by chance Kingsley was here. I'm lucky he was."

"From what it sounds like, you're incredibly lucky. Frank would have bled out otherwise. It was a shoulder wound, wasn't it?"

My already tenuous patience began to fray. "You know, he's your stepfather, Emily. You might show more than a clinical interest in how he's doing. This isn't a lesson you teach in your classes. You know, how to survive a shooting."

"Actually, it is something I teach." My sharp words had no effect. "Accidents can happen even to the best of hunters. They need to be prepared for it."

"If it turns out this was a careless hunter, I'll make sure that person never carries a gun again."

"It would be hard to prove, I suppose. How can you narrow it down?"

"Forensics," I said, more confidently than I felt. "Kingsley mentioned something like that. He used to be a detective. He said they can match a bullet to a gun."

"They won't go around testing all the guns in the county." Emily looked at the report I was still anxiously tapping against my leg. "Is that the housing proposal Kingsley put out?"

"Yeah, he gave me a copy to review. I figured I'd do it at the hospital." Hint, hint. I moved toward the truck, but she shifted position so I had to push past her to get to the driver side door.

"I know Frank won't be able to attend Mara's service, but you'll be able to attend, won't you? It's tomorrow at the cemetery at four o'clock."

"I have no idea if I can attend or not." I managed to work my way around her to open the door. "I'll have to see how Frank is doing."

"You're family. You need to attend."

I swung up into the cab, and she slammed the door behind me. "I told you, Emily. I'll try, but I can't guarantee I can get there."

"Mara never told me about the housing idea of Kingsley's. She only talked about a car dealership and a big store going in on our land. I think I like the housing thing. It's more pleasant, more forward-thinking. Do you remember when Bryan was alive, we talked about it once?"

"We did?" I paused, my hand on the key in the ignition. "A co-housing project?"

"Well, not co-housing. Back then they called it a commune. I remember he said it would be fun to try." She scowled at some memory. "Don't you remember? I wanted to run away from home and join a commune. Bryan talked me out of it."

Oh, crap. Yeah, now I remembered. It was when she

was in high school or just graduated. She had a crush on a kid who was in a religious cult. That sort of shit happened where cult people would come to campus and recruit unhappy kids. Emily came out to the farm and told us she wanted to live somewhere in Nebraska. It was after her mother died when Emily was seventeen or eighteen.

Instead Bryan went with her to meet the guy and somehow managed to open Emily's eyes to what was happening. She ended up transferring to community college and took a succession of uninspired jobs until Bryan died. Frank gave her a portion of the money we got from Bryan's settlement, and Emily was able to start her business.

If what Aden said was true, the business wasn't doing well if Emily had to borrow money from Mara. I considered asking her about it, but I wanted to get going and didn't have time for chat. "I forgot about that." I started the engine. "I need to read through his proposal. It might be a good use of the land. I'm sorry, but I need to get back to the hospital."

"I hope you'll come tomorrow." She moved to her SUV and got in, backing out quickly and driving off. I followed her, noting the crime scene tape was gone. Had it been gone earlier? I was so preoccupied with events, I guess I didn't notice.

Emily made a right turn on Goldfinch Drive and headed west, probably going home. I watched her go, seeing the mayor's house across the cornfield. Damn. Aden's car was there. I saw it across the cornfield. I slowed and stared. Yep, it was his.

So much for him caring about me. He left me and went to her house. I sighed. Had romance changed so much I didn't know the rules anymore? Maybe I was too old-fashioned for today's romantic world. I still believed in monogamy and honesty. The idea was depressing.

I drove to Iowa City, bemused by my past. It seemed like every time I turned around, I bumped into Bryan's memory. He died at this time of year, in November. He had faded to a significant but far-away part of my life. Yet this new construction site made him more present than he had been for a long time.

What would we be doing now if he was alive? I seldom thought about it anymore, but now I wondered. Would he have wanted Fairy Tale Endings? Would he still be working in the landscape business? For that matter, would I have stayed in a high-tech field? For some reason, I was questioning things I used to think were fixed and unchangeable.

I was questioning because of Aden Kingsley. I parked at the hospital and made my way through the labyrinth of corridors. Aden had opened my eyes not only to changes where I lived, but how I lived. Even if he was a duplicitous, flirtatious scoundrel, he made me remember how much fun it was to mingle and laugh with a man. What an odd intersection of events and people had brought us to this place.

Frank was propped up in bed when I arrived, sunlight filtering into the room. "Well, there she is," he whispered when I came into view. His voice was slurred but strong. "You're a sight for sore eyes."

I dropped my knapsack on the couch and went to his side. "How are you, old man?" I leaned over to enfold him in a tentative hug.

"I'm doing fine now my sweetheart is here." He tugged gently on the braid that swung down toward him.

"This place is like a palace. I have folks jumping up every time I press this button"—and he raised a small remote control—"I got TV whenever I want it, and I got a nice view out my window. What did I do to deserve such good treatment?"

I kissed his cheek. "I'm so glad to see you awake and sassy." I pulled over the recliner chair and sat, still holding his hand. His left arm was bandaged against his side and a bulky lump sat atop the shoulder. "You were shot. Do you remember anything about it?"

"I remember you singing to me." He turned his head to view me, smiling faintly. "I thought it was an angel. And I saw Aden, didn't I? Was he there?"

"Yep. He came to talk to me, and Cinders got loose. The dog led us to you. Maybe we need to keep him."

"I think you need to keep both of them." Frank looked past me to the doorway. "There's another angel come to visit me."

A nurse came in holding a large leather strap. "You won't say that when I'm done with you." She hefted it. "Time for your walk."

"Already? We just had a walk," Frank grumbled.

"And you'll walk every couple of hours until bedtime. We want to make sure you don't get any blood clots traveling around that manly body of yours."

"They said he was supposed to lie still." I moved aside so she could get close to the bed.

"That was then. This is now." Frank held up a leg. "Unhook me, honey." The nurse flung aside the bedclothes and I saw the compression devices strapped onto Frank's bony legs. "I hate those things," he said. "Feels like little hands pushing on me."

"That's what it's supposed to feel like." The nurse

helped him to sit up and swing his legs over the side of the bed where she could remove the pneumatic sleeves. I hovered nearby, worried he might fall.

The nurse got the belt on him and with her help, he stood, her hand hooked securely into the belt. They arranged his nightgown and robe then she said, "Get hold of your pole and let's see what you can do."

"Loop those tubes, would you, Ash?" Frank glanced at the lines attaching him to the portable stand. I tucked and looped, and they toddled off, Frank shuffling and the nurse chiding him to lift his legs. I followed behind, relieved to see him up and moving. He was still pale and he was shaky, but he was mobile.

"We'll be doing a couple of sprints up and down the corridor," the nurse said to me. "The doctor wants him to keep moving. He just can't move the arm."

"It'll put a damper on my guitar playing at your party," Frank said, peering around the nurse to me. "I'll ask Aden if he'll fill in."

"I won't be going to a party. I'm not going anywhere while you're stuck in here."

Frank stopped. "You will damn well go to the party, young lady, and the one tomorrow night. I'm not a weight to drag you down. You will go out and have fun, you hear me?"

"He might be going home by Saturday," the nurse said, tugging gently on his belt. "If he keeps this up, he will."

If he went home, I'd be at home with him. Frank resumed walking, pausing sometimes to chat with people. "He acts like he's been here for days," I commented to the nurse.

"He's one of those people who loves to socialize. I

can imagine him at the center of a group of children, telling stories." She nudged Frank to move along. He complied after complimenting a woman in a wheelchair about her slippers.

I followed behind them, smiling. Frank was such a social person. He would find any excuse to go into town and hang out at Herald's or drop by the coffee shop for a chat. He loved living on the farm, but he loved people, too, far more than I did.

I saw a map on the wall of the hospital while we were perambulating back toward his room. I made sure he was settled then I said, "I need to run down to the billing office and make sure everything's taken care of. I was so scattered yesterday I'm not sure I filled out all the forms."

"My wallet's in my pants in the closet there." Frank gestured vaguely toward a small cupboard near the doorway. "All my insurance cards are there." He lay back on the bed, frowning when the nurse wrapped the compression sleeves around his legs. "I might try to take a nap if those puffers will let me."

"Those puffers are necessary, so don't fiddle with them," the nurse warned.

I found Frank's wallet and left the room while they were still arguing. I followed the maps on the walls and soon was in the billing office, where I had to wait a few minutes before being ushered into the cube of a young man surrounded by computer equipment. I explained I was concerned about the cost of a private room.

"I was told it's common practice to put patients into private rooms after surgery like what my father-in-law had. We have high-deductible insurance, and I'm worried we might be out of pocket for a high cost."

The man accessed Frank's records. "The extra cost is being covered by the Kingsley company."

"I'm sorry." I blinked widely at him. "What?"

"Kingsley Development. They're paying for your father's care."

"My father-in-law," I corrected, my mind spinning. "What do you mean they're paying? They can't, can they? I mean, it's our insurance."

"Mr. Kingsley Senior was a generous donor to this hospital," the man said. "It might be somewhat unorthodox, but Mr. Kingsley has guaranteed any bills incurred will be covered by his company."

"Doesn't insurance cover things? Didn't everything get routed through insurance and we get stuck with the leftover bills?

"Yes, they do. We'll bill the insurance company but whatever insurance doesn't cover, the Kingsley company will cover. They're working with the insurance company to make sure that's done."

"That's stupid," I blurted. "Why would he do that?"

"I don't know." He kept his eyes fixed on me. I sensed he was evaluating me, as though measuring me like one of Kingsley's conquests. "You should discuss it with Mr. Kingsley. If you receive any bills, they'll be for a negligible amount."

"But I didn't ask him to—"

"As I said, you need to discuss it with Mr. Kingsley. He was most insistent, and we were happy to accommodate his request." He tapped the desk with one manicured fingernail. "As I said, his company has been a generous donor in the past."

I pushed away and stood. "Thanks. I'll contact him."

"He was most insistent, Miss Schone. It might be

hard to dissuade him."

I forced a smile. "I'll manage."

I stomped through the hallways and found a café where I got a coffee and a donut. Aden Kingsley was paying for Frank's hospital care. Why? I was halfway through my cup of joe when the realization hit me.

Lawsuit.

Kingsley was paying for Frank because he thought the construction site was at the heart of everything. He was doing a preemptive payment so we wouldn't come after him later.

That made sense. Well, if he was willing to fork out the money to make sure Frank was happy, we'd take it. I finished my donut and found my way back to the room where Frank was dozing. I got Aden's co-housing report and sank on the couch for an in-depth read-through.

The nurse came in an hour later and roused Frank for another round of walking. When he came back, he rested in the recliner, "for a change of scenery." "What do you think of that idea of his?" He nodded at the sheaf of papers I held.

"It's a suburb," I said dismissively. "Just a fancy one."

"It's a new kind of suburb. One that's planned in a good way."

"It's a bunch of strangers camped out on our back door." I pushed the report aside and went to the window to stare at the skyline. Night was starting to fall and lights were coming on. I glimpsed the stadium in the distance. Beyond it was where the new wildlife hospital would be built. A possible new job for me.

"But good strangers," Frank said. "Ones who have the best interests of the land at heart. It sounds interesting. Aden said—"

"I don't know if I trust him." I leaned against the windowsill.

"You know you don't trust him," Frank said. "But I do. I think this is a great idea."

"You and he talked about it?"

"Yes, we did. He explained how it would be set up. Listen to him about it, Ash. He has a good vision for the land, one involving us if we let it."

"Is it what you want?" I kept my eyes fixed on him and saw the telltale ducking of his head when he answered.

"I want you to be happy. This might be a good way to do that."

"Did he tell you about the job offer?" I asked softly.

Frank's cheeks flared bright red. "Yep," he muttered, still not meeting my gaze.

"Damn it, Frank. I don't want anybody making decisions based on a job I may or may not have in the future."

His head snapped up. "But don't you see? Even if a job doesn't pan out, we'll have options. We'll have people who want to help on the farm and maybe a chance to train or teach them. Who knows, maybe somebody there might want to help with FTE. It gives us options, honey. Options we don't have if a big retail center goes in there. It's time to move on, honey. Don't be afraid of change."

Someone knocked briskly on the door. "I'm here to take your dinner order, Mr. Goddard," an aide said cheerfully. "This is the menu you can choose from. You're on a somewhat restricted diet, but there are still a lot of choices." She smiled at me. "You can order, too.

It's covered by your room cost."

The room cost, being paid by Aden Kingsley. It still bugged me. It was one thing to have friends and colleagues help out at Fairy Tale Endings, but this was different. This was more like charity.

I scanned the menu and blinked in surprise. "This reads more like a restaurant menu."

"We've found if patients are happy, they get well sooner." The girl beamed at Frank.

He inspected the menu. "Good. Hooray. I'm not on the broth diet they had me on earlier today."

"Still soft foods, but more variety. How about a tuna salad sandwich and a cup of soup? The chicken soup here is excellent."

"Sounds good to me. Ash, give me a hand up, would you? I think I'll have dinner in bed tonight." I hurried to help him into the bed. "What do you want for dinner?"

"Same as his," I said. "That's fine."

"Add ice cream to the order," Frank said when the girl jotted down our selections. "And if there's any wine to be had, give my girlfriend here a glass, would you?"

"I'll see what I can do." She gave a jaunty salute and left with a giggle.

I helped Frank get arranged in the bed, making sure the covers were where they needed to be and his puffers were on his legs. "We can forget about those soon," he said to me. "The nurse said once I got up and moving regularly, I won't need them."

"That's good, because I always hated those things."

I turned. Aden was in the doorway, dressed in a dark topcoat over a gray suit. He looked amazingly handsome, his curly hair somewhat tamed except for the one curl that seemed to always bounce on his forehead. The collar

of his coat framed his oval face and his cheeks had a hint of color from the October night.

"You didn't have to get dressed up to come visit me," Frank said. "You look pretty fancy."

"I have to go to a meeting tonight and talk about the housing proposal," Aden said, coming into the room. "I'm trying to recruit other communities. I'm hoping they might be interested in working with us, perhaps in their towns."

"So you do this with the mayor?" I asked.

"Sometimes. Not tonight. Although I might see her later and update her on what goes on." He went to Frank's side. "You're acting good for a guy who was shot yesterday."

Frank eased himself up higher in the bed. "Hurts like crazy, but they keep me on these drugs so it's not too bad." He wiggled one of the lines connecting him to the nearby bags of fluid. "I hear I have you to thank for being there for Ash."

Aden smiled at me across the bed. "You need to thank the dog. He's the one who told us you were hurt."

"I guess he came in handy after all. We might have to keep him." Frank yawned and nestled among the pillows. "Have you talked to the police? Was it a stupid hunter out trying to get a buck out of season?"

Aden's stance changed. I couldn't tell what it was, but I got the feeling he stiffened. "The doctors retrieved the bullet. I think the forensics department here in town are processing it. I'm sure they'll have the results soon."

Frank yawned again, and I took his hand. "You're beat, aren't you? You've been running around this hospital all afternoon."

"I wouldn't mind a little nap before dinner," he

admitted.

"I wanted to stop on my way to the meeting," Aden said. He touched Frank's uninjured shoulder. "Get well soon. They miss you down at the hardware store."

"I miss them, too. You say hello for me the next time you're in there."

"Will do." Aden moved away from the bed, and I went with him to the door. "He's doing well," he said in a low voice. "I'm glad to see he's recovering so good."

"I was worried they were pushing him too hard, but I think he's doing fine. I guess I have to trust they know what they're doing." I left the room and faced Aden in the hall. "Why are you paying for Frank's private room?" I demanded. "Were you afraid we'd sue you or something?"

"What? No, it's nothing like that. I wanted to help. I figured you might not be able to afford a private room. Believe me, I know what it's like to recover from that kind of a wound. You don't want a noisy roommate sharing your room."

"It must cost a fortune. How can you afford it?"

He stuck his hands in the pockets of his topcoat. "If you're asking if I'm good for it, I am. I get paid well to run the company, plus I inherited money from my mother when she died. If you add in my pension from the police department, I can handle it."

"I didn't mean that, and you know it." I crossed my arms even though I longed to shake him. "Why are you doing this?"

"I like you, I like Frank, and I like to help. Wouldn't you like to have help now and then?"

"No, I don't need any." I remembered my manners. "But thank you for helping Frank. I'm sure he'll want to

thank you, too." I turned to go into the room.

Aden put his hand on my arm and held me back. "That wasn't what I asked. I know you don't need help. But wouldn't you like some?"

There was a hidden meaning in his words. I heard an underlying suggestion, a possibility. My initial response was *No, I don't want any entanglements.* I thought of Frank and what he said. *It's time to move on, honey. Don't be afraid.* Afraid? Me?

"I don't know," I said softly.

Aden pulled me to him until I was only inches away. "That gives me hope." He kissed me, his lips lingering on mine. "I like helping you, Ash," he whispered, his breath warm on my ear.

I savored the feeling of a strong male body against mine and the aroma of cologne, coat, and male. "I'm not good at accepting help," I said, my cheek against his.

Aden put his hand against my face, his thumb gently smoothing my skin. "I'll be happy to help you practice." He kissed me again then was gone, his coat swirling around him.

Chapter Eleven

Frank was dozing when I came back into the room. I got my little home-away-from-home area set up at the couch, plugging in my phone and tablet to charge. I kicked off my sneakers and put on the slippers I brought before flopping down to try to put my life in perspective.

My lips tingled from Aden's kiss. It was years since I had a lover. It seemed like every year, I considered jumping back in the dating game, and I'd try an online dating service. A few brief coffee dates would convince me to go back to my single life.

But Aden, he was different. First, there was his casual dismissal about finances. He said it without trying to impress me, so unlike other men I briefly knew. And his equally straightforward discussion about his past in the police. He didn't try to make himself out a hero or glamorize what he did.

He was, I realized, exactly what he seemed. He was a nice guy with a complicated past and an interesting future. Cop turned real estate developer; real estate developer turned environmentalist. What a complex man.

A man I wanted to know more about. But I wouldn't do it until I knew where he and Mayor Parralt stood. If Aden was involved with her, I didn't want to get involved with him. Maybe I was a coward, but I didn't want to be in competition with someone for his affection.

I didn't want angst in my life.

"He seems like a good guy," Frank mumbled from across the room.

"Yeah, he does seem so."

"You deserve happiness in your life, Princess."

"Tell that to whoever is in charge of the fairytale powder. I haven't been sprinkled lately."

"Your time might be coming. You mark my words."

"Suppertime," a cheerful voice called from the doorway.

I joined Frank at his bedside, helping him get into an upright position. He refused to let me help him with eating. "I can manage," he grumbled. "Cut it up for me so it's in a size I can handle."

I obediently cut his sandwich into smaller chunks. The soup was more problematic. I ended up holding the mug for him while he managed the spoon. The soft-serve ice cream proved to be the easiest to handle, "Although I wouldn't mind a little hot fudge," he said when he pushed his plate away.

"Let's not get carried away, now." I moved our trays to the rack in the hallway and had just settled down with my tablet when the doctor on call came in.

"The main concern now is to keep the arm immobile to allow the wound to heal," he told Frank. "You'll have extensive physical therapy later to determine how much damage might have been done to the brachial plexus. It was a tricky surgery. I think we kept the damage to a minimum, but it's critical in the first week or two to let things heal. So no using the arm until we say you can."

"How much longer do I stay here?" Frank asked. "I'm sure it's costing us a pretty penny."

"We never make any promises," the doctor said.

"We take it a day at a time. You'll be here tonight and maybe tomorrow. We need to keep an eye on your heart and to make sure you can get around okay without using the arm. So the more you work with your therapist, the sooner you can leave."

"You hear that?" I said after the doctor left. "Do your exercises, mind what the nurse tells you and quit fiddling with your puffers."

Frank glared at me. "I hate those things. I can't sleep with them puffing and pushing."

"You were dozing fine when I came back in before dinner." I picked up my tablet.

"How much is this costing us?" Frank asked, flipping channels on the TV remote.

"Insurance is covering it," I said. "I wonder what the WiFi password is here."

"It's all in this brochure." Frank tossed me a small pamphlet. "Insurance isn't covering all of it, is it? Maybe I should go to a shared room. I saw a couple of those when I was out walking. It wouldn't cost as much, would it?"

"I talked to the business office people and they said it would be covered." Not a lie, I reasoned. Aden was covering it.

"If you find out any differently you let me know. I won't have us wasting money on me lying in a hospital bed. How are things at the farm?"

I updated him on the volunteers working to help out. "I'm glad to hear that," he said. "I was worried about you going home and being alone."

"I'm sleeping here tonight." I pointed to the couch. "I slept there last night and it was pretty comfortable."

"You don't have to do that." He protested but it had

no energy behind it. I knew he wanted me to stay.

"I know I don't have to but I will. You relax and watch television and let me get caught up on email." I propped my feet up on the railing under his bed and skimmed through the emails that piled up.

When I looked up, Frank was dozing, the remote loose in his hand. I tucked the covers around him before going to the couch and lying down, dragging a blanket over me. The nurse came in a few minutes later. I assured her I didn't need to make up the bed. I fell asleep and woke up a few times during the night, when nurses came in to check on him.

By Friday morning, I was optimistic Frank might get released. A doctor came in to check on him, and he sounded encouraging. "The wound is healing, and you're doing what you're supposed to," the M.D. said. "Let's see how it goes today. Make sure to get up and walk with help. I want to make sure no blood clots form. That's a real possibility with inactivity."

Frank did as he was told, toddling about the halls with the nurses supporting him, doing the exercises the physical therapist gave him, and trying hard to manage necessary duties on his own. But I knew it was taking a toll. The nurses and I consulted. We agreed he needed at least one more day to recover before going home. That would be their recommendation, and I was relieved to hear it.

"You've got things to do," Frank complained when I told him. "You can't sit around here keeping me company."

"I'm happy to have a good excuse to miss Mara's funeral," I assured him. "I was dreading that."

He leveled an admonishing finger at me. "I know, I

know. Mara was no friend to either of us. But Emily needs support, and we're the only family she has left. You need to put in an appearance. Besides, you can go to the farm and check on things. Plus there's the party tonight at Aden's house." He shot me a knowing look. "You don't want to miss that, do you?"

"I should stay with you."

"All I'll be doing is taking a walk, eating supper, and sleeping. You go on and have fun." He made a shooing motion at me. "You've been cooped up here for long enough. Get on out there and enjoy yourself."

"A funeral is not a big occasion for enjoying myself."

"Yeah, but it's Mara's funeral, so it counts. Go on now."

I reluctantly left, stopping at the nursing station to make sure they had my phone number in case I was needed. "Call me," I insisted. "If there's anything wrong, please call."

They assured me they would and I left, driving to the farm in mid-afternoon. A vet tech from the emergency clinic was there. We talked about the patients, discussing each one's care. "Roberta is doing well," the tech said. "I removed the bandage and she's managing to get around with only a hobble now."

I hunkered down outside the stall to evaluate the small rabbit. She did appear good except for the nasty gash and the way her paw was twisted. Maybe there would be a fairy tale ending for her after all.

The woodchucks had put on weight, which was a good sign. The fox kit was much perkier than when he came to us a week earlier. We might be able to release them next week if the weather cooperated. We were getting to hibernation season for the woodchucks so we'd need to release them in the woodland. I knew where several dens were located and hopefully they'd find one.

After checking on the patients, I went to the house and rummaged through my closet for something appropriate for a funeral followed by a party. Black jeans and a black-and-gray checked sweater would be fine, especially if I paired it with a black leather jacket I splurged on years ago. That decided, I tackled my hair. I created four pigtails then I braided them and wrapped them into a crown. I stuck in decorated hair pins and called it good.

As I drove to the cemetery on the southwest side of town, I eyed the dark clouds piling up in the west. It wasn't unusual to get snow around this time of year. So far, we hadn't seen a flake. If I was lucky, there'd be a shelter at the cemetery in case of inclement weather.

I breathed a sigh of relief when I got there and saw the canopy set out above several rows of chairs. People were milling about, and I joined them, slipping in to sit in the back row. I recognized some of the people, mostly nodding acquaintances from town. Two of the men were vaguely familiar. I concluded they must be former husbands, although I wasn't sure.

Emily was in the front near the newly turned grave, talking to a man I presumed to be a minister given his somber attire. She wore a black, flowing sort of dress and uncomfortable-looking black pumps. When she glimpsed me, she gestured to me urgently. I moved through the crowd to join her.

"This is my sister-in-law, Ashley Schone," Emily said. "This is Reverend Verr. He's performing today's service."

I shook the man's hand and tried to make a hasty retreat, but Emily said, "Please sit in front near me, Ash. We're the only family represented here today. My stepfather is in the hospital," she explained to the minister. "Otherwise I'm sure he'd be here."

I wasn't sure at all, but I didn't quibble. I let Emily take me to one of the folding chairs in front and we sat, Emily nervously pressing her dress. "It's been so long since I wore nylons and a dress," she whispered. "I wasn't even sure I had anything."

"I know what you mean," I replied. "I've worn scrubs for so long I had to dig deep to find something acceptable." I crossed my legs and watched the people file into the area. It was a respectable turnout, especially given the fact Mara didn't live in town anymore but was only a frequent visitor.

I smiled at a couple of people I knew and was turning back to face front when I saw Aden come in, dressed like the day before in a suit with a dark overcoat. His eyebrows were drawn together to form a dark line, and his mouth set in a hard frown. The few remaining chairs were in the back and he sank into one. As he did, he saw me. I smiled, but he only narrowed his eyes, his frown deepening.

Emily tugged on my sleeve. "We're starting," she hissed.

I turned around. That wasn't the sort of reaction I expected to get from him. I tried to ignore my unease throughout the mercifully brief ceremony, but it was there at the back of my mind while the minister talked. We had a few prayers, and one of the husbands got up and spoke a few charitable words. The minister read scripture before Emily rose and went to stand next to the minster in front of the open grave.

"Although Mara and I were sisters, we led vastly different lives." Emily had a strong voice, and it filled the small space. "Our father died when we were young and then our mother married Frank Goddard." She smiled tremulously at me. "Ashley's father-in-law. Her husband, Bryan, became a brother to me. Ash was more of a sister than Mara."

I shifted uncomfortably. I had never been particularly close to Emily, but I suppose the fact Bryan was close to her made me seem close by proxy.

"I have fond memories of growing up here in Dasdorf, on Frank's farm and later in town. Mara always longed for the big city, but I was content here. It was another of the many differences between us. But despite that, I know she had the best interests of the town and our family at heart. She supported me and encouraged me, and I will miss that." For the first time, her voice wavered. I heard sympathetic sniffling behind me.

"I know Mara's death was a shock to many people. I'm confident the police will be able to find out who caused such a terrible accident."

A murmur of confusion broke out in the crowd. Emily ignored it and continued. "We're here to celebrate how Mara lived, not how she died. I hope you have fond memories of her. I know I do. And I know she wouldn't want us to dwell on the past but rather look to the future." Emily resumed her seat to more murmurs.

The minister finished the service with a homily about forgiveness and compassion, the gist of which was lost on me. We rose at the end. I hoped to escape, but Emily took my arm and I was roped into being in the reception line with her.

I tried to catch a glimpse of Aden, but all I saw of him was his back when he left the tent, his hands jammed into the pockets of his overcoat. I shook hands with people and murmured whatever seemed appropriate, but my brain was spinning. What was wrong?

It was an hour later that we wrapped up, the minister speaking with Emily at the gravesite, then gesturing to me to join them. I walked across the uneven ground and took the rose the minister handed me. "I'll wait here if you'd like to have a last few moments with your sister." He patted Emily's arm then left to stand with two men in work clothes whom I presumed would fill in the grave.

Emily and I stared down at the casket. Bryan had been cremated, and his ashes scattered in a cathartic ceremony Frank and I planned. It was less a funeral than a release for Bryan from the pain and horror of his disease. I tossed the rose into the grave. "Good-bye, Mara," I said softly. "I hope you'll find happiness. You never seemed happy in this life."

"I won't miss her at all," Emily said in a low, confiding sort of tone. "I'm glad she's gone. She lied to me and she cheated me. I doubt if anyone will miss her." She tossed the rose like she was throwing it into the garbage, then she went to the minister. "Thank you so much," she murmured, touching her eyes with a handkerchief. "I appreciate your support."

I gaped at her, my mind whirling. The minister approached me, hand outstretched, and I automatically shook it while he murmured condolences. He led us to our vehicles, still talking.

"Do you have time to talk?" Emily asked, her hand on her SUV door handle.

"I'm supposed to be somewhere," I stammered. "I

should be going."

"Just for a minute. Hop in. Let's chat." She slid into the driver's seat.

I went to the passenger side and clambered in. "I'm due to meet some people. I don't have much time. And I want to get back to the hospital."

"How is Frank doing?" Emily leaned against her side of the car to regard me.

"He's recovering, but it'll be a long time before he can use his arm again. The doctor said there might be long-term damage."

"It would be hard for him," she murmured. "He does love to play guitar, doesn't he?"

She made it sound like an inconvenience, not a major lifestyle change. "Yes, it would be hard," I snapped. "If you'd like to visit him at the hospital, I'm sure it would be okay."

"Oh, I'll wait until he gets home. I'd hate to tire him out. He's not as young as he used to be." She smoothed her skirt again, pushing it against her heavy thighs. "I wanted you to know I'll support you if you decide you don't want your land to be used for construction."

"Support me?" My decision regarding my land had nothing to do with her.

"Yes. With the town. We discussed this the other day. Several people in town are not happy about how you've managed this whole thing with Kingsley and the construction project. But I'll be happy to give you my support if you need it."

"Okay," I said slowly. "That's good to know. Thank you, Emily."

"Mara's will has been processed. I was her heir. So I have complete control about what is done with the construction site."

No one had control yet. It would hinge on the outcome of the environmental study. "Good," I murmured. "I hope we can come to an understanding for the best use of the property."

"I'm sure we will." She reached for the ignition. "I'm glad we had a chance to talk, Ash. I feel like we've always understood each other so well."

"You bet." I opened the door and slid out. "Thanks, Emily."

"No, thank you for coming today. Family is important."

I closed the door and stepped back when she drove away. What the hell was that conversation about? I wondered. I went to my truck and got in, driving after her. Did Emily think she could determine how the site would be used?

I considered it as I drove north to Nightingale Lane and Aden's house. Mara probably told Emily they controlled the development of the property. It seemed like it was always Mara who was involved in talks with Aden and the others. Emily was seldom there.

I had to park a block away because cars lined the street near Aden's house. I approached it in the twilight, enjoying the old neighborhood with its tree-lined street and the houses set back from the road. The homes were unique, two-story mixed with one-story, but all well maintained and cared for.

Aden's was a beautiful little house. I stopped on the sidewalk to admire the pale gray shingles and white trim around the windows and the wraparound front porch. The house was framed by trees arching gracefully overhead. Low hedges and flower beds provided a charming border. A bright red front door welcomed visitors onto the wide porch and into the house.

The door was open so I stepped inside, into a lovely foyer with a carved wooden staircase leading up. Stained glass windows were inset every two or three feet, leading to a landing out of sight.

Coats were piled on a built-in bench so I added mine to the stack and moved further inside. On either side were rooms, each with people standing and talking. Straight ahead down a short hall was what appeared to be a kitchen, where more people stood. I went left and entered what I assumed was a small, cozy living room. Built-in shelving, painted white, was against the far wall flanking a beautiful fireplace framed in stone. Windows above the fireplace let in the last of the fading light as did doors leading out to the porch. The chairs were wood framed with cushions, grouped around a square coffee table.

I nodded to a few people I knew from this year's Heavys event. Many of us had participated before so were familiar with each other. We didn't compete, but we did have a certain amount of bragging rights, I suppose. I passed through the room and into a small dining room with a round table and chairs. A built-in cupboard against the wall held dishes.

Everywhere was beautiful woodwork and detailing, from the crown moldings to the polished oak floors, inlaid with a dark border that was very art nouveau. People moved from room to room, drinks in hand, and in every room was a tray of appetizers.

As I passed through the dining room to the kitchen, I heard someone say behind me, "...surprised she showed up. It takes guts to come here."

I peeked over my shoulder, but I wasn't sure who was talking and about who. I smiled at a couple of folks I knew, but no one seemed inclined to chat. The rooms were small enough that if Aden was there, I'd see him, but he was nowhere in sight.

"…bedroom is amazing. The mayor said she's seen it and it's been fully restored. There's a private little balcony overlooking the backyard. The bathroom has a clawfoot tub and one of those rainforest showerheads."

"Well, she would know. She's been in on the renovation every step of the way."

The two women who were speaking moved away, and I longed to follow them and eavesdrop more. Why had the mayor been involved?

Unless Aden had included her because it might be her home someday.

The thought made me stop in the middle of the room.

Wait a minute. The man kissed me.

But he also spent the night at the mayor's house.

He said he wanted to help me. He was helping me. Well, he was helping Frank.

But he was seen around town and at functions with the mayor.

I shook my head. I had to have a talk with him about his relationship with the mayor if I wanted to have any kind of relationship with him. It was simple. No more beating about the bush. I needed to flat-out ask him. And if he wouldn't tell me, I'd push him out of my life. I was not going to get involved with someone who was already with someone else.

I felt like a weight had lifted. Easy. Talk to him and figure it out. I entered the kitchen and stopped in amazement. It seemed to glow with an inner life from the wood cabinets, the glass covering the upper cabinets, and gleaming marble countertop on the big center island where trays of food sat out.

"Quite the place, isn't it?" someone said behind me.

I turned. I recognized the man but didn't remember his name. He was from the "V" group of the Heavys, representing veterans. He was a Vietnam vet and came to the farm a couple of times to talk with Frank.

"Yes, it's amazing. I've only seen homes like this in a magazine."

He sipped the beer he held, nodding. "Yeah, I heard the guy spent a bunch of money fixing it up. He mostly shopped locally, too, so I guess I got no reason to complain." The man pointed to wine bottles on the opposite counter. "Food and drink is on the house. A bunch of the judges are here, and we're supposed to mingle. It might be tricky for you, hmm?"

I spied Aden through a doorway, talking to people. "I don't enjoy mingling, and I'm pressed for time because my father-in-law is in the hospital."

"Yeah, I read about that. Sounded pretty terrible. I'm surprised you're willing to show up after what's happened." He took another sip and watched me as though waiting for my reaction.

"I won't stay long. I need to get to the hospital to be with Frank." I caught a glimpse of the other Heavys, eyeing me from across the room. It was like I was in a searchlight or under a spotlight. People seemed to be watching me. I glanced down, wondering if maybe I had toilet paper stuck to my shoe or something.

"Well, good luck tomorrow. I'm not much for costume parties, but this one might be a doozy." He wandered off and another of the Heavys, the woman working with the homeless, cornered him to talk, both of them shooting glares at me.

"I'm surprised you have the gall to show your face here."

I turned and almost knocked into Mayor Parralt, immediately behind me. She wore a dark blue short jacket with a bright red silky top that clung and outlined her large breasts. Her blue pants were loose and flowing, covering the top of her bright red stiletto shoes.

"Hello, Mayor." I forced a smile.

"I'm surprised to see you here." She took a sip from the glass of red wine she held, her eyes fixed on me.

"My charity is one of the ones being represented tomorrow at the ball." I figured she was a relative newcomer to town and maybe didn't know how these things went.

"I know that. What do you have to say for yourself?" She was so angry I backed up, my butt pressed against the kitchen island.

"I'm not sure what you mean." I looked past her. Aden was watching us, standing a few feet away. He wore a dark sweater and pants and his face was partially in shadow. Then he moved into the light. I saw no glimmer of recognition in his eyes when he met mine. It was like meeting a stranger.

"You know exactly what I mean. I think it's not only deceitful. It's ungrateful. The Kingsley company has done a great deal for this town. It's rude of you to show up here." The mayor glared at me so hard I expected to see little lasers shooting from her eyes.

I realized the room had gone still. Everyone was staring at us. "I don't understand," I stammered. "If I'm not wanted, I'll leave. I thought this was open to all the groups who were entered in Harvesting the Future. If I misunderstood, I apologize." I tried to move past her but she blocked me in. I had to turn and walk around the island to where Aden stood.

I stopped to look up at him. "I apologize if I'm crashing the party." I waited for him to explain but he moved aside so I could get past. I went back the way I came, through the dining room and the living room.

I snatched my coat from the stack and went out the front door. I was to the sidewalk when someone called my name. I turned and saw Aden standing on his front porch. "I wanted to tell you I've withdrawn my name as a judge for the charity ball tomorrow," he said, coming down the steps to me. "I don't want anyone to think I have a vested interest in how you fare."

I pulled on my coat, using it to give me a chance to corral my crazy brain. "If you feel that's necessary, you did the right thing." I tried to decipher what I saw in his eyes. Disdain? Anger? Sadness? It was an emotion I wasn't sure how to interpret.

"I'm sorry I'm not the kind of person you can trust."

"I don't under—"

He was gone, moving quickly up the steps and back into the house. I stared at the door closing behind him. "What the hell?" I muttered. I hurried to my truck and got in, driving toward home through town.

I spied Harold outside the hardware store and on impulse I pulled into a parking spot. "How's it going, Harold?"

He smiled when he saw me. "Ash, it's good to see you. How's Frank doing?"

"He's making progress. He might be able to come

home tomorrow. Are you coming in or going home?"

"Came by to pick up some chain. I need to fix the tie-out for my backyard. Your dog is stronger than mine." He unlocked the door. "You know, I don't like to criticize and I know you feel strongly about land use, but your wording was a tad rough," Harold said. "Aden Kingsley seems like a nice guy and he isn't to blame for what his father did the past."

"I agree." I watched Harold go to the end cap where the chains were hanging. "I've read his proposal for land use and it's interesting."

"Then why did you do it?" Harold pointed at a newspaper lying on the counter.

"Why did I do what?"

"Write the letter." He joined me at the counter and tapped the paper. "Folks are talking about it."

"What letter?"

He thrust the newspaper at me. "This one."

I took the paper and skimmed over the page. Headlines about the idiots in Washington, D.C., a story about water quality, Letters to the Editor. Wait a minute. I focused on the one with the *Local Citizen Threatened* headline.

Most people in Dasdorf know me and know my father-in-law, Frank Goddard. We've lived here most of our lives and have been active members of the community.

What you may not know is we have been the victims of harassment since Kingsley Development began working on the job site situated on the land owned by Frank's stepdaughters.

I've also been a subject of criticism because I refuse to allow the use of land deeded to me by my late husband,

Bryan Goddard. The first home Bryan and I shared is on that parcel of land and it has enormous sentimental value to me. I refuse to allow it to be desecrated by development.

Aden Kingsley has sought to convince me otherwise, but I have refused. My home has been the target of malicious pranksters, and Frank was shot by persons unknown and remains in the hospital, recovering from his wound. Simply put, I'm not sure Kingsley Development is the best choice to manage the land adjacent to our town. Our land is sure to be tainted and our water fouled by any construction project, regardless of the type.

My convictions and my actions may prejudice my standing in our Heavys event, but I'm not concerned about that. My work and my home are more important. If I must sacrifice a competition to maintain my moral compass, I will.

Please join me to protect our homes and our environment. When asked to support Kingsley Development, refuse. It's the right thing to do.

It was signed *Ashley Schone.*

Chapter Twelve

The terrible thing about it was that it sounded exactly like me. Or, rather, the me I was a week ago, before I met Aden. I reread it and decided it was *almost* like me. I wouldn't have put in the sentimental attachment because of Bryan. I didn't have any particular memories about the land. My memories weren't tied to the place, just the person in the place.

"I didn't write this," I said.

"What?"

"I didn't write it. Somebody wrote it and used my name." Everything made sense now. The mayor's snide comment, the way the other Heavys acted, the way Aden glared at me and gave me the cold shoulder.

"People can't do that, can they?" Harold took the paper and shuffled through it. "Here. It says they don't print stuff that's sent to them anonymously."

"It wasn't sent anonymously. Somebody forged my name. Or signed my name." I grabbed the newspaper. "They can't do this. They can't print something just because somebody sent it to them." I opened the paper, scanning the inside page. "Who publishes this? It's not printed in town anymore, is it?"

"Nope. The local paper folded three or four years ago. It's run by an office doing news for a bunch of small towns. I think they're in North Liberty, or maybe Coralville."

I located the small box ad at the bottom of the page. There were several different editors listed, one for each of the small towns served by the version of the newspaper produced for their town. I didn't recognize the name of the one for Dasdorf. I showed it to Harold.

"Don't know him," he confirmed. "Must be an out-of-towner."

"He's going to hear from a townie," I fumed. I dialed the number listed and was routed immediately to voice mail. "My name is Ashley Schone and you printed a letter supposedly from me. But I didn't write it. I want you to print an immediate retraction." I rattled off my phone number, email address, and home phone and added, "If I need to write another letter to offset the one you printed, you let me know ASAP."

"You tell him," Harold said with a grin. "The problem is the next paper comes out on Monday, so folks will be talking about this all weekend."

"Well, shit." I rolled up the newspaper and whacked the counter with it.

"Who would do such a thing?" Harold's eyes narrowed as he focused, staring at the paper as if it might give him answers. "I wonder if it's because of the contest. Do you think one of the other Heavys is trying to make you look bad?"

"Oh, I don't think so. I mean, I hope not. What can I do about it, though?" I longed to rip the paper to shreds. "I can't deal with this. I have to get home and check in with the volunteers there, and I have to get to the hospital. What can I do?" I was mortified to hear my voice crack and felt tears burning my eyes.

Harold straightened. "I'm finding out who's behind this," he stated. "And I'll make sure the record is set straight." He nodded, wispy gray hair waving like tentacles. "You leave it to me, Ash. I won't let you lose that contest unless it's a fair fight. You leave it to me."

"What are you going to do?"

He lifted the old landline phone receiver. "I'm putting the party line to good use. You go along and do your business. I'll handle this."

"Are you sure? Maybe I should—" Do what? What could I do?

Harold reached out his arm and I went to him for a hug. "You go take care of Frank and let me take care of this. Go on now." He gave me a little shove.

I stumbled from the store, wiping tears when they rolled down my face. Who in hell would do that? It was downright malicious. It was illegal. It was Not Right.

I drove to the farm, a jumble of emotions tumbling around. Anger, sadness, hurt, grief, fear. I pulled into the drive and rested my head against the steering wheel, exhaustion hitting me so hard I wanted to tip over on the seat.

Instead I dragged myself from the truck and went to the lane to get the mail. I went inside, shucked off my party clothes and pulled on jeans and my *There Is No Planet B* sweatshirt. I shied away from thinking. I didn't want to think. If I did, I'd know someone was trying hard to sabotage my life. I didn't want to know that somebody hated me so much.

I went to the barn and checked on my patients. Marky Mark was on duty, and he proudly showed me logbook updates for the critters. "I'm holding down the fort until the vet gets here at seven," he assured me. "We're keeping an eye on things. The real pros come on duty, do their thing, and leave it to us to monitor."

Shoed

I sank down into a chair. "You don't know how much it means to me to have you guys here. You've been real troopers, and I mean that. I'll write a letter to your teacher and tell her how much your work helped me."

"Hey, it's been good for us, too. Gave us a chance to try out things. Tammy thought she wanted to be a vet until she had to clean out a stall." Marky grinned at me, raking his long hair out of his face. "Once you get shit on your shoes, it gives you a different perspective."

"It does," I agreed.

"You look beat. How's Frank doing? Everything going okay with him?"

"He's recovering, but it's hard."

"Man, a bullet wound. I mean, that's tough. He's lucky you found him, isn't he? Everybody is talking about it in town. I found your shirt."

I shot him a blank look. "My shirt?"

"Yeah, the one with the blood. I threw it away. I figured you wouldn't want it anymore. It was gross."

"I forgot about that." Aden gave me his shirt. My chest hurt at the thought of him, at the way he stared at me at his party. I needed to call him. Needed to tell him I didn't write the letter.

Later, I decided. If I called him tonight, he wouldn't take my call. He'd probably hang up on me.

I picked up Frank's kalimba from the table next to the chair. It was a beautiful little finger harp made of mahogany, the tines well worn and shiny. I ran through the scales, the music rolling softly through the barn.

"Frank will be okay, won't he?" Marky watched me play, his young face somber. "He'll play guitar again, won't he?"

I closed my eyes briefly to squeeze back the tears.

"I don't know. I hope so. The most important thing is he keeps his arm immobilized so the wound can heal. It'll be weeks before we know how much damage was done."

"We can still help out when he comes home. He shouldn't be out here working in the barn if he's got a wound. You know, infection." Marky waved a hand. "Yeah, we'll still be around to help."

"I'll pay you." I wasn't able to pay them much, but I needed to pay them something.

"Get Frank home, and we'll see how much you need us. Speaking of needing us, we're meeting at the gym tomorrow morning to set up the dioramas. Can you meet us there? We need you to give final approval for the setup."

It took me a minute to process what he was saying. "Oh, yeah. The charity ball. Sure, I can meet you there. What time?"

"Nine o'clock. The decorating committee will be setting up, plus all the charity groups can get in and set up their stuff, too. Ours is awesome. You should see what we've come up with. It's so cool."

I had totally forgotten about it. I wouldn't be able to attend if Frank was still in the hospital. Maybe I could go for a few minutes. I pushed out of the chair. "I'll meet you there. I need to get back to the hospital now. If the evening shift needs to talk to me, call, okay?"

"Will do. Say hi to Frank for us."

I paced through the barn one last time then left, stopping at Frank's house to make sure everything was okay. I touched the Fender, resting on his kitchen table. Would he be able to play again? At his age, with a wound like that, could he?

One day at a time, I reminded myself. I pulled out a

small duffel bag. He'd need fresh clothes when they released him. Be optimistic. I tucked in clean underwear, an old T-shirt, and pants, and a cardigan I'd wrap around him and his sling.

I went to the hospital, stopping by the cafeteria for a half of a ham sandwich and chips. When I got to Frank's room, he was sitting in the recliner, glaring at the television.

"You're pissed off at the world," I said, stuffing the duffel bag into the little closet near the doorway.

"That's because all I see is crap." He tossed the TV remote on the bed. "How was your day? How did the funeral go?"

I pulled over the guest chair and updated him on the ceremony. "It was odd," I said. "Emily acted like it didn't matter her sister was dead."

"Those children were never close," Frank said. "I remember when they were little. Mara would never let Emily play with her or her friends. Emily was such a pudgy little thing and not girly. Some of Mara's friends made fun of her." He hesitated. "I always wondered if maybe they weren't really sisters."

"Huh?"

"Miriam was a wild one when she was younger. I always wondered if Emily wasn't a child of another man. I know her husband thought that."

"What? It sounds like a regular Peyton Place."

"Oh, you'd be surprised what went on back in the day. Miriam's first marriage was contentious, to say the least. I think she breathed a sigh of relief when he died. I wouldn't be surprised if Mara had one father and Emily had another one. I wondered if that's why Miriam treated Emily differently than she treated Mara. Miriam always favored Mara, because Mara was so pretty and feminine." Frank blew out a disgusted snort. "Mara was good at acting, that's all. There wasn't anything pretty about her."

"It's not polite to speak ill of the dead," I pointed out.

"I've never been accused of being polite." Frank sighed. "I suppose that's why Emily latched onto Bryan. He was good to her."

"He was easy-going. He got along with everybody. He's like you, Frank. A guy without an enemy in the world."

"Oh, I have enemies," Frank said with a grin. "I just don't pay much attention to them."

"I think Emily still misses Bryan. I've been thinking about him lately. I realized I don't miss him."

"I know. I feel the same about Grace. I love the memories I have, but that's all they are. They're memories, not times I want to relive. I wish we had more time together, but I'm happy for the times we had." He tapped my hand. "How was the party at Aden's house? Tell me about it. I heard he's done a spank-up job remodeling it."

I described the charming little house in as much detail as I remembered given the short time I was there. "Lots of people were there, so I didn't stay too long."

"But you did talk to Aden? I have the feeling he's sweet on you, honey. We talked about this. You're a beautiful woman. You deserve to have a good man in your life."

"I have you," I said with a laugh. "That's more than enough."

The nurse came in and bustled around, taking his

blood pressure, checking his bandage, and ordering him to bed. "See what happens," he complained. "You get old and people start to boss you around."

"You don't act old," the nurse said. "And you don't act like somebody with a bad wound. You need to take care of yourself." She helped him into the bed and got him tucked in, then asked me, "Are you staying tonight?"

"You bet. I'll camp out on the couch."

"Oh, honey, you don't need to do that," Frank said.

I dimmed the light above the bed. "There's no place I'd rather be. I love you, old man." I leaned over to hug him.

"I love you, too, baby girl. Sing me something to give me sweet dreams," Frank whispered. "Play me a tune."

I settled in the recliner and picked up the finger harp. "I'll be glad when you're back on your feet and playing guitar."

"I might be able to sing some. How about this one?" He hummed a tune and I picked it up on the finger harp. "You Aint' Going Nowhere." His voice was raspy and wavery, but he managed to get through two of the verses. He was smiling when we finished. "Sing 'Since You Asked.' "

I lowered my head to hide my tears. I used to sing that song with Bryan. It was too full of loss for me, loss of Bryan, loss of Aden. "Not tonight," I whispered. I plucked a few random notes then I did "Bird on a Wire," "After the Ball," and followed it with "Heart of Gold." By the time I finished, his eyes were closed and he seemed peaceful and relaxed.

I eased away from the bed to go to my couch. That's when I saw the three nurses in the doorway, watching. I joined them at the door. "He used to play guitar with me," I whispered. "Will he ever play again?" I looked at Frank and the tears I'd been holding back suddenly came out. "He loves to play guitar. What will he do if he can't—"

One of the nurses enfolded me in a hug and then others were around me, surrounding me. "He'll come through it," someone murmured. "Don't worry. People adjust if they need to. The main thing is he's strong and he's mending well."

"I know I should count my blessings, but it's hard to see him like this."

One of the nurses put an arm around my shoulders and gave me a squeeze. "It's hard to see our parents like this, I know."

They left, murmuring words of encouragement. I took my sleep sweats and went into the bathroom to change. When I came back, I lay down and tugged the blanket over me, staring at the ceiling and listening to the wheeze and thump of the machines in the room.

Was there any way to repair the damage done by that stupid letter? Anything I could say or do to undo the ill will it created? Who would do such a thing? Who hated me so much they'd try to derail—

Derail what? A fleeting thought tugged at the edge of consciousness. All the letter did was create a chasm between Aden and me. Who cared about that? The mayor? No, she had no reason to think I was any threat. She and Aden were obviously close. Who else?

I tossed and turned, having one of those sleep cycles where I dreamed I wasn't sleeping but was awake and trying to sleep. I woke in the morning groggy and disoriented. I shared a breakfast of scrambled eggs and toast with Frank, then dressed in yesterday's clothes. I pulled my hair into a ponytail and went to meet Marky at the gym.

The parking lot had a dozen or more cars. When I entered the gym, it was a hive of activity, with people carrying tables, streamers, something that may have been a throne, and other props with a romance theme.

I spied Marky and his cronies, near the windows. Our display was in the middle of the side, two long tables pushed together and covered with a green tablecloth. Binny was smoothing out the cloth and three teenagers were setting up what I thought were big mushrooms. Binny was so skinny and tall and with her dark hair tucked into pigtails, she looked about eighteen or so. She fit in with the kids.

I went to join them, but before I'd gone a dozen feet, the guy from the party the night before hurried from his location on the opposite wall to intercept me. "I want to apologize," he said immediately. "What a terrible prank somebody pulled. They oughta be tossed in jail."

Another Heavy, the coach of the Youth tumbling team, joined him, adding his commiseration. "It's a crime, that's what it is," the coach said. "I hope they're punished."

"How did you find out?" I asked.

"Oh, a friend called and told me. It's all over town, how somebody forged your name to print that. This is a fair competition, but it made you out to be somebody who was whining and complaining."

"Nothing is farther from the truth." Binny joined us, her skinny arms akimbo on her hips. "It's a terrible joke, that's what it is."

"I wish we could work together." This came from

the woman representing the Homeless in the Heavys. "I hate this kind of competition when we're all trying to do good in the world. I feel like I'm taking money from a good cause, but I need the money for a good cause." She held out her hands. "It's weird."

"I know. I hate having to beg people for money when I know you guys need it, too." I gestured to the other displays in the process of setting up. "I wish we could combine it all."

"Well, if you figure it out, you tell us," the Vet guy said. "You let us know if you need any help. We're not letting a malicious prick besmirch one of the Heavys."

The others murmured agreement and returned to their displays. Binny and I went to where Marky and the others were working. "Word got around town?" I asked.

"Oh, yeah. You've heard of prayer chains? Harold did a phone chain. He called five people and asked them to call five people and before you know it, everybody in town knew." She shot me shrewd look. "I'll bet Aden Kingsley was called at least a dozen times."

"Oh, Lord. I didn't know what Harold meant when he said he was getting the party line going. Aden told me last night he asked to be removed as a judge."

Binny nodded. "It put the organizing committee in a tizzy. It's hard to find objective judges in a small town like this." She tugged me to the display and the teens who were swarming around it. "What do you think?"

I surveyed the vignette taking shape. There were six mounds making the table surface appear like rolling hills. Nestled in each "valley" was a stuffed animal, each holding a placard. "Aren't we doing iPads or something?"

"We decided to have one cohesive overview rather

than six small ones." Marky peered up at me from under the table. "All of their stories would compete. I'm still editing the final version. Stacy, hand me that extension cord," he said to one of the teenaged girls who were arranging animals. He disappeared back under the table.

I examined the raccoon. It had a bandage around one paw, and its ear was bedraggled. "What happened to him?"

"My dog got him," the girl said. "He kind of chewed up the ear before I got him away. I think it adds to the appeal, don't you?" She handed me the placard.

I'm Rocky, one of the current patients at Fairy Tale Endings. My paw is broken because I was caught stealing food when I was hungry. I was shot and hurt pretty bad. But Frank and Ash have taken care of me and I'll be going home soon.

People think I'm a nuisance and they want to kill me. But I eat a lot of pests that might harm you. I eat wasp larvae (yummy!) and can destroy wasp nests. I also eat little rodents and help keep them out of your house. Yes, I do get into the trash now and then (which is why I'm called a Trash Panda by some people).

I'd rather be living in the woods. But the woods are vanishing because you people are building houses where I used to live. Where am I supposed to go? Once I'm healed, Frank will take me to the woods near his house and I'll go back to where I belong. Believe me, I'd rather be there than in your backyard!

"That's the theme," the girl said, tapping the last paragraph. "See?" She pointed to the large sign in the middle of the display.

Urban development has pushed animals out. Fairy Tale Endings is needed to help those animals who are injured in the process. We owe them. We need to share the land.

"It's marvelous," I murmured. It wasn't what I envisioned, but it was creative, interesting, and far more elaborate than anything I might have done.

"Let's get the rest of them in place." This came from Gordy with the mohawk. He and Bart appeared to be directing traffic, helping the girls place the animals and arrange placards.

"Who did this?" I lifted the stuffed possum, which was the most adorable thing I'd ever seen. "Where did you find this?"

"Amazon Prime." This came from Tiff, the girl with the bright pink hair and the tattoos. "The others are borrowed. We're keeping track of expenses."

I blinked. "Expenses?"

"We're up to about fifty dollars." Binny handed me a clipboard. "I think we're a cinch to get the Favorite award. We're putting little baskets in front of each animal and we'll ask people to vote for their favorite one."

"But people are supposed to vote for their favorite project," I said. "So we should only have one basket on the tablet for Fairy Tale Endings."

"That's the genius of it," Tiff said. "People will walk by and they'll see this adorable little rabbit—" and she showed me what was, truly an adorable stuffed bunny with a bandage on her poor little paw, "—and they'll have to vote for her. Or they'll vote for Rocky or the squirrel."

"The squirrel?"

She pointed to the big box in front of the table. "We don't have it staged yet. It was hard to find cute ones. My brother had one he used as a lure to train his dog, but it was too beaten up. Thank God for overnight delivery." She consulted her clipboard. "Let's keep moving, people. We need to do a test run by noon."

"They seem to have it under control." I skimmed through the itemized list on the clipboard. Three stuffed animals, a green tablecloth, display boards, photo paper. "I don't know what I would have done without you. Between Frank in the hospital and Mara dying and the funeral and everything else going on, I would never have come up with anything."

"Everything else going on?" Binny took the clipboard. She put it on the table and drew me to one side. "Is Aden Kingsley part of everything else? I heard you and he adopted a dog together. Or rather, you stole a dog from Cox."

"The dog was running loose, so we didn't steal him. And it's not exactly our dog. Or maybe it is." I tugged on my ponytail, trying to jumpstart my brain. "I'm not sure, Binny. There are times when I think Aden is interested in me, and everything is fine. Then I drive by the mayor's house and his car is there."

"So? His car is there, big deal."

"At six thirty in the morning?"

"Oh. Well, have you asked him about it? Don't beat around the bush. Ask him if he and the mayor are involved."

"It seems kind of weird. I mean, it's not like he and I have even been out on a date. And maybe I'm old-fashioned, but if somebody is spending the night or, well, you know—"

"Having sex with someone," Binny said. "Let's be blunt."

"Spending the night," I repeated with a frosty look. "That means they're serious. Unless he's, you know, a slut or—" I searched for a comparable male term.

"Fuck 'em and shuck 'em," she said.

"Language!" I glanced furtively at the teens.

Marky peeked out from under the table. "Ditcher."

"Hooker upper," Gordy added.

"O.N.S.," Tiff chimed in.

O.N.S.?

She saw my confusion. "One Night Stand. But he's not that kind of guy. I mean, yeah, he's hot. In an older guy kind of way. I've seen him around town, and he is definitely hot. But older." Tiff styled as she spoke, poking at the fabric, unaware we had stopped to stare at her. "He's one of those sincere ones, the kind that's a one-woman man." She moved a faux tree branch and stepped back to evaluate the display. "Yeah, if he loves you, it's forever. I know the type."

"So says a sixteen-year-old," I muttered.

"Out of the mouths of babes." Binny winked at me. "Ask him. Quit running away from the future, Ash. This is your chance. Take it."

She made it sound so easy. I shook my head and turned to evaluate the other displays, more to avoid her than to view them. The Homeless one had a big picture of a lonely man, looking into a window where a family was gathered around a table. The Vets had a similar theme, a solitary man on a bench, staring at the ground. Behind him on the display table were pictures of combat and soldiers.

"I wonder," I whispered. "What do we have in common?"

"Hmm?" Binny gestured to Tiff. "I think we need

more greenery on the side, around the fox. It'll make him stand out."

I looked at the groups represented. We needed money. We needed support. We were trying to help a certain niche. What if we work together around a common purpose? Seniors, Vets, Homeless, Youth, Environmentalists. How to tie them together?

I snapped pictures with my phone of our display and the others, making sure to get a picture of Marky under the table and one of Tiff with all her tattoos so I could show Frank.

As though called from my thought, "This Land is Your Land," my ringtone for Frank, chimed. "Is everything okay, Frank?"

"More than okay," he said cheerfully. "I talked to the doctor, and he said I can go home today. I just have to take it easy and not strain."

Oh, crap. If he was home, I had to stay with him. I could not come to the party and leave him at home alone. I looked at the kids swarming around the display and guilt hit me, hard.

"That's great," I managed. "What time do I pick you up?"

"They said I need to be ready to leave by one or two." He chuckled. "I'm getting lunch before I go. You come here and we'll eat, and you can spring me."

"Sounds good. The kids have everything well in hand here. They don't even need me. In fact, they won't need me tonight, either, so there's no problem with me staying home with you." I tried to sound confident and upbeat.

"You'll do no such thing, you hear me? I already talked to Harold. He'll bring Cinders back tonight and stay with me while you're at the party."

"No, Frank, I should be there."

"Harold will stay with me at my house. He'll swing by his son's place and drop off his dog and bring Cinders to me. We figured two men and two dogs in my place might be too tight. You've got medical folks coming in to check on the patients, so if anything goes sideways, they'll be around."

"I can set up a place for you at the farmhouse, in the living room. I'll make up the couch there and you—"

"No way. I want to be in my place. You listen to me. I bought that costume for you special. Binny has worked to get it customized the way I wanted it. No, sir, you're going to the party and show them what real beauty is. I won't take no for an answer, young lady."

I looked at Binny, laughing with Marky and the other kids. *Quit running away from the future.* She was right. I needed to face Aden and find out what kind of a future I might have with him. Or not.

I guess I had a party to get ready for.

Chapter Thirteen

I left the setup crew at eleven and went to the hospital, stopping at the nurses' station on my way to Frank's room. "Not that I don't trust him, but I want to confirm the doctor agreed my father-in-law would go home today."

"Yes, he did." The nurse on duty laughed. "We'll be sorry to see him go. He has such a good attitude. The doctor feels he'll heal faster at home. Make sure he keeps his arm immobilized. We'll want him in for a recheck in a few days, so we can clean the wound and check progress."

"How long before he can leave?" I asked. "Do we have time for lunch?"

"I'm sure you will. We're waiting for his discharge papers to come in, so there's plenty of time."

I went into Frank's room, where he was sitting on the edge of the bed, his lunch on the roll-up table. "Chicken pot pie for me and tomato soup and grilled cheese for you," he said gleefully. "And salad and ice cream for dessert."

"You went all out." I surveyed the small feast. "Didn't somebody question why you were ordering so much food?"

"Nope. My insurance is paying for it, so I figured, why not?"

Insurance? Aden was paying for it. I shoved the guilt

to one side and sank into the recliner with the sandwich. While we ate, I showed Frank the pictures I took of the displays. "I wish we could work together instead of competing for money," I said. "I wish we could pool our resources somehow."

"All of the groups have a specialized niche." Frank deftly twisted his fork to catch an errant chunk of chicken that threatened to fall in his lap. "If you had a common denominator it might work."

"The common denominator is need. We need money to help people."

"And animals. We need money to help animals." Frank pushed away his tray. "Get me my clothes. I want to get dressed."

"There's no rush."

"Yes, there is. I'm tired of feeling a draft on my butt." He balanced on the edge of the bed while I fetched the duffel bag I'd packed. When I moved forward to help him, he waved me off. "I don't need you laughing at my dangly bits. Let me at least get my underwear on before you wade in and help."

"Oh, for heaven's sake. I've seen a naked man before."

"And I daresay you'll see one again. You will if Aden Kingsley has anything to say about it." He peeked sideways at me when he said it.

"I'm not so sure about that. I think that boat might have sailed."

"Why?"

I didn't want to get into the angst the stupid letter caused, so I just said, "He wasn't very friendly last night at his party."

"He was busy being a host. Mark my words. He has

his eye on you. Now you wait over there. Let me deal with this." Frank used the bed to support himself and managed to stick one foot at a time through the legs of his boxers and tug them up past his knees. "Okay, now you get behind me and catch me if I start to tip."

He tottered to his feet. I leapt to stand behind him while he tugged and pulled his shorts up with one hand. "Okay, well, that was more work than I thought it'd be." He sagged onto the bed, his nightgown tangled around his waist. I helped him escape from the fabric and handed him the T-shirt. "This won't work. We'd better cut it open."

"I think it's old enough and so stretched out we can make it on top of the sling. Let's give it a try." I helped him slide on the shirt, tugging it carefully past his injured side. Sure enough, the fabric was so flaccid it fit okay. I held out the cardigan, and he pulled it on one arm, and we draped the other over his shoulder. I tied it together with a strip of gauze bandage I found in a drawer. "There you are. You've got your cape on and you're ready to do your superhero thing."

"A superhero without pants. Give me a minute, and we'll tackle that." He perched on the edge of the bed, his face red. "Who would have thought getting dressed was such an effort? When the hell did I get so old?"

"Does anybody here need a ride?"

I turned to see Mark Byrd in the doorway. "What are you doing here?"

"Binny said Frank is coming home today. We figured a sedan might be easier to manage than a truck. How are you doing?" Mark crossed the room to Frank.

"I'd be doing fine if I could get my pants on. Can you give me a hand?" Frank held out his good arm. Mark helped him to his feet. He and Frank were about the same height, but Frank was swaying, so I stayed nearby in case I needed to help.

"Thanks for the ride, Mark. I never thought about the vehicle." I watched anxiously while Mark helped Frank slide on his jeans, holding my breath when they struggled to pull up the fabric.

"There you are." Mark knelt and tugged on Frank's socks and sneakers. "You're ready."

"Just in time, too." The nurse on duty came into the room, a sheaf of papers in hand. "I need to review your discharge instructions, then we'll get the wheelchair and get you on the road." Mark slipped away, and the nurse moved in to sit next to Frank on the bed. "Here's your medication list. We filled it initially at the pharmacy downstairs. We'll transfer it to your pharmacy when this prescription runs out."

She went over the pain pills, antibiotics, and interactions, then pointed to the appointment list on the last page. "You're scheduled for follow-up next week and one the week after that. Then you'll start physical therapy. We haven't scheduled it yet. It depends on where you want to do that."

"We'll figure it out." Frank shuffled through the papers on his lap. "This is well organized. Thank you." He smiled at her. She put her arm around him to give him a squeeze.

"We'll miss you, Frank. You've kept us on our toes these last few days. Let me get your wheelchair, and you're out of here." She bounced to her feet and I went with her to the door.

"I can't stay with him tonight," I confided. "A family friend is staying with him, at least until I get home. Is that okay? Do you think I need to be with him?"

"As long as someone's with him to make sure he doesn't overdo it. We like to have someone on hand for the first few days while he adjusts to the splint at home." She left the room and returned immediately with a wheelchair. "Load it up, Frank."

We bustled around getting clothes and things into bags, my overnight stuff as well as Frank's assorted hospital "freebies." This was anything he might have touched during his stay there, like tissues and toothbrush. He insisted on taking it all. "We paid for it, so by God, we're taking it."

Mark left to bring the car around while I juggled everything following the nurse and Frank through the corridors. We got Frank and our gear into Mark's car and they sped off. I retrieved my truck and followed, pulling into Frank's driveway as Mark was helping Frank from the sedan.

Harold was outside Frank's house, Cinders on a tight lead next to him. "Good to have you back, Frank." Harold gave Cinders some slack, and the dog snuffled eagerly at Frank, stubby tail going crazy.

"It's good to be home. It was fun to have those girls watching out for me, but there's nothing like your own bed." Frank managed to get up the steps into the house, Mark holding on to his uninjured arm. "I need to go to the barn and check on things. I'll do it once I've rested."

"You'll do no such thing," I scolded. "You are off duty for a few days, do you hear me?" I moved aside so Mark could leave the house, making room for Harold and the dog to go in. "I'll go do rounds and come back and report. You settle in for now."

Frank sank down on his daybed with a sigh. "I think

I'll do that. Come here, dog." He held out a hand, and Cinders bounded to him.

"Thanks, Mark. I appreciate your help." He and I went out to his car. "Tell Binny I'll be in for my costume and dressing in an hour or so."

"I'll tell her. She's excited. And so is Frank. He picked it out, you know." Mark slid into the car. "Hey, I meant to tell you. I ran into Emily in town. She said something about missing the party tonight. She's going out on a hunt and wanted to be in place at dawn."

"That's odd. I mean, it's not odd she camps out because she does it all the time. But she had a costume. I remember Binny mentioning something about it."

"Yeah. She was acting sort of distracted." He shrugged. "Usually she's straight-ahead, no nonsense, but she seemed disjointed. I hope if she's hunting she's going alone. You don't want a distracted hunter out there with a bow and arrow. I'll see you in an hour or two." He backed out and sped off.

No kidding. Hunters were bad enough when they focused. I went to the barn to check in. One of the local vet techs was on duty, a girl I'd worked with often.

"I'm worried about the rabbit," she said as soon as I entered. "She's taken a turn for the worse. I didn't want to sedate her before checking with you first."

I went to Roberta's stall. She was huddled into the corner, her back to the door. Everything about her said "forlorn and abandoned."

"She's going into what I call societal shock," I said softly. "That happens when they've been in treatment for a long time. She still remembers her life in the wild, but she's starting to realize she may not return to it." I was anthropomorphizing, but the gist of what I said was true.

Wild animals simply didn't adapt well to a caged life, especially those who came to us as adults.

"What do you do? Is there a treatment?" The tech leafed through the logbook.

"No. I'll remove her bandage in the morning. I'll release her tomorrow in the state park where she was found, down by the river. It's possible she'll be able to rejoin her colony."

"She's not fully healed."

"She'll be dead in two days if I don't. She'll quit eating, and it will become dangerous to treat her. At least this way she'll have a chance to return to her old life." I straightened, familiar grief washing through me. "We can't save all of them."

"It's not fair," the girl whispered.

"No. It isn't. You do what you can to even the odds, but sometimes it doesn't work out. And sometimes it does. She may make it after all." I went to Rocky's stall. He was moving much better, with no limping. "This guy is ready to go home. I can release him tomorrow, too. Busy day tomorrow."

It would be especially busy because Frank wouldn't be there to help. He was the best when it came to releasing our patients back to their homes. He had a soothing, gentle touch with them. Well, I'd have to manage.

The baby squirrels were doing well, but their weight was down. I reviewed their diet and made an adjustment in nutrition. The fox was coming along nicely and could be released next week. The two woodchucks had put on weight. I had to release them in the next day or two because they needed to hibernate and would have to get burrowing soon.

I checked the weather forecast on my phone, wincing when I saw freezing temperatures coming up in the next few days. I went back and adjusted the nutrition for the woodchucks and the fox. I'd give them a little boost before release.

"I'm going to the charity ball in town tonight, but if anything comes up, you can call," I told the girl.

"I'll be here until six, then Dr. Cindy is checking in. I think the high school kids are taking turns watching things until the morning. You've got a good group of volunteers."

"I'm lucky to have them. I can't do this on my own." I left and went back to Frank's house, peeking inside. "All okay here?"

"We're fine. How are things out at the hospital?" Frank lay on the daybed, a pillow supporting his injury.

"Rocky is ready to go. I'll release Woody One and Two and Red in a few days. They're doing okay. Roberta needs to leave, too. I'll take her back to the park tomorrow."

"Shock?"

I nodded.

"I was afraid of that." He sighed. "I'll ride along with you." I began to protest but he raised his good hand. "Nope, I'll ride along."

"What's wrong?" Harold asked. He was in Frank's minuscule kitchen, stirring a pot on the stove.

"I'll explain," Frank said. "You go on and get ready for the party, honey. Make sure to get plenty of pictures. I want to see you in your finery."

I kissed his cheek. "Thank you," I whispered. "For everything."

"We'll handle it together like we always do. Don't

worry. Go off and have fun." He gave me a little shake. I moved to the door.

"Don't party too much tonight," I warned. I shook a finger at Cinders, who lounged on the floor near Frank. "You keep an eye on them."

He woofed at me and wagged his tail. I went to the farmhouse and dropped my hospital bag on my bed. I longed to drop down with it and take a nap, but I needed to get to Binny's. Instead of sleeping I emptied out my bag and repacked it with a bathrobe and my minuscule makeup kit.

I was heading out the door when my mobile phone rang. It was Billy Grimm. "I wanted to update you about Frank's shooting. I called the hospital, and they said Frank was sent home. I don't like you out there alone. We might want to have a deputy with you."

"I'm going to town for the party tonight. Harold is staying with Frank, and we have volunteers at the barn. So he's not alone. Did you find out any more about who might have shot him?"

"It was a hunting rifle, but that's about all we know. I was hoping we'd get fingerprints off the bullet, but whoever loaded the shells was wearing gloves."

"Is that normal?" The few times I loaded a gun I did it with bare hands. However, I wasn't a hunter for sport, so I had no idea what they did.

"It's not unusual. Are you sure you folks will be okay out there? We're short-handed here, but we can send somebody by for a wellness check every few hours."

"Short-handed? Did somebody call in sick?" I tossed my bag in the truck and pulled myself in by the strap.

"No, it's Halloween, so there's always the chance for pranks. Plus there's the fire at the construction site."

"Fire?"

"Somebody set the chipper on fire, the one used on Mike Parsons. It exploded and caused damage."

"Damn. I didn't hear about that." I had a sudden horrible thought. "Was anybody hurt?"

"No, Kingsley had the site shut down so no one was there."

"Shut down?"

"Didn't you hear? No, I suppose you didn't, you've been busy. He shut down the site last night. There's a sign out on the gate that says it's closed until further notice. The guys working there were given two weeks' pay. They were told they'd be called when the site is open again, but they weren't told when."

"I wonder what's going on."

"Maybe if you see Kingsley at the party you can ask him. Take care, Ash, and don't be alone tonight, okay? I got a feeling this isn't over."

I started for town and considered doing a drive-by at the construction site. But it was out of the way and it was four thirty, so I decided not to. Binny would have the gossip, anyway.

I parked in the drive outside Binny's "shop," a detached garage next to their home on Mockingbird Lane. The building was used for her tailoring business and what she called "Binny's Bling Boutique." I entered through the side door, the little chime overhead tinkling through the scale.

Binny was sitting in front of her sewing machine at the long table in the middle of the room. Her dark hair was pulled back from her face to hang down her back.

Her pale face and hands stood out in sharp relief against the dark fabric she was working with. She had gained weight when Marky was born and fought hard to lose it and keep it off. Now she was tall and skinny and the perfect model for the clothes she designed.

The walls of her shop were lined with shelves full of the most amazing assortment of fabric and buttons and ribbon and frills and lace and things I had no words for. Despite the overwhelming amount of Stuff, she knew where everything was placed and could put her hand on a thing within seconds.

"Hey, I'm glad you got here. How's Frank doing? Mark said he was okay, but he was weak." She pushed away from the machine to join me in front of a mannequin draped in a white sheet.

"The doctor thinks he'll heal faster at home." I shucked off my jacket and hung it on the coatrack. "I think he's right. Frank was getting antsy."

"Mark said he was in a private room. That's kind of pricy, isn't it?"

"Aden Kingsley is paying for it. Or his company is."

"What?" Binny wiggled her eyebrows. "My, my. He's certainly making his intentions known, isn't he?"

"Is he? I don't know what to think." I circled the mannequin. It was surprisingly bulky, narrow at the top and flaring out at the bottom. "So what kind of costume is it? I warned you, it has to be comfortable. I won't suffer through a party in a costume I can't breathe in."

"You can breathe in it," she assured me. "Just breathe carefully."

"Carefully? What does that mean?"

"You'll see. Are you ready?"

I sighed. "Yes, I'm ready."

"Close your eyes. Cover them."

I glared at her.

"Do it."

I covered my eyes. "What did Frank buy?"

"Okay. Open your eyes. Ta-da!" She swept off the sheet and tossed it to one side.

O.M.G.

It was a Cinderella dress. Pale blue with yards of gauzy fabric and a puffy collar outlining a deeply plunging neckline. I peered closer at the neckline. There were butterflies in the gauzy stuff. It was fluffy, puffy, girly, and over-the-top. The skirt was voluminous, flaring out from the waist for at least three or four feet.

"Frank, you rat," I muttered.

"He was so excited when it came," Binny said. "He ordered it from a catalog or something. He said it would be perfect for you. Of course, I had to make alterations. I knew you wouldn't want to wear high heels, so I shortened it. We may need to alter it more once you try it on."

Try it on? I shot her a disbelieving look.

"I knew if you saw it ahead of time you'd find a way to weasel out of wearing it. And Frank was so happy with it. He said he wanted you to have a gown that matched your personality."

"Matched my personality? What did he think I was, a ball of fluff?"

Binny frowned at me. "Ash, please. He thinks you're a beautiful person. You deserve a beautiful ball gown." She ruffled the skirt.

"So that's why you never wanted me to have a fitting. How did you get my size?" I prowled around the mannequin, eyeing the elaborate gown.

"Oh, Frank snooped around for me. He's a crafty old dude. I'm so glad he'll be okay. He's such a big part of this town."

I evaluated the gown's neckline. "My bra won't work with this."

"That's the beauty of it." Binny spun the mannequin. The back of the dress had ribbons running from the waist to mid-back. "We lace you in and it's like a corset. Only not as tight, of course," she hurriedly said when she saw my appalled expression. "You don't need a bra."

I looked down at my breasts. Granted, I wasn't extremely large, but the girls were not as firm as they used to be.

"Trust me," she said. "I added built-in cups. And the dress is lighter than it seems. It floats. Try it."

I ran my hand over the skirt. "How'd you do that?"

"It's only a few layers of organza and chiffon on the petticoat. So it swirls and moves like air. You won't have any trouble dancing in this." She rummaged in the box next to her sewing table and pulled out a pair of blue shoes. Flats, like ballet shoes. "See? Made for dancing. And I found this. I think I can do it." She thrust a folded page at me.

It was a magazine picture of a woman with an upswept hairdo. Her hair was in a loose half-braid at the nape of her neck and pulled up into a sort of loose bun at the crown with the remains of the braid tumbling down. "It might be doable," I said. "With a bunch of pins."

"Pins I got." Binny rattled a small box. "And makeup. You'll be a princess when I'm done with you."

"But you have your own costume to do."

"You hop in the shower. Don't wash your hair,

though. It'll take too long to dry. I'll do my makeup while you're showering. Then Morticia Addams will come in and help you dress for your big night on the town." She beamed at me. "Mark has arranged for a car and a driver. Marky wanted to do it, but he thought he should stay at the school in case something needs adjusting on your display. Rod is one of our usual limo drivers. You'll like him."

"With a dress like that, I should go in a pumpkin pulled by mice or something."

Binny laughed. "You'll have to settle for a bronze-colored Crown Vic and Rod. Go on now. Use the guest bedroom. I'll be waiting for you. I can't wait to text Frank a picture of how you look."

I went into the house to the guest room, a space I'd used in the past when the weather was terrible and I stayed overnight in town. I found a towel in the linen closet and went into the tiny bathroom, which was barely large enough for a shower stall, toilet, and sink.

I washed away a day of hospital and nervous energy and emerged, wrapping my bathrobe around me. I pulled my hair out of my ponytail and massaged my scalp, luxuriating in the feeling of freedom. I picked up my makeup bag and went back to Binny's Boutique.

Morticia Addams was waiting for me, complete with a long black dress slit up the front, black hair falling down her back, pale complexion, and bright red lips.

"You're fabulous," I said. "You're the spitting image of Angelica Huston."

Binny laughed. "The scary thing is I didn't have to do much except part my hair down the middle and put on red lipstick." She waved one hand, her black nail polish standing out in stark relief. "Let's do your hair first. You can step into the gown so it shouldn't mess up anything we do."

I plopped down in a swivel chair and she arranged pins, brushes, and combs in front of me on the sewing machine table. I lifted one decorative comb, an enameled blue butterfly with wings outstretched. "Where did this come from?"

"Frank asked me to use it in your hair. He said it belonged to Grace."

I rubbed my finger on the well-worn design. "I love that old man," I murmured. I set the comb down. "Billy Grimm called me before I came over. Did you hear about the fire at the construction site?"

"Head down," Binny commanded. I obediently dipped my head and she began to brush and comb. "I heard. Somebody sure has it in for Aden Kingsley. Do you still oppose it? The co-housing thing? Pin."

I handed her a hairpin. "I don't know. I'm not sure how it would work."

"I'll tell you how it'll work." She briskly braided my hair and secured it with a twist tie. "It means Frank and you won't be alone out on the farm. Oh, you'll be alone, but not isolated. Pin." I held up a pin. "He'll have access to other people not far away. And a new road will be built so you don't have to go halfway around the county to get to your place. Raise your head and tilt."

I tilted my head. "Do you think Frank would want that? He seems happy enough as we are."

Binny focused on my hair style, frowning while she gently tugged on the braid. "I think he'll love it. Tip forward." I lowered my chin. "You and Frank will both enjoy it. Oh, it's a change, but—Pin." I gave her another pin, and she jabbed it into my mass of hair.

"Ow."

"Sorry. You have a lot of hair. Okay, give me the comb."

I stretched for it and managed to nab it. "Frank, you sentimental old fool."

Binny slid the comb in at the back. "Almost done. It didn't take as many pins as I thought it would." She came around in front to regard me. "Adjustments needed. Hang on. I think the beauty of the co-housing thing is it's a good use for the land. It's not another stupid shopping center. It'll have people there who want to live environmentally responsibly. And they'll be people who want to be a part of the community." She poked and pinned while she spoke, walking around me to check her work.

"I never considered the possibility," I admitted. "I read through the proposal, and I have questions."

"Well, ask them. Kingsley said he wants to have public meetings about it, so go and ask your questions. Oh, wait." She put her hands on my shoulders. "This isn't about Bryan, is it?"

"What?"

"You know. What that stupid letter said. You don't have a sentimental attachment to the land, do you? I never thought you did, but the letter said you did."

"No, not at all. Whoever forged my name sure didn't know me very well, did they?"

"I didn't think you felt that way." She poked more and stepped back. "Okay, I think that'll do it. Give your head a shake."

I tossed my head to and fro. "It's okay."

"I think you need more pins. It's wobbly." She took the pins I raised and tucked them in here and there.

"Okay. Let's do your makeup next." I reached for my makeup bag, but she shook her head. "This requires the real deal, not dime store stuff."

"Hey, it's okay stuff."

She pointed to a box next to the sewing machine. "Check it out."

I opened the plastic container decorated with a smiling sheep. "A sheep?" I eyed the assortment of pigments, colors, and Lord knows what.

"It's cruelty free, so you don't have to worry. I asked a couple of ladies who come in what was the best brand around here and they said to use this one." Binny regarded the contents with a frown. "Let's see what I can do. Lift your face."

I sighed but did as she asked, closing my eyes, pouting my lips, and tilting my head here and there. "You're so beautiful," Binny murmured, dabbing my cheeks. "You're beautiful, but it doesn't matter to you. Mara wasn't beautiful, but she always acted like she was."

"I'm not beautiful," I murmured. "I just have good skin and hair."

"And a gorgeous figure and beautiful eyes and a glowing personality. You're beautiful. You just don't know it."

"If I'm so beautiful, why are you fussing around me like I'm a mannequin that needs improvement?"

"I'm gilding the lily, that's all." A few minutes later she stepped back. "Perfect."

"It doesn't feel like you did anything. Usually makeup feels gunky."

"Not this stuff. It's the good stuff. Now let's get the dress on. Oh, wait. Stockings." She plucked a brown bag from the table and handed it to me.

I pulled out a pair of thigh-high white stockings with elastic at the top. "Good. I was afraid I'd have to wear panty hose or something."

"Nope. Stockings, your panties, and the dress. That's it. Get 'em on and let's do this."

I pulled on the stockings and joined her at the mannequin, eyeing the dress skeptically. "I'm not sure it'll fit."

"It'll fit. Come on." She loosened the lacing at the back of the gown. I slipped off my bathrobe, holding on to her to step into the frothy pile of fabric. Binny pulled up the gown and tugged on the lacings. "Let me know if it's too tight."

"That's comfy." And it was. My breasts were supported, the fabric was snug around the middle, then it floated around the rest of me.

Binny peered over my shoulder. "Like I said, don't breathe too deeply."

"Good Lord. My breasts haven't seen this much daylight since I was a teenager."

"It's too bad we don't have a diamond necklace or something," she muttered, fussing around with the lacing. "Oh, wait. I know." She went to one of the shelves and dug into a box, emerging with a length of thick blue ribbon. "This is perfect." Humming softly, she put it around my throat and tied a big bow off to one side. "Try the shoes. See how it feels."

I stepped into the shoes, which were a soft faux leather, and took a few cautious steps. "There's a bunch of fabric to manage," I muttered, keeping my arms down at my side to maneuver the skirt around the shop.

"It looks good. Is it too long?"

I tried a tentative twirl and didn't step on anything. "I think you nailed it, Binny. What about a coat or something?"

She settled a gauzy piece of chiffon around my neck. "That's all I'm doing. I refuse to spoil the effect with anything as mundane as a coat."

Someone pounded on the door. "Hey, ladies. The chariot is waiting. Time to go. Speed it up in there."

Binny threw open the door. Mark stood outside, his hair slicked back and a fake mustache framing his lips. "Ah, Morticia, you are beautiful." He swept Binny into his arms. "Fly away with me, my love." He turned and caught sight of me, almost dropping Binny. "Holy shit, Ash. Look at you."

I twirled slowly. "It's Frank's doing. And Binny's. Thanks to her, I'm passable."

"Passable?" Mark stared at me, eyes wide. "Holy shit, Ash."

"Not exactly the reaction I want, Mark."

"You know what I mean."

Binny handed him her phone. "Take pictures. I need to send them to Frank."

I obligingly posed for photographs, insisting that Binny be in several as the perpetrator of my style. Then we bundled into one of the biggest cars I've ever ridden in for the five-block ride to the school.

We got there just as the Heavys were being introduced by Jacob William, who always emceed the event. I paused on the threshold of the gym. I'll ask him, I decided. I'm going to find out if Aden is sleeping with the mayor. I'll find out if—

"Ash. Come on. It's your turn." Binny pulled the chiffon "shawl" off and gave me a nudge.

I stepped toward the spotlight.

Chapter Fourteen

I paused at the doorway.

Jacob's mouth dropped open. "That's a costume," he croaked.

"Yeah, it is, isn't it?" I fluffed the skirt. "Are you supposed to announce me or something?'

"Oh, yeah." He went to the doorway and banged a gong set up near the entryway. The crowd in the gym quieted. Jacob strode to the microphone a few steps ahead. "May I present Ashley Schone, representing Fairy Tale Endings and her escort, Frank Goddard—wait a minute." Jacob turned to me, mic still held in his hand. "Frank is in the hospital, isn't he?"

The crowd near the door parted. Aden moved forward, dressed exactly like Colin Firth channeling Fitzwilliam Darcy in *Pride and Prejudice.* Frock coat, cravat, vest, riding breeches, and boots. He was a romance novel hero come to life.

O.M.G. How did he know? How did he know it was the sexiest costume any man could wear? And he wore it so well, right down to the errant curl on his forehead.

He bowed deeply. "I'll be your escort for tonight if you'll have me, Princess."

A collective sigh came from the onlookers. I looked at Jacob, my eyes so big I thought they'd pop. He gulped, his eyes equally big.

"Thank you, sir," I murmured, holding out my hand.

Aden took it, held it for an instant and pressed a kiss onto my fingers. Another sigh came from the crowd when he pulled me to him. "I'll escort you anywhere, anytime," he whispered, bending down to brush his lips against my cheek.

"Anywhere?"

He smiled. "As long as you promise not to throw your boots at me."

I laughed. "I promise."

He led me forward to the other Heavys, who were gathered together at the front of the gym. Aden bowed again and stepped back to join the onlookers gathered in a semicircle around the microphone and our group. There was a moment of hesitation, then the Heavys surrounded me.

The Vet guy, dressed as a pirate, grabbed my hand. "That's a hell of a costume," he said, pumping my arm.

The others crowded as near as they could with the voluminous skirts I wore. All were talking excitedly or laughing, and that's when it hit me—the gist of an idea.

Jacob joined us. "Time for you guys to give your pitches. Who wants to start?"

I raised my hand. "I have an idea I want to float. It's not really a pitch."

"Okay," he said doubtfully.

I turned to survey the other Heavys. "No pressure on you, but I have an idea that might work for all of us."

"Go for it, Princess." The Vet gestured to the microphone. "We're willing to listen."

I stepped forward, struggling to put my ideas into words. I took a deep breath, but not too deep, lest my breasts escape the dress. I frowned at the microphone which was, of course, far out of my reach. Aden stepped forward and adjusted it for me, smiling as he did so. Then he moved back to stand with the crowd, his gaze focused on me.

"Hey, folks. I'm Ash Schone and I manage Fairy Tale Endings with Frank Goddard, my father-in-law." I spoke slowly, figuring out what to say while I went along. "You know what we do. We help injured or orphaned wildlife and get them back to the wild where they belong. As I was preparing for this event, I thought about how much we have in common." I raised my arms to encompass the whole group of Heavys.

"I tried to think of a thread connecting us, something besides the money we want to raise to help our various groups. You know what I came up with?" I looked around the crowd and turned to smile at the Heavys. "Animals. Maybe it can be a common thread to connect us. Here's what I thought. We can use the Homeless folks to help at the wildlife rehab center. If anybody knows what it's like to be displaced, they do."

The Homeless representative appeared surprised, then frowned thoughtfully.

"The young kids can work at the Humane Society to walk dogs and help get their energy levels to something manageable. The energy levels for the kids and the dogs."

The Youth coach nodded and kids at the back of the room hooted in agreement.

"Maybe some of the Vets could work with abused animals and help them get socialized. They understand trauma better than anybody. What if we set aside land for a dog park, a place where humans and animals play? And maybe the seniors can help out by doing publicity for the animals waiting to be adopted. They can write press releases or—" I stalled, not sure where my idea was going.

"We can do photography and write up bios for the animals," someone called out from the crowd. "We could learn about their personalities and find ways to make them adoptable."

"We've never done anything like it before," the Homeless lady said doubtfully.

"Doesn't mean we can't think about it now," the Vet guy said. "It's a good idea. Seems to me we're diluting the charity effect because folks donate a little here and a little there. Maybe if we put the money in a big pile, we can all draw from it."

"Let's talk about," the Youth guy said. The Senior advocate broke away and joined several people around his display, talking excitedly.

"Let's do this," I suggested, raising my voice to be heard above the others talking. "Let's have a party and let's celebrate. There are so many nifty displays here. Please, donate to anything you support, but let's not vote on one standing out from the others. Let's all be winners tonight and dance." I turned to look up at the stage and the young D.J. there. "How about playing the theme song?"

"Give me a second. I wasn't ready to play it at the first." He frantically tapped his computer screen.

I took a step toward the dance floor, and Aden appeared in front of me. "May I have the first dance?"

I twitched my skirt. "I hope I can manage it."

He winked. "We'll figure it out."

"The Iowa Waltz" began to play. People moved into the clear space in the middle of the gym. Aden held out his arms. I moved to him, his left hand on my waist and his right hand holding my arm up.

"Let's start out slow," I cautioned. "I'm not accustomed to this much fabric."

"And I'm not accustomed to having such a beautiful woman in my arms." He began a sedate waltz, piloting us around the dance floor in small sweeping moves.

It had been a long time since I danced, but Aden was a strong partner and led me surely around the floor. My worries about tripping on my skirt eased, and I began to relax. "Binny mentioned you closed the construction site," I said. "I heard about the fire there."

He steered us around the other couples on the floor before answering. "I checked the purchase logs," Aden said. "Mike Parsons did use an excessive amount of herbicide early in the project. Your concern about toxicity is valid."

"I knew something was wrong. I was seeing the effects of it downstream."

"I'll file a report with the E.P.A. Kingsley will be responsible for the remediation." He turned us, moving past the Vet guy who was enthusiastically piloting a white-haired woman around the floor.

"You'll do that?"

"Despite what you might think, I'm an honest businessman. My father was willing to cut corners, but I'm determined to be environmentally responsible going forward."

"Why?" I blurted.

"Because it's the right thing to do."

"No, I mean, why did Parsons do it?" I followed Aden's lead, my mind working furiously. "Earlier in the summer, he worked on clearing the site as fast as he could. With so much herbicide damage, would it stop your project? The co-housing project?"

"It'll slow it. I won't put in housing at a contaminated site. We'll need at least a year to do remediation."

"But a commercial development can go in?"

"It depends. If we planned it correctly, yes, it could. There would be a lot of concrete and fixing the problem wouldn't be as critical to be done immediately."

We did another turn around the dance floor before I began to see the pattern. "When did you discuss the possibility of a housing project with Mara?"

"Midsummer."

"When did he poison the soil?"

Aden met my gaze. "Midsummer."

"She did it," I said. "Mara. I'll bet she hired Parsons to poison the site. Then you'd switch to a commercial development, which would be more lucrative for her. I'll bet she had them do the firecrackers and the prank calls and all that crap. That's the kind of thing she'd do."

"Did Parsons kill her?" He shook his head. "No, it doesn't make sense. Why would he kill her?" The music stopped, and we moved to stand near the displays.

"I need to go talk to Marky and the crew," I said. "They did so much work for me these past few days. I owe them big-time."

"I need to check on a couple of things," he said. "I'll be back in a minute." He moved to the exit, pulling a cellphone from his frockcoat pocket, an incongruous sight that made me smile.

I swayed over to Marky, who was hovering near the FTE display. The table was transformed into a forest-like setting with the stuffed animals in their little niches. A video was playing on an iPad set up in the middle of it all. People were crowded in a small circle, viewing the film.

"You did a great job," I said, watching the onlookers who were oohing and ahhing at the display.

"We had good stuff to work with." Marky looked at me then away. "Nice dress."

"Oh, thanks. Or rather, thank your mother. She's the one who transformed me."

"Nah. You're pretty no matter what." He ducked past me to join Tiff, who eyed me with an evaluating stare.

"Ah, jealousy." The mayor moved into place beside me. She wore a flapper outfit complete with fringed dress, sparkly shoes, and a sparkly headband with a big red flower.

"Jealousy?" My face began to get hot. Was I so transparent?

"You have most of the men here gaping and groveling. Some of the ladies may be worried." She smiled faintly at Tiff, who glared at the display table as though it had mortally offended her. "It's always tough at that age."

"It's tough at any age," I admitted.

She held out a key ring. "Can you return these to Aden? I meant to give them to him last night, and I forgot. It's not for me." The mayor beamed at me. "I'm glad you and Aden have made up your differences. He was so hurt. He didn't want to believe you wrote that letter. But your sister assured him you did it, so what was he to think?"

"My sister?"

"Sister-in-law," she amended. "He spoke with her. She said you talked about those things. Well, what was he to think?" She waved to someone. "Excuse me. I need to talk with some folks."

Emily. Damn her. What did she do? I scanned the crowd. What costume was she wearing? Star Wars, wasn't it? Wait a minute. She wasn't here, was she? She told Mark she was out hunting. Why would she lie to Aden?

I wandered to the next table, the one for the Youth. The tumblers were gathered around, talking excitedly. "I want to play with dogs," one of the littler ones said when she saw me. "It would be more fun than balance beam."

"I think so, too," I said. "Although I'm sure you're learning a lot in your classes."

"Yeah, but—puppies!" She scampered off, laughing.

Aden rejoined me, two glasses of wine in his hands. I took the one he handed me and gave him the keys. "The mayor gave me this. Said she forgot to give it to you." I swallowed some wine. "Look, I don't play games. If you and the mayor are, you know, together, I'd like to know about it."

He stuck the keys in his pocket. "She's interested in a car like mine. I let her borrow it for a few days."

Borrow a fifty-thousand-dollar car? I stared at him before the import of what he said sank in. "What?"

"She drove mine for a few days. I had a company SUV, so it didn't matter. I didn't think she'd like it. She's not a sports car kind of person."

"So she had it at her house?" I asked.

"I suppose so. Where does she live?"

The D.J. was playing "Shake It Off." All of my anger, my fear, my worries fell away. I didn't care about Emily, I didn't care about the letter, Frank was recovering and safe with somebody to look after him, my animals were cared for, and Aden wasn't sleeping with the mayor.

Damn it, I deserved fun.

I set my glass on a table and crooked my finger at Aden. "Come on."

He laughed, handed his glass to Marky, and followed me out onto the floor. It seemed to be the signal for everybody to swarm out and join in. The whole place started jumping. We spun, we laughed, we changed partners randomly for song after song after song. Line dances, the twist, the stroll. You name it, we danced it.

I finally had to take a breather, making my way to the end zone where the buffet table was set up. The Vet guy had the same idea, and we both filled plates with snacks. "If I was ten years younger, I'd give that guy a run for his money," he said to me.

"What guy?"

Aden held up his wine glass from the other end of the table. "This guy," he called.

I laughed and winked at the Vet. "Any time you want to dance, you let me know."

"You get in touch with me about the idea of yours. I think we can work out something to help everybody involved."

"Thank you. I'll give you a call."

"You do that, Princess." He moved to the dining tables set up nearby.

I joined Aden at the end of the buffet. "This is turning into one hell of a party," he commented.

"There's nothing like a costume party to bring out the hidden personality in a person."

"Does that mean you're secretly a princess and

I'm—" He held out his hands. "An English country gentleman?"

"I doubt if I'm a princess, not unless somebody sprinkled me with fairy dust and didn't tell me about it." I made my way to a table and set down my plate before maneuvering my skirts into place so I could sit. "Man, I haven't danced this much in years. Whew."

He pulled a chair near me, resting his arm around the back of my chair. "I need to apologize," he murmured, tilting his head near mine. "I thought you wrote the letter to the editor. I should have known you wouldn't do something so public without chewing me out first. You're much more straightforward than that."

"I did not write it. I'm pissed off the newspaper printed it without checking with me first. It must be illegal or something." I punctuated my words with a celery stick dipped in ranch dressing.

"I'm glad you're not angry with me." He nabbed a grape from my plate. "I think you might be hard to seduce. If we toss anger into the mix, it might be darn near impossible."

I turned my head to look into his eyes. "Is that what you're doing?"

"I'm trying." He leaned forward. Our lips met in a slow, searching kiss.

"I think you're making progress," I whispered when we broke apart. "You know, I need to leave soon because I want to show Frank my costume. He's still recovering from surgery, so I don't want to wait too long." I met his amused gaze and fluttered my eyelashes.

"I like the way you think."

"Hey, Ash." Jacob appeared at our table. "You were going to sing a song, weren't you?"

"Oh, damn. I was. But Frank's not here to accompany me. I wonder if the D.J. has a version I can use."

"Frank suggested I bring along his Martin," Aden said. "Maybe I can fill in."

"When did you talk to Frank?"

"When you were getting dolled up at Binny's. I told him I needed to apologize. He said if I took his place it might help you forgive me. I know the song, but my playing might not be on the par with Frank's." Aden stood and held out his hand. "I hope I don't let you down."

I let him pull me upright. "I don't think that will happen."

"I wasn't necessarily talking about my guitar ability."

I looked up at him. "I know you weren't. I'm not worried." I slipped my arm through his. "Let's see if we can make beautiful music together."

Jacob grinned at me while we moved with him to the stage. "People might interpret that a couple of different ways."

Aden laughed. "I'm counting on it."

I approached the steps leading up to the stage, raising my skirt lest I trip. Aden steadied me with one hand on my arm, and we made it safely. The microphone was already set up and a chair was nearby, Frank's Martin resting against it. Aden sat with the guitar. I leaned over to listen as he tuned.

He looked up and whispered, "You'd better not do that again or I'll have heart failure."

Oh, dear. My bosom was perilously close to tipping out of my dress. I hastily straightened and tapped the microphone a few times, eventually getting the attention of the people milling about in the gym.

"Hi, folks. Ashley, again. You know I usually sing a song or two at this event. Usually my father-in-law, Frank, is with me for backup, but some asshole shot him and he's at home recovering. Aden Kingsley has agreed to help me out. I hope you'll join in, too." I turned to Aden and nodded. "Whenever you're ready."

He strummed the opening chords and I joined in with John Lennon's "Imagine." Aden's tempo was slower than Frank's, but he soon caught on to my pacing. By the time we got to the chorus, people were singing with me. We sang through the verses, and I repeated the chorus once more, letting the final words fade out in the still air before I stepped away from the microphone.

I turned and held out my hand to Aden. He put the guitar on the chair and took my hand while I curtseyed to the applause. He bowed once, then stepped back while I took another curtsey. He escorted me to the stairs. "It's getting close to midnight. Do I need to get you home before you turn into a pumpkin?"

"I don't know about a pumpkin, but I would like to get home and see how Frank's doing. Do you mind leaving?"

He held my hand while I cautiously made my way down the stairs. "I don't mind at all, Princess." He tucked my arm through his. We moved through the dancers and the onlookers to the exit. I glimpsed Binny out on the dance floor with Mark. She waved wildly at me and I waved in return before Aden whisked me from the gym into the cold October night.

"Binny wouldn't let me wear a coat," I complained when we hurried to the parking lot. "She insisted on style over practicality."

He tugged off his frockcoat and put it around me. "God forbid you should catch a chill."

I snuggled into it, reveling in the warmth and the faint aroma of cologne. We got to the lot, and Aden led me to an SUV, but then he veered to the right. "Since my car is here, let's take it." He clicked the key fob in his hand, and the car's lights came on. "Your carriage awaits you, Your Highness."

I settled into the soft leather seats, laughing while Aden corralled my skirts and piled them in with me. "Hang on a second. I need to get something." He closed my door and went to the SUV, reaching in and pulling out a large sack. He hurried back to me and slid into the driver's seat, handing me the sack. "This is for you. I was hoping I'd have a chance to give it to you tonight." He pressed the starter, and the car purred to life.

"Can I open it now or later?"

He extended his hand and touched my face, rubbing the back of his fingers against my cheek. "Let's save it for later." He took the sack and put it in the back then pressed a button on the dash. My seat immediately began to get warm. "Let's show Frank your party clothes."

I rested back, soaking in the luxury around me. The car was so quiet I barely heard the motor. I was accustomed to my old truck, which wheezed and thumped. This was like being cradled in a soft chair molded to my body. Aden touched a button, and music came through the speakers, Eric Clapton playing softly.

"It's a beautiful car," I murmured, running my hand on the inlaid wood on the dash.

"I like it. After riding in squad cars and police sedans, it's fun to have something nice for a change. I guess I take after my father in that, at least. I like good cars."

I looked at him in the flickering glow from the streetlights. "You didn't like your father, did you?"

"I respected him. I respected what he built. He had a tough life as a young man. He learned the construction trade from the ground up and made a good business. But he was hard on the people around him. I had a younger brother who ran away from home. He was a teenager when he came out as gay. My father couldn't tolerate that."

"What happened to him?"

Aden turned onto Hazel Lane, the headlights cutting through the blackness ahead. "He's happily married and living in Maine. He and his husband adopted two great kids. My mother had a chance to have her grandma moments before she died. He's a great father."

"Bryan was such a free spirit, a dreamer. Neither of us were grown-up enough to raise a child. And by the time I might have wanted to raise one, he was dead and I was alone."

"Do you regret it?"

"Not at all." I put my hand on his on the gear knob. "I don't regret anything in my life. It's brought me here."

He glanced at me, his face mostly in shadow. "You're a beautiful person."

"Thank you."

He grinned. "Wow. You accepted a compliment. What's the world coming to?"

"It must be the company I keep. I'm learning." I looked through the moonroof to the stars glittering overhead. "Full moon tonight. A harvest moon."

Aden made the turn onto our lane, slowing to a more

sedate crawl. "The gravel helps, doesn't it? But a paved road would be even better."

I tapped his hand. "Quit trying to sell me on your housing proposal."

"You have to admit, a paved road would be nice."

I spied lights ahead. "You can pull in at the farmhouse. We'll walk to Frank's."

"Are you sure? I can park there."

"I'd rather surprise him. Besides, you'll have to move the car once we show him our outfits. I mean, I assume you'd like to come to my house for a nightcap?"

Aden drove into the first drive, parking in front of the garage. "Your assumption is correct." The car rolled to a stop, and he reached into the back for the bag. "Hold on, and I'll help you with your skirts."

I was happy to let him. I had no idea how I would gracefully manage an exit from his low-slung car. He came around to my side and opened the door. He set down the bag, and before I knew what was happening, he reached in, slid his arms around me, and lifted me out, my skirts billowing out around us.

I put my arms around his neck, and he lowered me. His coat slid off when he pulled me against him. "The next big challenge will be figuring out how to get you out of the dress," he murmured, his lips against my neck.

I tilted my head so he could kiss my throat. "Where there's a will, there's a way."

"Oh, there's a will, so I'm sure we'll find a way."

I reluctantly moved from his embrace. "First we need to see Frank."

Aden cupped my face in his hands. "First we need to do this." His lips met mine in a long, lingering kiss ending with his hand on my breast where it popped out of the dress.

"Come on," I said, moving back a step and adjusting my gown. "Frank knows we're here because he saw the headlights. If we don't visit him, he might visit us." I shimmied my shoulders. "Let's not get too busy, or we might give him a heart attack."

"Lead on, my lady."

"Light the way, would you? I left my phone at Binny's house."

Aden put his coat around me again, then got out his phone. Soon we were picking our way through the trees to Frank's tiny house. I led the way, Aden laughing behind me. We got near the door, and Cinders began barking.

"It's me, Frank," I called. "Open up."

Harold peeked out the door. "Who's out—look at you, Ash. My oh my, what a dress. Frank, come here and see." He held open the door, and Ciders bounded out.

Aden intercepted the dog before he jumped up on me. "We thought you'd like to see the costumes in person."

"Binny sent us pictures and video, but this is better! Come here, Frank." Harold moved to one side. Frank tottered into view, holding the door to keep his balance.

"Come here in the light, and let me see you. I knew it would be perfect for you."

Harold reached behind him and switched on the outside light. I handed Aden his coat and pirouetted, turning slowly so Frank could see The Gown in all its fluffy glory. "What do you think?" I patted my hair, which had amazingly kept its style. "Doesn't Binny do a fabulous job?"

"Oh, honey, forget Binny. You're beautiful. I love

it. I'm glad I bought it." Frank leaned against the doorframe. He looked so happy, so delighted.

"Thank you, Frank." I lifted my skirt and climbed the steps to join him, enveloping him in chiffon and a hug. "I had a great time tonight."

"Who won?" Harold asked.

"We all did, kind of." I gave them an abbreviated summary of my speech and idea. "We'll talk about it and come up with a plan." I put my arms around Frank and gave him a hug. "That's for tonight. You need to rest. I'll tell you more about it in the morning." I looked behind me at the darkness. "I need to go out and check our patients."

"No need to," Harold said. "The vet stopped by about two hours ago. All quiet. One of those teenagers is staying out there tonight." He lowered his voice and smiled conspiratorially. "I think he might have a girlfriend staying with him." He winked broadly.

"Yep, there might be hanky-panky going on tonight," Frank said with a grin. "You kids go on now. Me and Harold are going to turn in as soon as I beat him in this hand of poker."

"You and who else?" Harold put his hand in Cinders' collar and tugged the dog back to the house. "Come on with us. You had your last walk tonight." He disappeared back inside.

I kissed Frank's cheek. "I'll see you in the morning."

He put his hands on my shoulders. "You have fun, sweetie."

I went down the steps and joined Aden, turning to wave goodbye. We made our way back along the path to the farmhouse. Aden got the sack he left by the car. I led the way into the kitchen, flipping on a light. "I have wine and I might be able to make a liquor drink if you're not too fancy."

Aden pulled me into his arms. "How about we take the wine with us upstairs?" He held up the sack. "I think maybe it's time for you to unwrap your present." He ran his finger over my collarbone, dipping close to my breasts. "And maybe I can unwrap mine."

"I like the sound of that." I reached into the fridge for the wine while he picked up two glasses from the rack on the counter. We went out to the front hall and I went up the stairs, holding my skirts high so I didn't do something stupid like tip backward.

We got to the top and I went down the hall to my bedroom door. "If I'd known I'd have company, I would have—" Whatever I wanted to say was lost when he took me in his arms.

Good Lord, it was so good to have a man with me again. I didn't realize how much I missed it until his guy parts pressed against me. Before I knew it, my gown was halfway off and Aden was kissing my breasts, his mouth hot on my skin.

He turned me so my back was to him. "I need to figure this out," he whispered, his hands busy on the lacing on my back. "Oh, it's easier than it looks. It's a bow and some ribbon." The dress loosened as he spoke, the fabric gradually giving way. "Bless you, Binny," he murmured. "You made it simple."

I looked up at him while he pushed the dress down until it pooled around my knees. "I may need help escaping all the fabric." I turned, mindful that all I wore now was white stockings, ballet slippers, and panties.

He waded in and lifted me, carrying me to the bed. "You are the most beautiful woman I've ever seen." His voice, always hoarse, was positively husky now.

I wiggled until I was underneath him. "You unwrapped your present. What about mine?"

"I'm not sure I'll be able to maintain my composure."

I ran my hand along his pants, which were straining at the zipper. "I trust you can."

He pushed me against the bed, his hands on my breasts. "You're teasing me."

"I'm trying," I agreed.

He gazed into my eyes. "Okay. But don't blame me if I go a bit crazy when I see you with your present."

"Ooh. That sounds like fun."

He kissed me then released me, turned, and scooped up the sack from the doorway. With a deep bow, he handed it to me.

I sat up on the bed and peered inside. "What?" I pulled out the big box.

"Open it." Aden watched me, smiling.

I opened the present and pulled out a new pair of cowboy boots. "You want me to model them?"

He nodded. "I need to know if it's a good fit."

I tossed the boots to one side. "Come here and let's find out."

Chapter Fifteen

Maybe I was sprinkled with fairy dust after all because the night sure seemed magical to me. We made love, we laughed, we drank wine. I undid my elaborate hairdo and Aden brushed my hair, plaiting it into a loose braid. We made love again and fell asleep in a tangle of arms and legs.

I woke at some point and went to the bathroom and came back to snuggle with him. It was getting light outside when I woke again. I opened my eyes. Something was wrong. I couldn't figure out what it was, though.

Aden leapt from bed and reached into the pile of clothes he left by the doorway. I sat up in bed, leaning on my elbows. "What is it?"

He turned and that's when I saw the handgun he held. "Engine outside."

I heard it. The distinctive sound of an ATV.

We didn't own an ATV.

"Who's out there?"

Aden was at the window, the curtain pulled back, his handgun pointed at the floor. I don't think he even realized he was naked. He was totally focused on the view outside. "Two people. One looks like Frank."

"What?" I rolled out of bed, almost tripping on the gown which took up a large amount of floor space. "He shouldn't be out in an ATV. He's supposed to be home recovering."

"It's Emily." Aden spun away from the window and went to his clothes. "Where would she take Frank?"

"*Where* would she take him? I don't know. Why would she take him?" I stared out the window in the gray light of dawn. The ATV was skittering down the lane. "She's insane. What's she doing?"

"Where's she going, Ash? What's in that direction?" Aden sat on the bed and pulled on his pants. "Talk to me. What's there?"

I spun around. "The cabin. The cabin I had with Bryan. It's out there. What's going on?"

"Emily has Frank, and she's taking him there." Aden lifted his white shirt. "I can't wear this. It'll stand out like a spotlight."

"Here." I tossed him his black and white flannel shirt I had washed. I found a sweatshirt in my dresser and dragged it on.

"Tell me about it. Describe it." Aden pulled on the shirt, buttoning it as he spoke.

"It's a quarter-mile northeast of here. Cut across the cornfield, and it's over the top of the hill. There's a stand of trees on the west side with a stream north of it and a windbreak on the east of evergreens." I hopped on one foot, pulling on a pair of jeans.

Aden tugged on a boot. "Stay here. I'll go see what's going on."

"Are you kidding? I'm going with you."

"No. It might be dangerous."

"It's my family, fucked up though we might be." I was still wearing the white stockings so I only had to get my boots on and I'd be ready.

"It's not your family. It's your husband's." Aden

picked up the gun he set on the nightstand and went to the door.

I dropped the boot I held. "Bryan," I whispered.

"Stay here." Aden pulled open the door and disappeared into the hall.

I jammed my feet into my boots and raced after him. We burst from the house, cold night air wrapping around us. "Go check the barn," Aden shouted. "Check Frank's house. I'll follow Emily."

I hesitated, then followed him out to the drive and pointed north. "Go that way. She's probably on the road. It ends in about a hundred yards, then it's a dirt path the rest of the way. She'll have to go slow. If you go overland, you might beat her to the cabin."

"Be careful." He kissed me, hard, then he was off, running down the drive. I went in the opposite direction, dodging through the trees separating Frank's house from mine. My breath puffed out in tiny clouds through the cold air. I paused at the tiny house. The door was open, and lights were on.

Harold was stretched out on the couch, Cinders on the floor next to him. Both of them were unnaturally quiet. I paused in the threshold, afraid to move forward. I saw Cinders' paws twitch and Harold's labored breathing. They were alive. I touched Harold's neck and felt his pulse. I did the same for Cinders, checking the underside of his uninjured front paw.

Drugged? Gas? They were alive and that was what mattered. I ran, reaching for my cell phone—

Which was on the table at Binny's house. Damn. I considered going back to Frank's but instead went to the barn. Better to know the totality of what I was facing before calling for help. I threw open the side door and stumbled inside. The night lights were on, the low lighting showing me the two shapes under a blanket in the old recliner in the corner.

I approached slowly, not sure what I'd find. The shape split apart and a head poked up to regard me sleepily. "S'up, Ash?" Bart mumbled. A girl with tousled short brown hair peeked over the blanket and ducked back under.

"I need your phone." I snatched it from the table near the chair. "I'm calling the police. Get up and get dressed." Oh, thank God. No password.

"Whoa, wait a minute. No need to call the police." Bart flung the blanket aside. "Nothing happened, come on. No need to call the cops."

They were both dressed. Maybe not fully dressed but they were dressed. I ignored their incoherent protestations and focused on dialing 9-1-1. When the dispatch officer came on, I said, "Kidnapping underway at the Schone farm, off of Hazel Lane. Frank Goddard has been taken. He's injured and in danger. We're in pursuit. Me and Aden Kingsley. I'm Ash Schone. We think they're going to the old cabin at the end of Hazel Lane. Send backup."

I whirled to leave the barn but paused. "Get to Frank's house," I told the wide-eyed kids. "Take care of Harold and Cinders. Don't follow us. It might be dangerous. And make sure the animals are cared for this morning out here. Get help."

I thought they'd balk or protest. Instead Bart jumped off the chair. "We'll handle it," he said, flapping his arms. "Go."

"Thank you." I dropped the phone back on the table and went to the gun safe in the office. It took two tries, but I got it open. I loaded the small handgun I kept there and pulled on the shoulder holster. I ran out the door and headed for the field.

A light drizzle was falling, more like a heavy cloud blanketing the earth than rain. I ran into the cornfield, thanking God the farmer we leased the land to had cleared the field rather than leave knee-high stubble. There is nothing harder on the body than moving through a harvested field. The clods of earth tossed up were still friable, not frozen yet, and that was another thing to thank God for. Otherwise I'd break an ankle.

I picked my way up the field. When Bryan and I lived in the cabin, this was pastureland. It had been a cornfield for ten years. I used to know the way, but my memory was faulty because when I crested the hill, the cabin was to my right. I came out at the trees, not south of them. I saw someone moving ahead of me.

I crouched, trying to keep a low profile while approaching the trees. I was to the outlying shrubs when I saw Aden waiting for me, inside the tree line. I joined him. "Bart is at the barn. He'll help Harold and Cinders."

"Are they alive?"

"Yeah. Drugged, maybe. Unconscious."

Aden inched forward, further into the strip of trees flanking the cabin. He moved cautiously, watching each step. I tried to follow suit but I was clumsy compared to him. "Stay behind me," he whispered. "Watch my back."

"No one is behind us. It's only Emily."

He turned. "Just do it, Ash."

I saw the memories in his eyes. He'd been here before.

I hadn't ever been in a place like this, though. This was Emily. What was it Jacob said about her? Volatile.

Emily was volatile. Emily didn't like to lose. What was her purpose? What was she doing with Frank?

Aden stopped in front of me. I saw the edge of the small woodland ahead. "How much further? What's on this side of the cabin?"

"The woods aren't deep. Maybe fifty, seventy-five yards." I tried to visualize the distance. A football field. "Fifty yards. Once you get out of the trees, you're at the top of the hill. The cabin faces northeast. It's at an angle so we got the best sunlight through the back windows. Those face us." I pointed ahead. "The building is down-slope from here."

Aden peered through the trees, which still had a lot of leaves. We were relatively well hidden, especially because of the foggy morning. "Does Emily know the lay of the land?"

"Yes. She spent time here, hunting and trapping with Bryan. She knows it better than me. I mostly stuck to the cabin."

"Single room? Nowhere to really hide?"

"No. But I'm not sure what condition it's in. It's been maybe five or six years since I've been here."

"Someone's been here. Look at the roof." He moved forward, his gun held in both hands. A hunter's stance. A predator's stance.

I followed and finally saw what he saw. The roof was patched. There were shingles on this side a brighter color than the other shingles. The grass was trimmed around the foundation and the remains of flowers drooped along the back wall, victims of the last frost. "Who's maintaining it?"

He glanced at me. "Emily."

"Emily? Why?"

Aden moved from the trees. "Let's find out." He scurried ahead.

I caught up to him at the top of the hill. A faint light came from inside the cabin, a soft glow from one of the two big windows overlooking the short expanse of lawn. The back door was open but it was dark there.

"Is there any way to approach without her seeing us?" he asked.

"No. There are windows on all sides."

Aden stood. "Stay here." He tucked his gun into a holster on his belt and went forward, hands raised.

"What the hell are you doing?" I followed him, a pace or two behind.

"Stay there!" The voice came from the cabin. The muzzle of a rifle poked out of the doorway.

Aden paused. I moved past him. "Emily, it's Ash. What's going on? Is Frank okay?"

"I'm fine, honey." Frank's voice drifted out to me, wavery but recognizable. "I should have known better. She dropped by last night and gave us some cider. Turns out it was stronger than I thought."

"Jesus, Emily, you drugged him? Don't you know how dangerous that is? He's on medication for a damn gunshot wound." I stopped, knowledge flooding me. "You shot him? What the hell are you doing, Emily?"

"They were supposed to trace the bullet to Parsons' gun." Her voice was as wavery as Frank's. "I took it after I killed him."

"Oh, my God." I looked at Aden, but he appeared unsurprised. "Did you know this?" I whispered.

"I suspected. I made a couple of calls last night. I knew Parsons had a gun the same caliber as the bullet found in Frank. But he was dead before Frank was shot.

That's what Grimm confirmed for me last night. It meant there was another shooter."

"Why did she think it would work?"

"She's not thinking clearly," Aden muttered.

"No shit, Sherlock. Who is?" I followed him toward the cabin.

"Stay there," Emily called.

"Emily, you know me. There is no way in hell I am staying here if Frank is in any danger. So shoot me now or shut up." I stomped down the short slope.

"Stop it, Ash." Aden reached for my arm, but I managed to evade him.

"Everybody is telling me to stay safe. What about Frank? He's in the middle of all this. I won't let him die so I can stay safe." I reached the small patio behind the back door. The rifle muzzle had vanished, which I hoped was a good sign. "Emily, I need to come in and check Frank. He's just out of the hospital. I need to make sure he's okay."

"Only you. I don't want that guy inside here."

Before Aden could reply, I called, "That's bullshit and you know it, Emily. He's worried about me so he won't let me come in without him. Put your gun down and let us come inside."

Silence. Then she said, "Okay. But I won't put down my gun."

"Shit," I muttered. "Now what?"

"Now we go in. Keep your hands where she can see them. Keep her talking. I'll try to work my way around her to see if I can get a shot."

"Get a shot?" I began moving forward. "You can't shoot her."

"If she threatens you or Frank, I will." I drew breath

to speak, but Aden didn't let me. "She's not the person you think you know."

"That's crap. This is Emily. I watched her grow up. She stayed overnight at my house."

Aden put his hand on my shoulders. "She's not anyone you know. She's a dangerous murderer. She's kidnapped an old man, and she's using him as bait to get you into the open."

"Me? This isn't about me."

"It's always been about you. It's about you because it's about Bryan." Aden gave me a little shake. "This is what I used to do. I've seen this before. There are people out there who want to die, but they don't know it. All they know is they feel pain, and they want it to stop. Those people are the ones who pull guns on the police because they know the police will shoot them. Do you understand what I'm saying?" He stared intently at me, willing me to understand.

"I've heard about that, but Emily isn't—"

"Listen to me. I may need to shoot her. I won't let her harm you or Frank. I know what I'm doing. Don't get in my way, Ash." Aden studied my face. "I know you don't like to accept help, but trust me in this."

I didn't want to believe him, but this had been his job. Maybe he was right. I had no idea what the hell was happening, so I moved to the door, my hands outstretched. I inched my way inside. Luckily it was gloomy outside so I didn't have much adjusting to do to the lower light inside.

It was eerily familiar. That's what stunned me the most. To my left was the built-in desk and bath. Beyond it was the wall hiding the bedroom. The fireplace was straight ahead of me with the built-in couch to the left on the bedroom wall. To my right the kitchen took up the south wall. In the middle of the space were the only free-standing pieces of furniture we had, two armchairs and a kitchen table and two chairs.

Frank sat immediately inside the door opposite me in an armchair similar to the one we used to have. Emily was to his left with her back to the kitchen. I hurried to Frank but stopped when Emily raised her hands. She held an automatic handgun, big and heavy. "He can't come in. He stays there."

I turned. Aden was in the doorway, his hands up.

"He has to come in," I said. "I need his help. Please."

Emily shook her head, her brown hair a matted mess, her face blotchy and red. Her outfit was field camo: gold-green-brown pants tucked into green rubber boots and a camo jacket covering a black T-shirt. The gun was pointed at Aden. At this distance, she wouldn't miss. Hell, she wouldn't miss at any distance. Emily was an experienced shooter.

"I need to examine Frank," I pleaded. "Aden can help me."

She frowned at Aden. "He can come in but stay away from me."

Aden joined me where I leaned over Frank. "How are you?" I whispered.

"Tired as hell and my owie hurts." Frank peered up at me groggily. He wore a cotton pajama top haphazardly buttoned on top of his sling with baggy sweatpants and slippers. "I should never have trusted her."

Aden moved so he had his back to Emily, a move that made me cringe. "Keep her talking," he said in a low voice. "Try to get her to move away from the wall."

"Let's move him to the couch," I said. "He needs to

lie down." I put my arm under Frank's good arm and helped him up, Aden providing additional support. As I expected, Emily followed us while we made our tottery way to the couch adjacent to the fireplace. "Can we start a fire? He's cold."

Aden moved so he was nearer the back door where we entered. Emily took a couple more steps. I sank down on the couch next to Frank, helping him rest against the wall. We were protected by the bedroom wall behind us and the fireplace to our left. Emily was in the center of the cabin in front of Frank and me.

Aden had circled until he was on my right with a clear shot at her. I think she realized it the same moment I did. Her arms came up, gun raised.

Aden's gun was leveled at her, held in both hands, unwavering. "Drop your weapon," he said softly.

"Do it, Emily," I pleaded.

Her gaze shifted to me. "I didn't mean for any of this to happen."

"I know." I longed to reach out to her, but I was afraid of distracting her, afraid of drawing attention. "I'm sure you didn't."

Tears streamed down her face. "I have nothing left. I'll lose my business. I lost my family. I didn't want to kill anyone, but I had to."

"Why?" Aden asked, inching forward.

"Because Mara betrayed us."

"Us?" I asked.

"Bryan and me."

"Bryan," I whispered. "Oh, no."

"Emily, this won't end well," Aden said. His voice was soft and calm, reasonable. "Put down the gun."

I knew what she would say before she said it. "I

don't care. I want it to end." Her eyes met mine. "You know."

I did. I understood her torment, her grief. I felt that when Bryan died. The months after his death were filled with self-doubt, fear, anger, and such a crushing sense of loss I wasn't sure I'd ever feel anything else. I did, of course. I eventually found purpose, found a new life and maybe, just maybe, I might have found a new love.

Emily had felt a horrible loss for twenty years, with no one to commiserate with her, no one to understand her. She loved him, too, with the hopeless, unrequited love that she had to keep hidden. She could only grieve publicly as a sister. Good Lord, what a hell she lived in.

I saw a world of pain in her eyes. I'd seen the expression before, in the eyes of a deer lying on the side of the road. Confused, frightened, resigned, and done with it all. I saw it in their eyes when I had to shoot them. I always—*always*—second guessed myself. And I always knew, after a time of grief, I'd done the correct thing.

Even if I had the chance, I wouldn't shoot her. This was Emily, not an injured stray animal. This was a human. We could find help for her. Surely it was an accident. Surely it was all an accident, wasn't it?

Aden approached from her left. "Drop the gun, Emily. We'll talk about it. Please. Don't hurt Ash."

She wouldn't hurt me. I was her connection to Bryan. Aden didn't get it. He couldn't. He was thinking like a cop.

"I didn't want to hurt Mara," Emily said, her voice choked with anger. "She pissed me off so much. We were at my house, and she told me she hired Parsons to poison the site. She went ahead and did it without so much as consulting me. She was trying to force a stupid commercial development to go in. That's not what Bryan would have wanted."

I looked past her at Aden, who was moving cautiously to keep her in his sights. *Keep her talking,* he mouthed.

"I know," I said. "Bryan would never have wanted another shopping center. Bryan loved the land. You need to honor his memory, his legacy. Why are you doing this? He wouldn't want you to hurt Frank."

"Frank never loved Bryan." Emily's gaze shifted to Frank, who sagged against the fireplace wall on my left.

"Of course he did," I said.

"No, he didn't. They argued all the time. Bryan told me."

"Is that why you shot him?"

"I told you why I shot him," Emily said impatiently. "It was all about Parson's gun."

"You might have shot me, though," I said. "Why did you shoot Frank? Was it because you thought he didn't love Bryan? I didn't hear them argue."

"It's true." Frank's voice was faint, exhausted. "I thought he could do better for himself than a stupid landscaping job."

"You never understood his creativity. You never supported it. He was a free spirit, a creative spirit. You wanted him to bury it under a desk job somewhere."

I finally saw what I'd been blind to for so long. Hero-worship. Selective memory. She was a clumsy, unattractive child, ignored and ridiculed. Unappreciated by everyone. Everyone except Bryan. He was endlessly patient with her, he shared his interests with her, never made fun of her. Big-boned, chubby, ungainly, Emily.

Manic Emily. Volatile Emily.

"What happened?" Frank whispered. "What happened to Mara?"

"She came to talk to me. I got so mad I threw my hatchet at her. It was blind luck it hit her leg like that. She was dead in a couple of minutes."

Emily recited this like a disinterested bystander discussing a car accident. I didn't believe what I was hearing. My disbelief must have shown because she said, "It's a good thing I'm a hunter. I knew what to do."

"What was that?" I managed to croak.

"Get rid of the body, of course. I knew Parsons broke the law when he poisoned the site, so I forced him to take Mara. I didn't know where he'd take her. I thought maybe the river or the state park. I didn't know he'd toss her out on your road, Ash."

I swallowed hard, struggling to keep my stomach from rebelling.

"Parsons decided to try to blackmail me." She smiled grimly. "A crowbar to the head and a chipper, and he was done."

Her matter-of-fact voice washed over me, and I had one of those ah-ha moments. I suddenly understood exactly what Aden meant. This was no longer someone I knew. This was a woman who had, perhaps, accidentally killed one woman and cold-bloodedly murdered another a man.

I fought to figure out an argument she understood. "I need to save Frank. He's all I have left of Bryan. He's all that remains. Please, Emily. We're all family here."

"He isn't." She glared at Aden. "I saw you together last night. Maybe he'll be family someday. Will he?"

"Emily, please. I don't know what the future might

hold."

"Do you love him? Has he replaced Bryan?"

How to answer that? Anything I answered might be wrong. I saw Aden, stock still, his gun leveled at Emily's head. "I don't know," I said. "I barely know him. It's hard to know what might happen."

Emily regarded me, her head tilted as though she evaluated my response. "You love him. I can see it. You love him, and you don't want him to be hurt."

"Of course I don't," I snapped, my patience fraying. "I don't want anyone to be hurt."

"You can't love anyone else. You need to honor what Bryan wanted. He wanted the farm to stay as it is. We don't need strangers. We don't need anyone else here."

"Emily." Aden's voice was like an electric wire, forcing her to stare at him. "This won't end well, Emily. Put down the gun."

"I can't," she whispered. "I can't." Her finger, resting on the trigger, began to move.

"Please." I stood, drawing my pistol out of my pocket. "Emily. Put down the gun." I raised my arm.

Her attention swung back to me. "I don't have anything, Ash. There's nothing left." She turned, her automatic pointed at Aden.

I pulled the trigger.

****

It was springtime before all the legal bullshit began to clear. The first complication was that I was legally the heir of the woman I shot. And it was further complicated because Emily killed Mara, but she was Mara's heir just like I was Emily's heir.

But my bullet wasn't the only one to hit Emily. The medical examiner couldn't say decisively who killed her since both Aden and I fired shots. I had aimed low but when Aden's bullet hit her, she twisted. The shot I aimed at her shoulder ended up entering through her side. Aden insisted it was his shot that killed her, but I think he said that to help alleviate my guilt.

I admit, I did struggle with it. I had never aimed a gun at another human being, much less fired at someone. But I knew she meant to kill Aden. A few sessions with a psychologist helped me to understand that I made the only choice available to me in that split second.

Eventually it was decided I could dispose of their property as long as what I did was approved by a board of trustees. I promptly deeded the land that was in contention to the city of Dasdorf. They in turn voted to support the co-housing project Aden had proposed. The rest of Emily and Mara's estates—the homes and the other assets—were all sold. I split the money between all the Heavys, including Fairy Tale Endings.

Once the co-housing project began to take shape, we had further legal fuss because our farm would be incorporated into the overall project. But by then I was living with Aden and we had to be careful it didn't appear I was being given favored status.

I should say I was sort of living with him. I stayed at his place in town several nights a week, and he often stayed at my house. I was working with the university on the design for the rehab center they were building. I had interns staying at the farmhouse, working with our patients to see how we managed things.

I also was on the Harvesting the Future board of directors, mapping out new strategies for charitable cross-funding. Frank was on the board of directors for the co-housing project. He was busier than ever between that and overseeing the interns and the homeless folks who were working with our patients at the barn.

Everything was going fine, or so I thought. It was mid-summer. I was sitting on the front porch at Aden's house. He sat nearby, idly picking out chords on an old Fender Parlor guitar. I always knew when he had a tough day at the office. He came home, changed to a T-shirt and faded jeans, and came out on the porch barefoot to play guitar. I'd kick off my boots and settle in on the wicker loveseat, listening to him and sometimes singing along.

Tonight he picked and plucked then said, "I learned a new song. I've been practicing it for a while."

I set aside the notebook where I was jotting ideas for a new possum poultice. "Let me hear it."

He strummed a couple of chords and launched into "How Long," by Dire Straits. His husky voice infused the words with melancholy. He kept his eyes on me while he played, and it dawned on me he chose this song for a reason.

I forced myself to stay quiet until he finished, then I asked, "Will that happen? Will I wake up and find you gone someday?"

He set aside the guitar. "I love you, Ash. I want us to be permanent. But I'm not sure how you feel."

I longed to get up, to pace, to do anything but meet his dark brown eyes. It was time to be honest with him and myself, but it meant I had to face what I was afraid was a terrible truth. "I love you, Aden, but I'm not the right person for you."

He leaned back in surprise. "Of all the things you

might have said, I did not expect that." He joined me on the wicker love seat, putting his arm around me. "Why are you not the right person for me?"

"You're a businessman. You have to entertain clients and talk to civic groups. You need someone with you who can support that. I'm not a little-black-dress kind of person. I can't shake hands and schmooze."

"Did I ever ask you to do that?"

"No, but I know it would help you if I would."

He was shaking his head before I finished my sentence. "It would be great if you did help, but if you don't want to, that's fine. I hope the last few months have shown you that being part of a pair is all about helping each other." Aden's arm tightened around me. "You help me in other ways more important than standing around at a cocktail party with a drink in your hand, chatting with clients."

"I do?"

"You know you do. I can come home and sit down here, and we talk and we play songs and the world falls away. This is what's important, not crap happening at the office. This is what's real. I hope I do the same for you."

A world of worry began to seep away from me. "You do."

"I know you hate to admit it, too," he whispered against my ear.

I smiled. "I do. I guess I'm still getting used to the idea I can live in a beautiful home like this and be a partner with someone like you." I looked into his eyes. "It still amazes me you're with me."

"Oh, Ash, I love you because you're strong and beautiful and independent. You don't need me, but I hope you want me."

"But I'm still worried." I held up a cowboy boot as though it proved my point. "I have obligations. You don't want to spend nights in a barn, singing lullabies to possums and foxes."

He took me in his arms. "What I want is you. We'll work out the details about what it entails later."

"Later?"

"Later, Princess. First—" He lowered his head. "First you need to kiss your prince."

A word about the author…

J L Wilson writes mysteries with a touch of romance—and romance with a touch of grey.

Keep up with all her doings at https://www.facebook.com/jayeAtplay and all her books at https://bit.ly/JLWbooks.

Please consider posting a review at the site where you purchased this book. Reviews help authors in so many ways.

Thank you for purchasing
this publication of The Wild Rose Press, Inc.

For questions or more information
contact us at
info@thewildrosepress.com.

The Wild Rose Press, Inc.
www.thewildrosepress.com